A Mother's Deceit

Caroline Rebisz

No part of this book may be reproduced, scanned or distributed in any printed or electronic form without permission in writing from the author, except for the use of brief quotations in a book review. Please do not participate or encourage piracy of any copyrighted material in violation of the author's rights.

Any trademarks, service marks, or names featured are assumed to be the property of their respective owners and are only used for reference. There is no endorsement, implied or otherwise, if any terms are used.

A Mother's Deceit is a work of fiction. Names, characters, places and incidents are either the product of the author's imagination or are used fictitiously. Any similarities to persons, living or dead, places or locations are purely coincidental.

The author holds all rights to this work.

Copyright © 2022 Caroline Rebisz

All rights reserved.

ISBN: 979-8-4144-4710-8

DEDICATION

For My Mum.

CONTENTS

1	Chapter One	Pg 1
2	Chapter Two	Pg 7
3	Chapter Three	Pg 15
4	Chapter Four	Pg 23
5	Chapter Five	Pg 28
6	Chapter Six	Pg 32
7	Chapter Seven	Pg 37
8	Chapter Eight	Pg 42
9	Chapter Nine	Pg 46
10	Chapter Ten	Pg 53
11	Chapter Eleven	Pg 57
12	Chapter Twelve	Pg 62
13	Chapter Thirteen	Pg 68
14	Chapter Fourteen	Pg 74
15	Chapter Fifteen	Pg 78
16	Chapter Sixteen	Pg 81
17	Chapter Seventeen	Pg 86
18	Chapter Eighteen	Pg 94
19	Chapter Nineteen	Pg 98
20	Chapter Twenty	Pg 103

21	Chapter Twenty-One	Pg 110
22	Chapter Twenty-Two	Pg 115
23	Chapter Twenty-Three	Pg 122
24	Chapter Twenty-Four	Pg 130
25	Chapter Twenty-Five	Pg 135
26	Chapter Twenty-Six	Pg 142
27	Chapter Twenty-Seven	Pg 148
28	Chapter Twenty-Eight	Pg 154
29	Chapter Twenty-Nine	Pg 158
30	Chapter Thirty	Pg 165
31	Chapter Thirty-One	Pg 171
32	Chapter Thirty-Two	Pg 175
33	Chapter Thirty-Three	Pg 180
34	Chapter Thirty-Four	Pg 186
35	Chapter Thirty-Five	Pg 192
36	Chapter Thirty-Six	Pg 200
37	Chapter Thirty-Seven	Pg 211
38	Chapter Thirty-Eight	Pg 214
	Afterword	Pg 219
	About The Author	Pg 220

ACKNOWLEDGMENTS

Thank you to my family who indulge my passion for writing. Alan, Danuta and Beth, my lovely family who support my work and encourage me throughout.

A special thank you to my friend Helen Mudge who has proof-read my document . Her attention to detail is invaluable. We make a great team when editing..

CHAPTER ONE
1875

A fiery spark hissed as it hit the cold grate, waking the woman from her slumber.

She coughed; her throat dry. All too often these days, Mary was found slumbering in her chair with her mouth open. Her jaw was slack as she ran her tongue across her dry lips. Picking up a glass, she took a sip of cold water. Her fingers shook, spilling a few drops of water on her chest.

The days dragged so slowly now.

She slept most of the day, especially if left to her own devices, and then dozed during the long, dark nights when she was always alone. It was hard for her to keep awake once the evening chill sneaked into the room. But all too often she would wake in the cold light of early dawn before the family was awake. It was then that her mind swirled around the past.

Slowly shaking her head from side to side as she came out of her reverie, the woman became more aware of her surroundings.

Mary had the use of the front parlour whilst the rest of the family worked together in the warm kitchen. Her padded chair had seen better days. Its straw stuffing sagged in places, making equal mounds of soft and hard padding. The fabric was fraying but was all so familiar to its owner, like a favourite child, one could not let it go. It was her favourite and had travelled with her from the inn. She spent most of her days on its bulging cushions which had moulded to her shape.

Soon she would make her slow shuffle to her bed. Hannah would come and help her settle down for the night. Unfortunately, that really was the extent of her movement now. Her world revolved around the bed and chair in a slow dance of solitude and quiet reflection. There is little dignity with age. Even her private needs were supervised by Hannah, as the old woman struggled to dress and wash herself.

The parlour room was her domain.

It was her sanctuary, where she met her grandchildren when they made their obligatory visit to see Grandma. It was not always a lonely existence, as John and Hannah would often sit with her after the children were abed. John always had a good story to tell which usually involved one of his parishioners. The local vicar heard most of the village tittle-tattle. Mary delighted in his stories. He was a great raconteur. It was light relief from the boredom which ruled her life these days.

Her body was the main barrier to her making more of her life with her daughter and grandchildren. It was slowly wearing out with the passage of time. The aches and pains of middle age had developed into a stiffness of body and a slowness of mind. Her memory worried her. She struggled to remember what Hannah had told her the day before, but her thoughts of the past hit her with such clarity. A clarity which, sometimes, she wished she didn't see. She could recall the detail of a conversation some twenty years before as if it were the present. And many of those memories troubled her deeply.

Mary was happy and fairly content in her family life with her daughter and son-in-law. It hadn't always been the case.

Fortunately, she had no complaints about her present circumstances. She realised she was lucky that Hannah and lovely husband were willing to care for her in her frailty. Mary certainly respected John. He was a good man and clearly loved her daughter. He was everything she had hoped for Hannah. Mary had warmed to John Greening when she first met him. He was so similar in character to his namesake; her first love.

Sometimes when it was warm, she would treat herself to a trip outside. John would take her chair out to the garden so she could feel the warmth on her skin, although she found it increasingly hard to feel comfortable anymore. Another peril of age. Mary was all skin and bones. Gone were the ample curves of middle age. Her life was draining from her far too fast. Mary knew she had to grab hold of those moments spent under the willow tree watching the children play and remember good times.

As the nights drew in, Mary liked to be alone.

On evenings of solitude, she could be silent with her thoughts. She didn't have to make conversation with her beloved daughter and her kind husband. Perhaps that was one of the only benefits of becoming old. Your family understood if you wanted to be a miserable sod. You didn't have to be polite. They forgave your moans and groans and happily left you to it. In fact, the look on Hannah's face when relieved of her duties confirmed that assumption.

And Mary had become an objectionable old lady.

She should really feel guilty. Hannah and John were too good to her. They had taken her in, to live with them these last five years. Hannah had cared for her, fed her, and put up with her obstinate nature. Her grandchildren accepted living with a grumpy matron in their home. In fact, Matthew and Gwen hadn't known anything different. Matthew at four years old and his sister, so recently walking at two years of age, had been born while Mary lived with her daughter. She hadn't been able to support Hannah, like her own mother had, when her little ones were born. Her only value had been a lap to hold a crying baby on, as her daughter completed her household duties. It did worry Mary that the children's memories of her, after she had gone, would not be pleasant ones.

And she would be gone soon.

She knew it deep down. The fight was leaving her body. Her mind wandered too frequently these days. She had heard Hannah talking to her husband about her mother's forgetfulness. They didn't know she had been listening. Mary wished she was truly forgetful. Unfortunately, her ancient memories were still too powerful. They obsessed her during times of quiet. If only she could forget everything. Or maybe not everything. Just those dreadful memories that tapped incessantly on her forehead, like an angry woodpecker. Tap. Tap. Tap.

Those thoughts tormented her.

She longed for peace.

To forget.

She knew the day of reckoning was approaching fast. One day soon she would stand before her maker and account for her actions. One day soon she would be reunited with Sarah and beg her forgiveness. She yearned for that day. But at the same time, she was scared for that day. Would Sarah forgive her? Would the torment continue after death or would the past be laid to rest? The pain in her heart niggled at her, reminding her that it wouldn't be long now.

Tonight was Sarah's morbid anniversary. Fourteen years ago her beautiful firstborn had died. Taken too soon when she had not had the chance to taste the delights of this world. The fever which took her daughter was the fire which stoked Mary's hatred for her husband Jack. That monster had destroyed her beloved child's future.

Jack Whiting, may he rot in hell when his time comes. Even hell may be too good for that evil bastard. Mary hated her husband with a passion. He was the reason she had left the family home to come and live with Sarah's blood sister. It was the similarities between the two elder daughters which Mary had craved even after one was lost to her.

Sarah would have had the world at her feet. She could have married, had children, made a home. Within the space of a few months, she had changed from a loving, enthusiastic daughter to a shell of herself. She became moody and argumentative. As her mother, Mary should have spotted the changes. She should have enquired further into her daughter's troubles rather than ignore what was happening right under her own roof.

By the time she knew what was happening, it was too late.

Her eldest and favourite child had been damaged. She was to bear her stepfather's child. That child would kill her when childbed sickness carried her off. Fourteen years ago she sat at her daughter's bedside, holding her sweaty hand. Her heart had simply broken at Sarah's passing. The grief had overwhelmed her and her anger had turned on Jack. She had been determined to make him pay. She promised to protect her daughter Hannah from his dreadful behaviour. A promise she had failed to deliver for Sarah.

Unfortunately, Mary was not without guilt.

She had allowed the sin to take place in her home. She had brought this man into their lives. She had known his nature before she married him, although she could never have imagined his indecent desires would stoop so low. She had seen the warning signs. She had watched Jack's eyes follow Sarah around the kitchen, just as he had done with her when she was young and comely. She should have seen him pursue Sarah with his fanatical passion to possess, in the same way as he had ground her down when she was married to John.

Her stupid jealousy had prevented her from examining what was really happening. She had even secretly accused her own daughter of seducing her step-father, thankfully never putting it into words. But in her mind, she had found Sarah guilty, not her husband. To her shame, she had not been shocked when she finally found out the parentage of her first grandchild. She had been angry but not shocked.

The fear of scandal and shame drove her to the most heinous crime. A crime she had never admitted to a soul. She could not share her sin during her lifetime. It was one she would pay for when her time of reckoning came.

Unfortunately, that monster, Jack, was still very much alive.

Unlike Sarah.

Mary had not spoken with him for years; and definitely not since she had moved to Eye with Hannah and her new husband. From her son Tom's letters, it was clear that Jack spent most of his time in his cups now. Haunted by the destruction of his family and business, brought about by his own evil hand. Serves him right. He was a broken man, mocked by the community. The close-knit village would never know the reason behind his self-destructive actions. It was a family secret buried deep. No doubt the community thought Mary was also at fault. She had kicked her husband from their home and denied him access to his children.

People always seem to take the side of the man wronged. If only they knew. But it was a family secret which must remain a secret. The shame would destroy her children and that was not a price she was willing to pay. The secrets of that time would go with her to her grave, where they belonged. Jack would never utter a word of it, she was sure. He would know the consequences if he opened the family to that dreadful shame. He had just enough sense to know that his own children, of his blood, needed his silence to hold true.

Where had it all gone wrong? At which point had her journey through life taken a wrong turn? Could she have seen the warning signs and changed course before the damage was done?

Mary had been happy once.

When she and John Cozen had been wed. That had been a magical day. When the children were small. She had loved all her children so much. They were the remaining joy in her life. John had made her so happy. Life had been tough but they had forged a path together, building their business and their family. Surrounding their world in love, they had been happy.

Still, she would see John again soon.

Her one true husband. He had been the love of her life. Everyone in the world is fated to meet one person in their life who is the other side of their heart. The perfect fit. The perfect match. Mary was lucky that she had met John. It was just so unfair that he had been taken from her far too soon.

She had been left alone to bring up his children and protect the business they had built together. Would he blame her for the damage wreaked on his family? Or would he see that she had to do it? In her heart she knew the man she remembered and cherished would understand her dilemma. He would understand the pain she caused which then came down threefold on her head.

In time she would know the answer.

The light was dimming as Mary gazed through the front window. Evening was drawing in. The fire was burning strongly, filling the room with its comforting heat. Mary stretched her feet towards the grate, feeling the warmth tingling her toes. She rubbed her fingers together, reaching them out to the fire. A huge sigh escaped as she shrank back in her chair.

Staring into the flickering flame, her mind wandered.

Back to the start.

CHAPTER TWO
SUMMER 1841

"Come on Mary. Hurry yourself." Her mother yelled up the stairs.

Mary pulled her brush through the ends of her ringlets, adjusting the new ribbon which her mother had presented to her this morning. A special treat for a special day. Smoothing down the folds of her pinafore, she pulled at her dress where it had hitched up behind. Doing a quick twirl, she was satisfied with the results.

Mary Cooper, at 17, was the prettiest girl in the village.

She didn't know it but everyone else did. That was part of her beauty. A lack of vanity existed within her caring character. Her dark brown hair fell to her waist and had a natural curl to it. She didn't have to spend nights with her hair wrapped in papers to achieve the required wave. Just the ringlets surrounding her cheekbones were created with a hot iron for special occasions. Her daily regime included brushing her hair one hundred times before bed, a discipline her mother had encouraged as soon as she could do it herself. That hard work paid off as her hair was one of her best assets. Unknown to Mary, most of her friends were jealous of her hair. Added to her crowning glory, she was fortunate to have a warm peach skin type which absorbed the sun's rays without making her burn. A natural beauty, which she had inherited from her mother, Anne. Her mother was not from around these parts. A foreigner.

Anne Cooper was French by birth. Her parents had escaped the French Revolution; servants to an émigré Marquise who had died during the Channel crossing. Arriving in England with no papers and very little money had been difficult. Her parents had picked up casual work, moving slowly from the south coast and finally ending up in Norfolk. The change in lifestyle had taken its toll on Anne's French parents. They had struggled with learning a new language and were often treated with distrust by those they met.

England was still at war with France. Rich landowning émigrés were accepted into society as the misfortunate victims of the Terror.

Commoners, like Anne's parents, were regarded with suspicion. Why would they have a need to flee from Paris? Surely it was the common people who were in charge of the Revolution? With their lack of expertise of the language of their adopted country, Anne's parents found it hard to explain their circumstances. Moving on often became the only solution. On one occasion, her father was accused of spying by a local landowner which had led to them fleeing away at night. It was this distressing event which had hastened their arrival in Norfolk. The farming community didn't ask as many questions. The couple could slip anonymously into the background to bring their only daughter up as English.

The turmoil of their early life had taken its toll on Anne's parents and they both departed this world before their time. Fortunately for their beloved daughter, she was settled before this came to pass. When Anne was 18, she met Benjamin Cooper, a farrier. Theirs was a love match and they married within the year.

Mary was their youngest child and the apple of her father's eye. Her upbringing felt like that of an only child, simply because her elder sister Victoria was ten years older and had left home when Mary was seven. Mary had grown up surrounded by love but without spoiling her nature. Her mother's strong arm was a steadying contrast to her father's favouritism. Mary was far too used to getting her own way which led to many an argument between the two women, especially as Mary started to blossom.

Unlike the other village children, Mary could speak two languages. Her French was basic but it added to the exotic image she portrayed to her peer group. It made her different. It made her special. All the children in the village wanted to be Mary's friend and the unwanted attention she received from the boys was particularly trying.

Mary wasn't interested in finding a husband just yet. She had big plans.

She dreamed of moving away from Little Yaxley and discovering the world. She would travel to London and live in a big house with servants to care for her every need. Her dreams were follies but she could dream. Her dreams came from the books she read, growing up. Stories of princes on white chargers, carrying off their true love to live happily ever after. It was a silly dream which would never come true.

In Victorian England, country girls married within the village or the surrounding area. Choice was limited and no boy had turned her head as yet, despite their extensive efforts. She struggled to see the boys in the village as anything but the annoying pests who had tormented her as a child, pulling her hair and calling her names. She had not shown any particular favour to any of the young men who came calling, so far.

Jack Whiting was the closest to piquing her interest but she was too young to think seriously about him or any other boys. He was the most grown up of her peer group; managing his own farm which had made him mature quicker than other boys. He was a handsome young man but there was something about his attitude which scared Mary. There seemed to be a hint of cruelty in his actions. He bullied many of the other young men with his arrogance and boastfulness. He took pleasure in reminding his peer group of his eligibility as a husband. But despite this, he rarely made any effort to court a girl.

What was he waiting for?

Or who?

The morning was moving on a pace as Mary rushed down the stairs, finding Mother and Father impatient to leave. Mother was shaking her head in frustration whilst Father was grinning with pride for his beautiful daughter.

"Finally. I wondered what you were doing up there," said Anne, adjusting Mary's ribbon as she surveyed her daughter. Mary was certain the ribbon was perfect but mother just had to rearrange it. "The fair will be starting soon. We don't want to be late."

"Sorry Mother." Mary's smile lit up her face as she squeezed her feet into her Sunday best boots. They would not last another winter, she thought.

Little Yaxley held a summer fair every year. Alongside the stalls selling local produce there were a number of fairground attractions for adults and youths alike, including apple bobbing, hoopla and ring toss. The centre piece was a beautifully decorated Helter Skelter which Squire Cole owned. The longest queues were always found there. Age was no barrier to having fun. The village children would split their sides laughing as they watched their parents floating down the slide on coarse sacks. The ride was short but exhilarating. Standing at the top, waiting a turn, gave the villagers the chance to see their homes from a whole new angle.

The village fair was an opportunity for friendships to be renewed as folk travelled from nearby villages to join in the fun. Anne had been brought up in a village some five miles away. A few old familiar faces would be interesting, especially if it meant catching up on a bit of gossip. It was a chance to meet old friends and make new acquaintances. For the younger villagers, there was the excitement of meeting fresh faces which may lead to new relationships.

It was at one such fair that Victoria met her future husband, Michael, which would lead to her moving away. Anne Cooper missed her eldest daughter and the distance between them was difficult to stomach. Mary had grown up knowing her mother favoured her big sister but she was not jealous of that fact. She was secure in the knowledge that her father loved her to distraction. A love which she reciprocated wholeheartedly.

She was definitely her father's girl. And always would be. It was at his knee that Mary developed the skill of winding any man around her little finger. It would be a skill which she would put to full use in the days ahead.

The fair took place just outside the village on one of the fields which was usually used for grazing sheep. The field was vast and ran alongside the main track from Little Yaxley towards the market town of Watton. Its position, just outside the village, was perfect as a meeting place and tradition ensured that the fair was a regular event, even when the weather was not clement. Today the village was fortunate. The sun shone down on the grass making it look even more lush. If it wasn't for her mother's attitude to deportment, Mary would have loved to pull off her boots and curl her toes into the soft grass.

Opposite the field was the Crown and Hare inn which had been closed for the last couple of months due to a family tragedy. The village workers were missing the chance to sup an ale on their way home each evening. Out of respect for the Cozen family, those complaints were kept behind closed doors. It did not seem appropriate to moan about the lack of beer when a family had been lost. They would just have to wait and see what happened in the future to the local inn. But secretly most residents hoped its future would be resolved as soon as possible. The men missed the joy of a pint of ale and the women missed the joy of time alone.

Richard and Elsie Cozen, who had owned the inn, ran it with their eldest son Tom, all of whom had tragically died in April from smallpox. The whole village had been petrified with fear when the rumours were found to be true that Tom had fallen ill. Especially when the rumours indicated that the dreaded disease was in their midst. The inn shut its doors as the community kept close to home. Smallpox put the fear of God into the hearts and minds of the villagers. Once it arrived it could sweep through a community, killing at will. Those who were lucky to survive would carry the scars for the rest of their lives. Fortunately for Little Yaxley, the only casualties were the Cozen family. Richard fell ill soon after his son and finally Elsie contracted the disease. The whole family was dead within a week.

Today's celebrations could be seen as being in bad taste. But not for the residents of Little Yaxley. Life was dangerous and could be cut short at any time. Life went on after tragedy. Prayers would be shared in church and mothers would hug their little ones a little more closely. That was the harsh reality of life in the Victorian countryside. Disaster could strike at any time. Accidents on farms were commonplace and the risk of illness could often lead to death.

But today was a chance for the village to come together and celebrate life.

Mary and her parents made their way amongst their many neighbours, who all seemed to arrive at the fairground field at the same time. The noise of conversations mixed with the clucking of geese and chickens. Many a prize bird would exchange hands before the day was over. Anne clutched a selection of preserves she planned to sell today. Their garden was surrounded by plum trees which provided the sweetness for both chutneys and jam.

"Mary." Emily, her best friend, ran across and grabbed hold of Mary's hand. "Quick, come and see. The inn is open again. Let's go and find out what's happening."

Emily was jigging on the spot, determined to be the first to discover who was now in charge. Her hair was tied up in bunches with pretty ribbons which swayed as the young girl shook her head with pent up excitement. She adored her friend Mary and could not wait to share the news with her.

Mary looked towards her father, knowing his permission would be more easily won over than her stricter mother's.

"Go on then girl," sighed Benjamin. He slipped a couple of pennies into her fingers. "Have a good time and don't eat too many sweets."

Benjamin smiled indulgently. He had no concerns about the girls being alone and unsupervised. Whilst strangers were rare at such an event, any new faces were watched by the regulars until they knew their backgrounds. The community looked after their own.

Mary took Emily's hand. The girls skipped across the grass taking care to avoid any animal waste. They both had their best boots on so the last thing they needed was to stand in a pile of steaming mess, especially at the start of the fair. As they skipped, Emily chattered non-stop. Mary loved her best friend dearly but she was exhausting. Emily charged through her life, packed full of energy and emotions and her constant chattering was an endearing, if not frustrating, feature of her character. At times, Mary definitely preferred silence. Being, to all intents and purposes, an only child was probably the main reason for that. She hadn't grown up in the cut and thrust of a huge family, like Emily, where you had to be loud or you didn't get your fair share of both time and of food to eat. Mary didn't understand the competition of sibling rivalry.

The door to the Crown and Hare was open, allowing the menfolk to spill out onto the front yard with their pints. The inn was a typical brick and flint building, most popular in Norfolk. The entrance at the front of the inn delivered its clients into the bar, which dominated the front of the building. The rear of the building was taken up with the household living accommodation. The front yard was small and ran alongside the track, although at the rear a large yard with various outbuildings led into an orchard, bursting with fruit hanging heavy in the summer heat.

Emily's father was nursing a beer when he spotted the girls hanging around the front gates.

"Emily, you know you can't come in here. Off you go, girl."

He was a hard man, Emily's dad George. Mary was a little frightened of him as he had a deep, growly voice so different from her own father. She also knew that he hit Emily, especially when he had too much beer. Her own father would never dream of hitting his daughter. Admittedly, Mary was not a naughty child growing up. If she did wrong her father's disappointment had a far greater impact than a raised hand. If he refused to speak to her, that became a stronger punishment. Emily had never complained to her friend about the beatings. It was the normal way of life in her family and with the number of siblings, was accepted as a way of keeping control in Emily's parents' eyes.

"Father, please. We just want to see who is in charge of the inn now. We won't come in. We will just wait out here." Emily's voice sighed as she pleaded with George.

"Girls!" he laughed. "Just want to see the new boy, is that it? Well, you will remember him. It's John Cozen. The younger brother who left here some years ago."

George had been one of the first into the bar as it opened. He had recognised John immediately, greeting him with a hearty handshake. It wasn't just a good neighbourly handshake. George was hoping for a free pint of ale from the new landlord. Not that he got it, unfortunately.

"Oh."

The disappointment in Emily's voice was noticeable. It was apparent that she had been looking forward to some fresh newcomer. Mary remembered John vaguely. He had been a tall, gangly youth when he left the village for King's Lynn. No doubt he was married with a brood of children by now.

Emily had lost interest instantly and was dragging Mary back towards the Helter Skelter. "Come on Mary. Let us have some fun." She laughed.

As they walked away, Mary did not see the eyes that watched her leave. A longing gaze observed the nubile young woman as she strolled across the field. The young man took in her comely figure, beautiful hair. He watched the way other men stopped and stared as she walked past. She seemed oblivious to the numerous glances and continued on her way with a beaming smile fixed on her face.

John Cozen stood at the door of his inn, watching the two young women.

Even though he had only just clapped eyes on Mary and not even spoken to her, John knew he had found his heart's desire. The most beautiful woman he had ever seen, strolling away across the field. The sun danced around her making a halo of her velvety hair.

Desire struck his heart, filling it with joy. He had never felt this way about a stranger. He had scoffed at the thought of love at first sight. Until now.

He must find out who she was. Because he knew who she was going to be.

His future wife.

CHAPTER THREE
SUMMER 1841

The closing hymn was sung and the congregation headed out to the welcoming sunshine.

Mary pulled on her gloves, walking beside her parents as they made their way from the church. Anne and Benjamin were greeting neighbours as Mary searched the crowd for Emily. She caught sight of her friend away across the graveyard with her mother, Edith. It was impossible to attract her attention from that distance. Shouting out across the graveyard was just not acceptable behaviour for a young lady. She would have to contain her excitement. She had been desperate to tell Emily her the news and she knew her friend would be disappointed not to be the first to know.

Mother had invited John Cozen to join them for dinner after the service.

And he wasn't married.

Emily would be green with envy that her friend had bested her in meeting the new owner of the inn. Mary was certainly not one to boast but she knew Emily would be overcome with excitement. She would be determined to find out all Mary knew before she had even had the chance to greet the man himself.

As Mary stood watching her friend, a stranger walked towards her. Stranger? Could this be John Cozen?

The world around her stopped still as she watched the man approach. He had to be the most handsome man she had ever seen. Tall, slim, with shoulder-length blond hair. His face was kind with a broad grin reaching from ear to ear. His walk was confident and he seemed oblivious to the admiring glances he was getting in all directions. The female population of the village stopped to stare at him. The men shook their heads in defeat.

Mary could feel her face redden as the blush crept into her cheeks. He could surely see her admiring him. How embarrassing. Shame was compelling her to lower her eyes. It was not decent for an unmarried woman to look so obviously at a man. Sneaking a peak under her full eyelashes, she watched him greet her parents, confirming she was right. He was the new innkeeper.

"John, welcome home," said Benjamin. He clasped the newcomer's hands between his in a gesture of peace. "I'm just so sorry it was in such dreadful circumstances. We mourn for your family. Richard was a good friend and I miss him greatly."

"Thank you, Mr Cooper. I appreciate your prayers. It was such a shock. I was not able to see them before their passing which was incredibly hard. And I am so grateful for your invitation for dinner." The men continued to clasp hands. "I know how important your friendship was to my parents. And without your invite, it would be cold cuts," he smiled. "I haven't had to cook for myself before so until I can engage some help, I will be relying on the goodwill of my neighbours."

John's smile lit up his face, making him appear even more handsome.

If that were possible.

"John, please call me Benjamin. You have met my wife Anne before, haven't you? Let me introduce you to our daughter, Mary."

Her father reached his arm around Mary's shoulders bringing her into the conversation. She could look on him now. It was surely now allowed. Her eyes drank in every detail of his beautiful face. She could feel butterflies trembling in her stomach as she tried to stop blushing. His eyes met hers and a spark ignited. Suddenly they were both unaware of her parents and the other villagers around them. They locked eyes, absorbing each other's face, committing them to memory.

Anne gulped as she observed their interaction. A secret smile touched her eyes as she realised that she had just found her future son-in-law. And what a lovely looking young man, she thought. Let's hope his character is as good as his looks. Before it became painfully obvious to everyone, Anne decided it was time to interrupt the chemistry brewing between the couple. It could wait until the privacy of their cottage.

"Come on then. Let's get back home so I can check on the meat. I'm famished."

Benjamin took his wife's arm as they walked the few paces back to their cottage. John motioned to Mary that they should follow. He couldn't touch her arm despite an overriding desire to do so. If he touched her, he would be lost. He knew it. Something had happened just now. He didn't know what it was but deep down he knew he had to make this woman his.

Mary was trembling as she walked beside him. They didn't talk. She couldn't say a word. When their eyes had met, she had felt something special. What it was, she did not know. It had started in her belly, a swarm of butterflies dancing a jig. Her legs felt like jelly and she could hear her heart banging in her chest.

She had never felt like this meeting someone before. Was this what love feels like, she wondered? No man had ever tugged at her heartstrings like that. Could he tell? Was he embarrassed with her childish behaviour? Did he see her as a child or the woman she felt she was blossoming into? Her mind whirled as she tried not to think about rejection. How would she ever deal with that? She would be devastated if he felt differently.

Please let it not be so.

Or did he feel something too? The way he looked at her had sent her emotions into a whirlwind. His smile had reached his eyes which glimmered with desire. Or was that desire? Her inexperience of love sent her into a maelstrom of confusion.

What if he didn't feel the same way?

She could not live with that. None of the boys in the village could come close to John Cozen. He had to want her as much as she wanted him.

No-one else would do now.

If she could have read John's mind, Mary would not have been disappointed. John had felt the spark and it bubbled away in his gut. He somehow knew that Mary was his future. He would take courtship slowly and carefully.

There was no way he was going to mess this up.

....

Finally, dinner was served, although Mary didn't expect to eat a thing. Her stomach had been jumping around for the last hour as her father entertained their guest. She could not sit there quietly observing the conversation between her father and John without giving herself away. And she could not have joined in. It just was not acceptable for an unmarried woman to enter a discussion without being invited. Both men had been wrapped up in their talk and didn't notice her.

So she thought.

John had been intently aware of the young woman as he tried to converse with her father. He watched every movement as she fidgeted in her chair. Her fingers played with the ribbon in her hair, slowly releasing its knot. A couple of times he missed Benjamin's question as his mind was devoted to Mary. He had to quickly guess the direction of the discussion to avoid embarrassment. Benjamin was not fooled. He watched with a wry smile as the young man in front of him tried to pretend he wasn't falling for his daughter.

Unable to bear the emotional tension any further, Mary had escaped to the kitchen with her mother to help prepare the food. Even in the kitchen there was no escape. Anne had chattered on about the qualities of the newcomer as she worked. It was as though her mother felt the need to matchmake. There was no need. Mary wasn't listening.

She was enveloped in her own little world of fantasies. She was dreaming of John Cozen and her future with him. He didn't need her mother to champion his qualities. Mary had already determined them.

Anne prepared a joint of ham with boiled potatoes and carrots alongside a rich meaty gravy, which she heaped on John's plate in recognition of his place as honoured guest. Initially there was little conversation as each of them paid deference to the tasty meal. John could not remember the last time he had enjoyed his food so much. Perhaps it had something to do with the company. He was sat opposite Mary and could watch her as she delicately cut her food and placed each morsel gently in between her lips.

It was seductive and mesmerising. The simple act of eating was driving him insane.

Eventually, Benjamin broke the silence. "John, tell us about your life in King's Lynn. Your father told me you were working in the port."

John laid his cutlery on his plate. "Yes, I think it's nearly five years since I left home. Father managed to get me an apprenticeship with a master boatman in King's Lynn harbour. I knew my future couldn't be in Little Yaxley, being a younger son, so it was good to have a chance to do something very different." Benjamin nodded, knowing the challenges faced for second sons. "It was hard manual labour, very different from pulling pints but I loved it. Being out in the sea air all day and meeting people from some very strange lands."

"Did you have lodgings in the town?" asked Anne.

"A boarding house near the harbour, so not far to walk to work." John smiled. "I was making good progress in the job, I think. My boss saw me as good worker and I oversaw a team. I just thought that would be my life. Until my parents and Tom passed." A shadow passed over his features.

"It must have been such a shock getting the news," said Anne. "It all happened so quickly. The village was desolate, both worried about your family but also worried about the risk of infection. Smallpox can decimate communities so there was a great deal of panic." Anne paused, remembering how scared she had been for her own child. "It must have been so difficult not being able to have a funeral. I want you to know that everything was done respectfully. The vicar took all required precautions but we were able to gather in the churchyard to pray for their souls. If that brings you any comfort?"

"It does, thank you Anne. I didn't get to hear of their passing until about a week later so I couldn't have made it here in time. I was then thrown into a quandary. I had to decide whether to sell the inn or come back home. I loved my life in King's Lynn but the chance to run my own business swayed my decision."

"Well, we are all so pleased that you decided to come home," replied Benjamin. "Your parents would be so very proud of you taking this on. It will be hard work on your own but there are many in the village who will be willing to help."

Mary smiled thinking that she was one of those pleased he was home. She wanted to know more about the man sitting opposite her. "John, you said you met people from all over the world. Please tell me more?" Her face beamed as she smiled across the table.

John could not forgo telling a tale. He loved to share details of his life in the big city which was so alien to country folk. It would make him a big attraction during the evenings in the bar.

"We saw boats from far flung places and often the sailors would drink in the bars with us locals. The sounds of lots of different languages would fill the room. Somehow they made themselves understood. Drinking ale is a universal language." John laughed. "The most exotic ship I ever saw was from China. That's far to the east and the people look so different to us. They traded some weird herbs and lotions which smelt horrific. But they also brought the most beautiful material. It was called silk and was being transported on to London. I wish I could have afforded a piece. But only for the very rich I'm afraid."

"Did you ever want to stow aboard and travel the world?" asked Mary.

Benjamin smiled indulgently, knowing where his daughter was going with that question. "I should tell you that Mary dreams of escaping Norfolk and travelling the world," he told their guest.

"Oh Father."

Mary blushed again. Why did her father have to embarrass her like that? John would think she was some sort of child with foolish dreams. And of course, now she had no desire at all to leave her home village. Prospects were certainly looking up. Her prince on the white charger had arrived in Little Yaxley. There was no need to seek him far and wide. Any sweeping off her feet would no longer require travel to foreign lands.

John looked her directly in the eye, sympathising with her dilemma. "I would have loved to travel the world, Mary. It would be so exciting seeing other lands and cultures. Working so close to the sea does give you a respect for nature though. I saw too many women widowed when boats sank in a foreign waters. And of course, the best things are always found close to home."

Mary sighed, understanding the secret message to his words. The atmosphere between the two young people was electric. Anne could sense the charge in the air. Benjamin would normally be oblivious to the emotional haze. He still saw Mary as his little girl and found it hard to contemplate the blossoming of a relationship right in front of him. But even he was picking up on the electricity between the two young lovers.

Conscious of the charge in the air, John changed the conversation in an attempt to throw Benjamin and Anne off the scent. It would fail to work.

"Anne, I will need to find some paid support to help me out. I'm thinking a few hours each morning to help me keep the place clean and perhaps do some cooking. Do you know of anyone in the village who may be looking for some work?"

Anne sat for a moment, thoughtful. "I am sure there will be someone, John. Let me have a think and if you are happy, I could ask around?"

"I could do it." Mary interrupted. "I could help John as well as keeping on top of my work on the stall."

Anne ran a weekly stall at the market in nearby Watton. Once Mary had completed her education, she had helped her mother preparing the produce they would sell. She would join her mother each week at the market, helping on the stall. The money they took helped to supplement the income Benjamin made at his blacksmith's forge. The family had enough money to buy the essentials and to keep Mary at home rather than put her into service. There were times when money was tight and, like most rural residents, the Coopers just about had enough, but no more than that.

Strangely, Mary had never shown any desire to take on any more work before and her parents hadn't pushed her to do so.

John looked towards Anne, waiting for her to give her blessing. The last thing he wanted to do was to come between mother and daughter. Anne looked at her husband, who nodded in silent agreement.

"If that suits you, John, I am happy for Mary to do some chores for you. Should we try two hours each morning except Sunday? She's a good worker so should be able to cook your dinner and clean for you. I am happy to take your wash in each month as part of the deal."

"Thank you, Anne. I certainly appreciate that. Should we say 2 shillings a week?" The conversation was going on without Mary's involvement. She simply observed as her salary was negotiated.

"That is very generous of you, John. Thank you. Mary can start tomorrow."

The deal was done.

Mary was floating on air with excitement. She could not wait to share the news with Emily. Her friend would combust with excitement and probably jealously. Mary would be spending every day with John and really couldn't be happier.

It would mean her days would be busier and that she would collapse into bed weary. But it would be a lovely exhaustion. She could play at being a wife and perhaps convince John that she was the one to take on that role officially.

All of a sudden, her dreams of running away to the city were dashing against the wall of desire. Staying in the village and marrying one of their own was now her ambition. Over the coming weeks she was determined to make that her mission. She was sure John felt similarly. That was half the battle won.

Now to execute the plan, before another woman set her sights on him.

CHAPTER FOUR
SUMMER 1841

Mary swallowed, desperately trying to lubricate her dry throat.

Reaching out a trembling hand, she lifted the knocker on the kitchen door. She had come round to the back yard thinking John was more likely to be there. All was quiet except for the clucking of a few skinny hens pecking in the dust. They need a good feed, Mary observed as she waited for an answer. That's a job for later. Obviously, her new employer hadn't worked with chickens before. Mary was responsible for her family's brood and was rightly proud of their egg production.

It was already mid-morning and, foolishly, Mary had thought John would be out working in the yard. No sign of him or any sound of work was coming from the house. Mary had left early and had run all the way down the main street of the village to Emily's house. The friends had managed to chat for a few minutes before Edith had dragged Emily back into the house to continue her duties. Emily was an unpaid housemaid, tied to the kitchen. She spent most of her days caring for the numerous Shephard brood. Edith seemed to produce another child every winter. Heaven knows how they all fit into the house, thought Mary.

"When I marry there will be more to my life than just children," Mary muttered as she strolled towards the inn.

As expected, Emily had been beside herself with excitement about the news. She was thrilled for Mary and could hardly contain herself. It was so typical of Emily to genuinely feel happy for her friend without a hint of jealousy. Emily was a good friend to have, Mary reflected. In recognition, Mary had promised to tell all later that day when the friends would meet for a short time before the bedtime rush in the Shephard house. Another reason why Mary didn't want a large brood. It must be exhausting.

The top half of the stable door swung open. John was naked from the chest up and his hair was dripping with water. He held a towel in his hand so it was clear what Mary had interrupted. Mary gasped, looking at the man. His torso was perfect with a fine downy matt of hair covering his breast and reaching down to his dark cotton trousers. It was as if the hair was signalling the route to the delights which lay below. Mary's eyes were fixed on the shiny buttons which held the fabric in place at the front. She couldn't look up. If she did, he would see the desire in her eyes, for sure.

She gulped noisily, trying to control the base desires she had not known were burning within her.

Mary had seen men stripped down to the waist before, but never someone this beautiful. It was common practice during harvest time for the menfolk to lose their shirts especially when the sun beamed down on their work. Women would provide the midday sustenance carrying large baskets of bread, cheese and ale across the fields. Gathering in the crops was a community effort and everyone pitched in to get the wheat or barley in before the rains. Mary had played her part, feeding the sweating men. She had never felt excited to see any of her fellow workers undressed. It hadn't stirred the feelings she was being overwhelmed with right now. These new feelings were confusing but exciting at the same time.

"Morning Mary." John worked at the lock, swinging open the bottom half of the door. "Forgive me for my state of undress. I was trying to change one of the barrels and it exploded in my face. Covered from head to toe in beer. Forgive my smell too. Come in. Come in."

John was stunned that his best laid plans for Mary's arrival had been so quickly ruined. He had been up since the crack of dawn tidying the kitchen. He had hardly unpacked his personal belongings since arriving back in the village. The place was in a state of disarray. John had been so desperate to make a good impression and then look what had happened. Sticky beer squelched under his boots as he led Mary into his home.

Unbeknown to him, he had not disappointed Mary. In fact, he had inadvertently created a wonderful first impression for Mary. She was trying hard to concentrate as John explained where everything lived in the kitchen and she knew it wasn't sticking in her brain. She would have to make do as she found her way around.

"Why don't I start by mopping the floor?" asked Mary. "You have left boot prints right the way through to the bar and if we don't get those up, this place will stink later."

John blushed then let out a guffaw of laughter. He stared at Mary as she took control. She had found the mop and bucket, filling it with warm water from the range. Ignoring her new employer, who was perched on the wooden table wiping the beer from beneath his boots, Mary set to work.

John could not help watching her as she moved with grace across the floor. Her body swayed in time with the mop in a seductive dance, entrancing him. John remained quiet, enjoying the opportunity to gaze on Mary. She really was so very beautiful.

Once the floor was sparkling, Mary turned her hand to making bread. She found it relaxing kneading the dough. Breadmaking was a skill she had learnt early on. It was also a task best completed early in the day so that fresh bread would be ready for the midday meal. The smell of cooking would bring its wonderful scent into to the home for the remainder of the working day. Mary threw the dough onto the kitchen table scattering flour around it. As she kneaded and worked the elastic dough, she hummed to herself, forgetting that John was there.

He was sat at the kitchen table watching her.

John had a long list of tasks he needed to complete including sorting out the barrel, the contents of which he continued to dry from his hair. Maybe having Mary working for him would not give him the much needed time to prepare the bar for the night ahead. She was a welcome distraction and one he couldn't ignore. He lapped up the moments together, capturing each in his memory to take out later and examine again as he lay in bed later that night.

As she worked, they talked.

Conversation flowed naturally between the couple. He talked about his life in King's Lynn. He shared more stories about the characters he worked with. John was a natural storyteller and had Mary giggling at many of his descriptions. He brought the port workings to life for her. Mary was transported to the hustle and bustle of Norfolk's famous port as John wove a thread of colour through his stories.

In turn, Mary shared the village gossip, bringing John up to date with his customers. Many of the young men who would frequent the inn after work would be old school friends of both of them. One such was Jack Whiting who had attended the village school with John many years ago. They had been close as boys but had lost touch over the years. Jack farmed Wood Farm which was just across the fields from the inn. John was excited to meet up with him to find how life had treated him. He knew that Jack's father had died some years ago and that he had full responsibility for the farm, including the care of his mother, Harriet.

Before they knew it, Mary's time with him was finished. She had the bread in the oven and a rabbit stew on the hob slowly cooking. John had bundled up a pile of laundry which Mary would take for her mother. She was reluctant to go but knew her mother would be watching the clock for her return. She departed in a rush, leaving a silence behind that spoke volumes.

John couldn't remember the last time he had enjoyed a morning as much. Mary was not only beautiful but great company. They had talked and talked. They had laughed, enjoying each other's company. They were getting to know each other's hopes and dreams for the future. Remarkably they shared many aspirations and it was clear to John that they would make a formidable team. He could imagine them making a success of the business and spending their old age sat either side of the warm range, enjoying the fruits of their labours.

As normal when it came to thinking about Mary, he was running ahead of himself, too quickly.

The thought of tomorrow morning together would get him through a busy night in the bar and a cold bed where he would toss and turn, dreaming of Mary. It had only been the briefest of encounters but he had enjoyed the morning more than he cared to contemplate. Being with Mary brought joy and excitement. He decided that moving back to Little Yaxley was probably the best decision he had made in his life to date.

Pulling himself up from the kitchen table he realised he should get back to work. He really couldn't allow his desire for this woman to affect his running of the business. He was even more determined now to make this a success and provide for Mary.

If she would have him.

CHAPTER FIVE
SUMMER 1841

Mary pushed the kitchen door open, using her buttocks, as she balanced the teacups in her hands.

"Cup of tea, John?" she called.

John had been splitting logs all morning for the winter ahead. As she spoke, he had raised the axe high above his head, bringing it down with force onto the piece of wood. The axe became embedded into the log. John lifted the axe and wood up over his head and crashed both down onto the stump he had been using. The log split cleanly into two and fell naturally into the two piles which had formed on either side of the stump.

Sweat poured from John's face through his exertion in the warm summer air. It was a job which needed doing but he had really picked the wrong day to do it, he thought. John wiped the sweat from his forehead across his shirt sleeve. That was another mistake. If it hadn't been for Mary working away in the kitchen, he would probably have removed his shirt. He was just not prepared to embarrass them both again so soon after the beer explosion episode.

"Thank you, Mary," replied John. "You are a life-saver. I'm gasping."

John perched his backside on the wooden bench which lay under the kitchen window. The bench gave an excellent view of the yard and orchard beyond. Mary joined him, handing over the steaming cup. For some time, the couple sat quietly in companionable silence. They supped their tea and watched the chickens rooting around for grain in between the flagstones. John could see the improvement in the hens' wellbeing since Mary had started working for him. They seemed to have gained weight and, judging by the number of fresh eggs available for him to break his fast, they were producing more eggs.

Something had been troubling John for some days now. Mary had volunteered to take on his housekeeping. But he could see how tired Mary was when she arrived this morning and didn't want to be the person at fault. He felt it was only right to release her from her commitment if it was too much for her.

"Mary, do you very much mind working for me alongside all your normal chores? I would hate it if you were finding it too much." John looked across at his companion, a serious expression evidenced by a frown.

Mary watched his face, trying to judge his mood. Was he not happy with her work? She had thrown herself into her duties with an enthusiasm she rarely showed at home. Her increased duties had added pressure to her day but she welcomed them, as it meant she could spend time with John every day. If she was a little more tired by nightfall then that was a burden she was happy to shoulder. The housekeeping duties were not really onerous and she loved having a kitchen to herself, without her mother watching her every move.

"Of course I don't mind, John. I'm happy to be helping. You are happy with my work, aren't you?" The last sentence was delivered with trepidation.

"You are a diamond, Mary. I honestly don't know how I would manage without you. You just looked so tired this morning and I really didn't want to be the cause of it."

Mary could not reply. She would have to lie so decided a smile would suffice. Of course John was the reason for her tired eyes. She had been awake half the night thinking about him, fantasising about him. She couldn't tell him that in case it frightened him off her completely. She was trying so hard not to come across as some love-struck fool. She was desperate for him to see her as a woman, not a silly young girl whose head had been turned by the first man who showed some interest in her.

John smiled back, a smile which reached his eyes, twinkling as he looked at the woman beside him. John could not imagine life in Little Yaxley without Mary Cooper. She had come into his world like a saviour, organising him, feeding him and keeping his home. It was almost as if her actions were designed to reveal the obvious to him. He needed a wife to care for him and support the business. And why not this lovely woman beside him?

Being honest with himself, John knew that the way he felt about Mary

Cooper was not just a business transaction. Oh, of course, life in the countryside was tough for a single man with a business to run. Arranging a suitable partner was often something agreed between families, a transaction with mutual benefits for both families. John was confident that Benjamin would support his suit. That was not arrogance but a feeling that Mary's father wanted a good man for his daughter and that he considered John Cozen to be a suitable catch for his precious child. The most important thing for John was that he wanted Mary to want him. He didn't want her to feel obliged to take on the role of his housewife rather than housekeeper.

He wanted her heart.

Mary broke the silence. "It must have been tough for you, John, since you came home. A new business to learn and a big old place like this to manage. People in the village are keen to help, you know that, don't you? We all feel sad about your parents and Tom."

Without any bidding a small tear made its way down Mary's cheek. John was struck by how adorable this woman was. She was emotional, lively and had the best sense of humour ever. She could even cry to order, he smiled.

"Thank you, Mary. I really miss my family. It was so cruel to not be able to see them before they died. I guess I haven't really had time to mourn since I came back. It has just been so full on and time to grieve hasn't really been a priority."

Mary was overcome with emotion, hearing John speak. In her little experience of life, men rarely talked about their emotional troubles. Her father left that to her mother to deal with. The lads in the village would laugh at someone's tears rather than console them. Here was a man with deep feelings who wasn't scared to share them. Mary gently took his hand and squeezed it affectionately.

"You are such a good friend, Mary Cooper," said John.

He looked deeply into her eyes, hoping that she could pick up on the strength of his feelings. The last thing he wanted to do was to scare her off. She was so young and so inexperienced. If he jumped in too fast with his big boots on, perhaps he would frighten her off. He needed to take things slowly and gently coax her forward.

He would be surprised to know that Mary was desperate for him to jump right in. She was trying her hardest to send him a sign that she was ready for romance, that she understood her own feelings and that she was falling in love with John Cozen. But a woman could never make the first move in a relationship. It just would not do. She would have to wait and follow his lead. All she could do was to remind him at every opportunity how important she was in his life. In time he would see her as more than a housekeeper and see the woman herself.

The woman who loved him.

John lent across the seat and kissed her cheek. It was the lightest of touches but it sent sparks fizzing into Mary's belly. She closed her eyes, savouring the moment. She could actually faint with delight, right at this moment.

"Oh well, better get on," cried John as he pulled himself to his feet. "These logs won't split themselves. Thank you for the tea, Mary."

As he picked up the axe, Mary continued to watch him for a while. She was in awe of his beautiful physic. He was a man in every sense of the word. Strong, powerful, and sensitive.

Shaking herself back to reality, she eased herself off the bench and headed back to the kitchen. There was much work to be done, especially if she had to show this man that he couldn't manage without her.

.

CHAPTER SIX
SEPTEMBER 1841

The harvest was in full swing.

A late summer sun had been beating down on the heads of the menfolk all morning as they sweated, driving their scythes through the ripe wheat. Harvest time was a village effort. There was normally a short window of time for the heavy heads of corn to be cut and thrashed. Each morning, eyes would turn to the clouds, willing them to stay away a bit longer. The whole village would be impacted if the harvest didn't bear fruit. It would be a tough winter for all if the crop failed.

The last week had been beautiful. Hot sunny days with a faint breeze and hardly a cloud in the sky. There were five fields to complete and the menfolk had cleared three already. As they worked, the women thrashed at the bundles, separating the wheat from the chaff. It was back-breaking work especially in the heat. Children ran between the women's legs gathering the kernels into baskets.

Whereas the men could strip down to their waist, the women were hampered by long skirts which stuck to their sweating legs. The younger women, including Mary and Emily, were less tolerant of tradition and wrapped their skirt ends into their work belts, giving some respite from the heat. They ignored the disgusted looks of their elders as they enjoyed the freedom of movement. Mary had considered donning a pair of Benjamin's breeches but realised this may be one step too far for her mother. The unfair restrictions on women were never more pronounced than in the hot summer sun as they laboured.

The youngest children rushed around the field passing out cups of water to the workers. A dangerous job, making sure they avoided the razor sharp blades as they swished through the thick crop. It didn't pay to dawdle. Many a near miss would be reward by a cuff of the hand on a child's head as they ran past. The men resented any distraction as they moved in an orchestrated dance across the vast field. Each person knew their role in this dance, designed to complete the task as soon as they possibly could.

Mary stretched skywards as the muscles in her back screamed in pain. Chaff was embedded in her hair, matting her ringlets into a complex weave. Her fingers stung from a series of small cuts, her skin irritated by the spiky shafts. It was undoubtedly the worst week of the year in Mary's opinion, but the reward would be the festivities which were planned for the weekend. It also meant not working for John all week. The loss of his one-on-one company had left her feeling bereft.

Looking across towards her mother, she spotted a couple of the older women arrive with the food platters. Trays were stacked with hot bread, fresh from the oven, and thick creamy cheese. Mary could feel her stomach grumble as it craved food. Her mouth was ablaze with anticipation at the smell of crusty bread and the need for sustenance.

The villagers dropped to the ground where they had been working as the food was passed around. Mary, keen to help, rushed to pass round platters to the men. She had an ulterior motive. John was working near the edge of the field and she headed in that direction with a wedge of bread and cheese and a flagon of ale. She had almost made it when an arm, grabbing at her, stopped her progress.

"Hello Mary, where are you off to in such a hurry?"

Jack Whiting moved in front of her blocking her path.

Jack was short and stocky with unruly, curly hair. His barrel-shaped chest was equally covered with springy, course hairs. Ruddy cheeks bore testament to his outdoor lifestyle and love of the ale. He was not an unattractive man but had an arrogance about him which was not pleasant. He liked to think he was in charge of the harvest despite him being just one of five farmers who worked the fields around Little Yaxley. His stubbornness with his fellows made him hard to like. He was tolerated rather than liked. Not that he seemed overly bothered by that. If anything, he encouraged a fear of him, to get what he wanted.

John had renewed his friendship with his school chum, the farmer, over recent weeks. They would be seen propping up the bar chatting most evenings. Jack was a frequent visitor to the Crown and Hare. The inn was left to its own devices this week as John got stuck in with the rest of the village to get the valuable corn in. Most of the village would be heavily involved with the harvest and would spend next week catching up on all other domestic chores. Mary yearned for the busyness of next week as it meant time alone with John.

Their budding friendship was a joy.

Mary smiled sweetly at Jack, hoping to avoid too much conversation. She liked Jack but right now he was the barrier between her and John Cozen. It was a distraction she didn't welcome. "Hello Jack. I was bringing John his food. I can see you have yours?" Mary nodded pointedly at the largest lump of bread resting on Jack's napkin.

Jack pulled at her arm as he slumped to the ground, bringing her with him. She settled her skirts around her as she tried to determine how to escape his unwanted attention. He was not to be pushed aside too easily.

"Just a word of warning, Mary," he started. "You are really making it a little bit obvious you know."

"What do you mean?" asked Mary with a confused expression on her face.

"You, hanging around John like a cow in calf. Mooning over the man; it really isn't seemly."

He smiled at her as he spoke but the smile did not reach his eyes. His icy stare chilled her to the core.

"That's not kind, Jack. John is a friend. And of course, I work for him. You know that."

Mary couldn't understand why Jack would be saying such nasty things. He was supposed to be John's friend and she thought he liked her too. Why would he want to interfere with their friendship? What could his motive be? In her innocence she was naive to his true intentions. It was as if he had read her mind.

"Mary, I can say this to you because I like you and I really don't want to see you hurt. John is playing with you. He's not interested. Do you really think a man of the world, like him, would be interested in a silly young girl?"

Mary gasped at the cruelty of Jack's words.

John was sending her completely different signals when it came to their friendship. Each day they would talk as she cooked. He appeared to enjoy her company and finding out that his attention was false, cut deep. Her head dropped as the joy of seeing her beau dissolved away. She had been so excited to eat her food sat with John and now that was ruined. Her lack of confidence stopped her from questioning the truth of Jack's words. Her innocent mind would not jump to the conclusion that Jack Whiting may be after her for himself. Unknown to Mary, he would do anything in his power to stop the budding romance.

"Come, girl. Stay here with me and share my food."

Jack took her hand as they sat next to each other on the freshly cut straw. Mary had no option but to comply. She looked across at John, seeing that he had been attended to by another woman from the village. Her services were no longer required. Mary sighed as she sank her teeth into the cooling crust. The joy of eating had been sucked from the day, but she was hungry. She chewed without enjoying the taste, simply making sure that she had enough sustenance for the rest of the day's work.

Jack continued to talk whilst he consumed his food. Pieces of bread fell from his mouth and nestled in the stubbly beard which covered his square chin. Mary wasn't really listening, just nodding at times to show her attention was on him.

It wasn't.

Jack was enjoying the trouble he had caused. Over the last few weeks, John had talked of nothing but Mary Cooper. Jack had to listen to his friend extolling her virtues. He didn't need to be told. He knew them. He had been planning his conquest of Mary for years and, just at the wrong time, in walks John Cozen and destroys all his plans. He had been too cautious, not wanting to frighten her off when she was so young. He had planned to approach Benjamin for permission to walk out with Mary but then John had moved back. He needed to work fast if he stood any chance of stopping this relationship in its tracks. Once John was out of the picture, he would move in and pick up the pieces.

Mary's gaze was fixed on John who was chatting to George, Emily's father. He must have sensed her eyes on him as, all of a sudden, he turned. Their eyes met across the tufts of wheat. He smiled, a grin which lit up his face. Slowly he raised his hand to wave at her.

Mary returned his smile.

It must not be true, she thought. Why is he so kind to her if he is playing games? John Cozen just didn't seem to be the type of man who would act cruelly with a maid's heart.

But then Jack knows him better than I do. They have been friends for years. Why would he say it if it wasn't true? Confusion took over as Mary tried to reconcile the man she spent nearly every day with as they worked together to prepare the inn for the evening ahead, with the man Jack Whiting was portraying.

She knew she would have to talk to John about his intentions.

I may be naïve, she thought, but I won't be anyone's fool.

CHAPTER SEVEN
SEPTEMBER 1841

A fiddle burst into life, reminding the villagers that the dancing was about to start. Its screeching tune rippled through the early evening air. Feet tapped in time with the tune and a few pairs of hands added to the crescendo of noise as they clapped along. The celebrations were set to begin.

Harvest time was over.

Huge bales of straw littered the landscape, climbing high in towering stacks. The grains of wheat had been bagged and stored. A rich treasure, which would keep everyone in bread throughout the cold months ahead. The successful harvest had produced a bumper crop. Everyone had worked hard over the last week, whether it had been as part of the team cutting the crop, thrashing to divide the grain from the straw, or supporting the workers with sustenance.

Nothing gathered would be wasted. The straw would keep sheep and cattle fed when a harsh frost covered the fields, making foraging difficult. Mattresses would be restuffed with what remained. The smell of fresh filling would pervade every house in the village as the old feisty stuffing was discarded. A ritual burning would take place soon, as a means of ridding houses of lice and bedbugs. Weary bodies would appreciate the additional softness after their labours. A good night's sleep was expected tonight after the celebrations, not just drink induced for sure.

Traditionally the whole village played a part in the harvest and the whole village would celebrate together. Many a relationship was forged at the harvest festival and tonight was no exception. John had been watching Mary as dinner had been eaten and knew the time was right for him to speak.

Over the last few weeks, he and Mary had spent more and more time together. They talked as they worked and shared so many stories. She made him laugh with some of her tales. He had grown to love her little mannerisms, her clumsiness when she bashed into furniture. She seemed to whirl through life in a dreamworld. John had decided he desperately needed to be at the centre of her dreams.

Tonight's celebrations would be the time to speak. Preparations for tonight were not just centred around John's desire to speak of his heart. The whole village had been getting ready to celebrate. Ovens had been working flat out to provide the harvest pies. As they were served, it was like a swarm of locusts had descended on the long benches of food. A few moments later, platters were covered with crumbs and nothing much else. Flagons of ale provided by the Crown and Hare inn were being passed around and a number of villagers were already showing the signs of a little too much of the strong beer. There would be a few sore heads in the morning. It would be the one morning when no-one would be reprimanded for their tardiness.

Emily grabbed Mary's hand as the young women headed for the clearing. A circle had formed, allowing the centre to serve as a dance area. Emily, never a wallflower, was first to enter the circle dragging Mary with her. The fiddle screamed as its owner picked up the pace. Someone had grabbed a barrel and they were thumping their hands on its base in time with the fiddler. The two young women lifted their feet to the beat of the drum and careered around the circle inviting others to join them.

Within minutes a group of the younger villagers were dancing, hands held in an inner circle, swaying to one side and then the other. The inner circle moved faster and faster and the sound of enthusiastic screams lit up the atmosphere. It was an expression of joy and celebration of a job well done. The outer circle was predominantly made up of mothers and young men who lacked the confidence to join the dance.

Jack was amongst them.

He was not shy. He did not lack confidence. His problem was dancing in front of him, exposing themselves to the world as future lovers, with absolutely no regard for his feelings.

He was watching John and Mary. He grimaced as he watched the young couple, who had eyes for no other. His attempt to put Mary off seemed not to have worked. He had to up his game soon or he would be beaten to the prize by his new friend. He enjoyed John's company but in the game of love there could be no friends.

Mary was his destiny. She just didn't realise it yet.

In the meantime, John had found his way to Mary's side and was clutching her hand as they twirled furiously. His face was alight with the depth of his feelings. Mary was oblivious to his gaze as she scanned her fellow revellers enjoying the celebrations. Her fingers clasped his as she laughed with delight in the dance. She was panting with the exertions and could feel perspiration running down her spine. As the music ground to a halt, Mary sighed with disappointment. The fiddler needed a break. His fingers were on fire and he deserved refreshment. The dancers took the chance to grab a swig of ale.

As the circles dispersed, spilling villagers to the makeshift bar, John pulled Mary away from the crowd. He ran towards the old barn at the edge of the field, which was only just visible in the evening gloom. Mary ran beside him, excitement building. Her head was still spinning from the twirling dance. Her feet were floating as she ran towards her future. She didn't stop to think about the consequences of being alone with John.

She trusted the man.

As they came to a halt, John turned and faced her, rubbing his hands up and down her arms in a gesture of reassurance. His eyes bore into hers with a heat which melted any fears which could have been bubbling to the surface. Slowly and deliberately, he lowered his lips to hers and very gently kissed her rosy pout. Mary's knees shuddered as she tried to steady herself. Grabbing John's shirt, not initially with passion but to prevent herself from falling. Blood rushed to her head making her dizzy with desire. Touching his chest, she could feel the heat rising from him. A faint smell of their exertions mingled, adding charge to the atmosphere.

"Oh Mary," John sighed. "You are the most beautiful girl in the world. I cannot imagine ever wanting anyone else."

He groaned as he kissed her again with a bit more force. His lips spoke of an urgency. Mary could so easily fall. Abandonment was possible.

Suddenly Mary thought about Jack's words. She pulled back, examining

John's face. She looked deeply into his eyes trying to see the honesty within his soul. John became confused and concerned. This wasn't the reaction he had expected.

"What's the matter, Mary? Have I got it wrong? I thought you liked me too?" The confusion was obvious in his stare.

Mary knew she must confront the worry which had taken over her mind in the last few days. "John, are you playing games with me?"

"What? How could you even think that?" John's voice was raised now.

"Jack told me."

"What do you mean Jack told you? Told you what?" John continued to stroke her arm as he would a frightened animal, coaxing her to relax.

"He told me that you were just messing with me and that I was making a fool of myself. That you couldn't be interested in me as I'm still a child." Mary was struggling to look John in the eye as embarrassment took over.

"Oh Mary. He's wrong. He's just jealous. Can't you see he is secretly in love with you and hates our friendship." John smiled.

"Jack loves me?" Mary grimaced. "Well, I certainly don't love him so he can get that idea out of his head."

John was laughing now watching the disgust flash across Mary's face. Her pompous answer was all he needed to hear to know where her heart truly lay. His fingers moved towards her cheek as he gently caressed her hair, wrapping it around her ear. As he did so, he stroked her lobe, sending a shiver down her spine. She was quivering with excitement.

"Mary, I love you so much. I want to spend my life with you. For ever." He kissed her again but this time her lips opened under his. Her arms wrapped around his shoulders as she fell deeply into his embrace. "Say you will be mine, Mary. Marry me."

"Yes," she whispered into his hair.

John's head moved back so he could look into her eyes. "Yes?"

"Yes, John. I love you and I want to be with you forever." She laughed at the shock in his eyes, tightening the grip on his fingers. "I will be your wife John and I'm going to make you the happiest man alive."

The couple enfolded each other in their arms, feeling their hearts beat in tandem. They knew this was the start of something special. They continued to kiss, not worrying about their absence from the party being noticed. John was careful to hold his emotions in check. She may well have agreed to be his wife, but he would not disrespect her and her family by rushing the delights of the marriage bed before he had walked her down the aisle.

Pulling back, he knew he had a responsibility to stop.

Gently he coaxed Mary back to the party. No-one had missed them as the music was playing again and most of the village was now dancing in the clearing. Mary re-joined Emily, desperate to tell her the news but knowing it was a secret to keep for her parents. For the rest of the dancing, she and John exchanged glances, following each other with their eyes.

Their happiness was private to them only. Their fellow celebrants were either too deep in their cups or too involved in their own merriment to notice any change.

Except for Jack, of course.

He groaned as he realised he may have lost the fight. Unbeknown to the lovers, Jack had followed them. He had watched as they kissed, the rage building in him.

John and Mary did not see him. They were completely oblivious to their watcher. The man who would do everything he could to stop their destiny.

For John and Mary were two souls enjoined forever.

Until death would part them.

CHAPTER EIGHT
APRIL 1875

"Mother, stir yourself." Hannah gently rubbed her mother's shoulder trying to rouse her.

Mary had slumped forward in the chair with her head resting on her chest. A most uncomfortable position but one that deep sleep had driven her towards. At her daughter's voice, the old lady started to wake. Confusion was her initial expression as she stared at Hannah, wondering where she was.

The dream had been so real in her mind. She had been back at the start when everything was new and exciting.

A time of happiness.

Hannah was knelt on the floor in front of her, gently stroking her hand. Her daughter's smile was wondrous, acting as a guide, helping her navigate her way back to reality. The mist of memories receded slowly. Her face glistened with the tracks of tears which had made their journey down her cheeks as she dreamt. Hannah touched her mother's skin, wiping away the tears.

"Are you in pain Mother?" she asked.

Hannah had taken to the duties of carer with the same dogged determination she applied to everything she had done in life so far. Daughter, housemaid, wife, and mother. All executed with a passion to do the best job possible. She thrived on praise for a job well done but not in a boastful way. It was an ingrained pride in helping others and following the shining example of her beloved older sister. It had provided Hannah with a purpose in life after they lost Sarah; a mindset Mary admired in her precious child.

Mary was fully awake now. "No. No pain."

Mary groaned as she tried out her voice. In her dream her speech was young and carefree. At 51 years, she certainly wouldn't be described as ancient. But life had been hard and the toils of time were written in her features. Her mind was no longer agile. She wandered through a fog of memories. She'd forget things which she knew frustrated Hannah. Mary was so ashamed that she added to Hannah's work because of her own forgetfulness and confusion.

Mary had become a burden over recent years. It should have been so very different.

Her decision to live with Hannah had been organised so she could help her daughter with the challenges of being married to a parish vicar. Helping Hannah with the house and children would allow her daughter to support her husband in his important mission. She had fulfilled her bargain in the first couple of years. Both women had enjoyed the company and Hannah appreciated having her mother on hand when Matthew was born. Mary was a lap for her new grandson to rest his head. Her experience of bringing seven babies into this world had supported Hannah through the early days of managing a new-born.

Soon after Gwen was born in '73, Mary suffered a mild stroke. She lost the use of her left arm which hung loosely at her side like some useless implement. It soon became impossible for her to assist and, unfortunately, Mary quickly became a burden. Hannah never complained and picked up the additional work but Mary was conscious of the added strain she was causing her daughter and her family.

It was after the stroke that her mind seemed to wander more. She spent more time in the past than having her thoughts centred in the present. Her confusion became more apparent. She knew Hannah worried about her and shared her concerns with her sibling, Tom. Mary's eldest son managed the inn now. He and his wife Jane were making a success of the business and would send Mary a cut of the profits each year. Hannah and John refused to take any money for her upkeep so her little nest egg was hidden away awaiting her demise.

She would leave the money to John after she departed this life. She knew he would invest it wisely for the good of her grandchildren. Not that it was a fortune but every penny would help pay for Matthew and Gwen's education. A vicar's stipend was meagre. Not that you would ever hear John

Greening moan.

"I was dreaming," Mary whispered. "About your father."

"Oh Mother, that must have been lovely."

Hannah smiled, encouraging her mother to continue to speak. She had been a baby when her father had been lost and she had no recollection of him. Her mother had told her that she bore a passing resemblance, which was a comfort, especially as she had not inherited any of her mother's features.

"He was a great man, your father. So handsome. So kind." The expression on Mary's face softened as she thought about John. "Things would have been so different if he hadn't left us. Sarah may still be with us." A tear burst from the side of her eye and trickled slowly down her cheek.

"Don't upset yourself Mother." Hannah pulled a chair next to Mary and reached an arm across her mother's shoulders. "What happened is in the past. Let it be now. It doesn't do any good dwelling on what happened."

Hannah's words were designed to comfort even though she didn't feel that peace herself. She had been angry for so long. Her darling husband had tried to help her forgive her step-father for his part in the death of her sister. She knew it was the Christian thing to do, but deep down in her heart, she was sure God would understand her fury. That man would rot in hell. She knew that with a certainty of faith.

Mary reached her good arm out to take Hannah's hand in hers. "You are a good girl, Hannah Greening. I don't know what I would do without you. I miss Sarah every day but you give me the comfort I need to continue."

Hannah kissed her mother's hand, resting it against her cheek. "I love you Mother. Now come. Let's get you dressed for bed. It's late. Time for sleep."

Hannah placed her arm under her mother's armpit and gently pulled to leverage the old lady from her comfy seat. Mary groaned as she slowly rose to standing. Her body was hunched with age and it seemed such a long time since she could reach up high to the sky. These days the best she could do was to keep her head up despite the pain in her shoulders.

Between them, the women shuffled across the room to the bed. Mary's bed was set against the front bay window facing east. In the early morning she could lie abed watching the morning sunrise. It was a cruel reminder of the passage of time but a blessing that she could welcome the day in peace and quiet before the household was active. Age gave the woman a chance to lie abed which she could never have imagined when she was running the inn and managing the daily routine of her household.

Mary sat heavily on the edge of the bed as Hannah helped her to undress. It distressed Mary greatly that she had to allow her daughter to change her into her nightdress. As a child, Hannah had been fiercely independent and was a fast learner, even if her mixture of outfits was often a thing of wonder. Now she was responsible for her mother's daily ablutions and she accepted that chore with grace.

She's such a good girl, thought Mary.

Once Mary was tucked within the comforting bedcovers, Hannah settled her frame on the edge of the bed, taking her mother's hand in hers.

"Try to sleep, Mother dearest," Hannah whispered.

She reached across and gently moved Mary's hair away from her brow. In a slow, soothing motion, she touched her forehead as she would her own children as they prepared for sleep. It is a strange anomaly that, as we age, we become more childlike.

"Sweet dreams."

Hannah was not to know that as she spoke, Mary was tumbling into the past. Her mind raced towards John and the excitement of their wedding day.

CHAPTER NINE
APRIL 1842

It was a marriage of love; plain for all to see.

The expression on John's face, as his future wife glided down the aisle, was a beauty to behold. His grin reached from ear to ear. There was clearly no evidence of nerves for the ceremony ahead. He spoke his words with confidence as he gazed at the vision of loveliness at his side, filled with pride that she had agreed to make him the happiest man in the world.

Mary was indeed exquisite, in the fine dress her mother had strained her eyes over. That too had been a labour of love. Benjamin and Anne Cooper's youngest daughter was indeed marrying well. John Cozen would provide for their daughter, giving her everything she could have hoped for: love, security, and a thriving business. Her parents had dug deep into their household funds to provide the best for Mary on her momentous day. Money was always in short supply but their special daughter would be a sight to behold.

The village would talk about the beautiful bride for years to come.

The dress complemented her natural skin colour and her assertive character, flaunting bold pink stripes. The bodice was cut to a point at both the front and back, nipping in to show off her tiny waist. Minute, white buttons lined the bodice to the neck, which was modestly high, emphasising her virginity. Long sleeves reached a point at her wrist with matching white buttons in a row stretching up to her elbows. The skirt was full, with a ruched bustle, which revealed a dark pink underskirt. A calico hooped petticoat gave the dress body, swaying in time with her footsteps.

In fact, Mary was floating on air with excitement.

Theirs had been a whirlwind romance. From the moment John had kissed her at the harvest festival, plans had been put in place for a spring wedding. Benjamin had given his blessing when John came asking. The relationship between her father and her future husband was delightful to witness. They bonded over their shared love for Mary. Benjamin was found many a night leaning on the bar talking to the young man he now regarded as a son. It was a relationship built on mutual respect. Benjamin filled a father-shaped hole in John's life.

The only jagged crack in Mary's brimming glass of happiness was Jack Whiting.

He was always there, hanging around on the periphery of their budding relationship. John had chosen him as his groom's man; a choice not popular with Mary, but what could she say? John and Jack had become firm friends since his return to the village. Jack was a regular in the inn. Likewise, John was always on hand to help his friend on the farm, when needed. The two men were inseparable.

Inexperienced in all areas of romance, Mary was conscious that she mustn't drive a wedge between the two men. She didn't feel confident enough in her hold over John to try and influence his friendships. John clearly did not see the looks his friend directed at his future wife. Those uncomfortable looks, which spoke of desire and jealousy.

But Mary did.

She would shudder at his gaze and tried her hardest to avoid being alone with Jack. The man just made her feel uncomfortable, especially now that she knew Jack was fond of her. Jack might well be supporting his new friend but was he developing that relationship to get close to her? Whilst Mary tried her hardest to avoid him, Jack on the other hand, tried his hardest to find time with her. It was a dance of avoidance of which Mary practised the steps to perfection.

Once the ceremony was over the happy couple left the church to the cheers of their friends and family. Rose petals greeted their stroll down the aisle as their neighbours smiled, sharing in the young couple's obvious happiness. The sun had beamed down on the pair of them as it sanctified their union.

Mary spotted Emily, beaming a smile at her across the crowds. She waved frantically at her friend with her bouquet. She would try her hardest later to make Emily the lucky recipient of her flowers. Tradition told that the first to catch the flowers would be the next bride and Emily was desperate to settle down now that her best friend had managed to catch the most eligible bachelor in the village. She had a couple of interested parties but, as ever, Emily was making hard work of choosing.

Benjamin was the first to reach their side, planting a kiss on his daughter's cheeks. Anne joined him as she congratulated her new son. The pride of her parents was plain to see. They liked John which was a bonus to the excellent station in life he would bring their youngest daughter.

"What a beautiful ceremony," exclaimed Benjamin. "I am the proudest man alive to see my daughter looking so happy. I just hope you are both as happy as your mother and I."

"Thank you, Father." John tested out the new name. After the loss of his own parents, he felt blessed to have acquired the love and support of Mary's parents. "I promise you that I will spend the rest of my life making your daughter happy."

"I never had a son," said Benjamin. "I always felt my two daughters were all a man could want. Until now. Welcoming you into our family, John, is very special to both of us. I hope you will come to look on me as your father."

Benjamin had never warmed to his older daughter's husband Michael. He was a bit of a cold fish. Fortunately, they lived some distance away so Benjamin didn't have to pretend politeness to keep the family peace. Victoria and Michael had travelled to be with them today, a fact which delighted Anne. Anne was especially close to her eldest daughter, which meant that, as night followed day, Mary was her father's favourite.

"You do me an honour, Benjamin," smiled his new son-in-law. "I couldn't wish for better." The two men shook hands. "Now we should make our way back to the inn. We have some hungry mouths to feed before I get to spend time alone with Mrs Cozen."

Mary smiled, thinking of the night ahead.

Her mother had sat her down last night to explain what to expect. Initially Mary was horrified to have the conversation with her mother. It was all too embarrassing but, on reflection, she wanted to be prepared so that she didn't disappoint her husband. She loved John with all her being and wanted to make him happy. She and Emily had speculated before about the secrets of the marriage bed. They were country girls so had a decent idea how offspring were made, although translating that into the night ahead made Mary blush.

The party adjourned to the Crown and Hare, where a wedding breakfast had been prepared. Cold meats and freshly cooked bread were passed around the guests. A whole cheese was being cut into chunks to be placed alongside spicy pickles. John was pouring flagons of ale for the men and Mary opened a bottle of fortified sherry for the ladies.

This is my home now, she thought, as she looked around the room.

It was hard to imagine that the house she had been helping to keep for months was now hers. She could make whatever changes she wanted to it, according to John. She already had plans for the kitchen, rearranging its contents. It wasn't especially required but Mary felt the need to stamp her own mark on the house. Make it hers rather than Elsie Cozen's. Mary had never seen upstairs so Jack had given her a tour of the bedrooms the other day. Previously all her household duties had been restricted to the downstairs living quarters.

John's bedroom was a large space at the front of the house. A magnificent oak bed dominated the room and a solid chest of drawers would be hers in which to keep her clothes. Tucked away under the eaves was a huge storage room which housed several personal items of John's parents. He hadn't the stomach to go through them yet. This would be a task Mary would help him with over the coming days.

Mary was excited to have control of the kitchen.

Since they had agreed to commit to each other, Mary had taken special care of her new domain. The huge black range had been polished to within an inch of its life. The copper pans gleamed and hung in regimented fashion across the fireplace, glistening in the light from the flames. Dominating the centre of the room was a large farmhouse table which evidenced the passage of time with its many cracks and marks of normal family life. Generations of Cozen children would have learnt their manners at this monstrous beast. In recent weeks, Mary had sat and contemplated filling the table with a whole bunch of their children.

She had talked to John about her desire to have a family.

Being, to all intents and purposes, an only child, she had grown up alone. Vicky had left when Mary was tiny so she had known the loneliness of a solitary childhood. Her parents had showered her with love but she missed the chance to cuddle up with a sister or brother at night. Having a fellow conspirator to play games with and get into trouble with, was something she craved as a child. That sense of disadvantage had driven Mary to want to fill her new family with a cradle of babies.

The thought of what she would have to go through to achieve that ambition had not really entered her mind. Childbirth was dangerous. Mary knew women in the community who had lost their babies or had been lost themselves during childbirth. A doctor was out of reach, financially, for most rural workers. They would rely on the local midwife, who was basically the most experienced woman but with no specific medical training. Thoughts of risk were for the future. For now, Mary was simply excited to understand the mystery of being alone with a man and to start a family of her own.

The wedding breakfast was in full swing.

The noise of conversations filled the bar area and a group of matrons had settled down in the kitchen with their knitting. The clatter of needles beat in time with the chatter of village gossip. Mary and John worked their way between the two parts of the house, entertaining their guests and ensuring everyone had a plentiful supply of drink and food. Sometimes they worked the rooms together but often they became separated as their attention was grabbed.

Stealing a few precious moments alone, Mary let herself out into the yard. Breathing in the fresh air, she surveyed her new kingdom.

The sun was setting slowly over the back yard sending out shimmers of light into the shadowy corners. The square yard was surrounded by outbuildings which housed brewing equipment and supplies. An ancient henhouse held prime position on the only area of grass which was being fought over by the mangy specimens. That was high on Mary's list of priorities. Whilst she had improved their laying skills over recent weeks, some fresh hens were needed to improve the stock going forward. Some of the older ladies were only fit for the pot.

Mary had her plans thought out. She would bring some fresh hens into the flock and move the hen house around to give the land time to recover. Animal husbandry was not top of her new husband's skills. Mary knew she could bring her expertise to the relationship. The hens she managed for her parents were expert egg-layers. Her husband would not go without a fresh egg to break his fast. She was looking forward to spoiling John with her cooking skills.

As Mary stood in the yard assessing her new domain, the door of the outside privy swung open. Jack Whiting strode out, adjusting his breeches with little consideration of who might be watching. He had no modesty. Wiping his fingers on his backside, he spotted Mary and grinned at the opportune meeting. Jack wandered over to stand next to her, leaning against the kitchen wall. Knocking his pipe on the wall, he filled the bowl with fresh baccy and struck a match.

Mary loved the smell of pipe tobacco. Her father enjoyed a pipe in the evening and the smell reminded her of sitting on her Papa's knee as he puffed away. She breathed in deeply taking the smoke into her lungs, tasting the strength of its drug in her throat. Jack continued to smoke whilst he watched Mary. She was deep in thought, he guessed, as she didn't seem interested in starting a conversation.

He watched her.

God, he groaned. She is the most delicious woman ever. Why the hell did John Cozen have to come back home? If her head hadn't been turned with his handsome looks then Jack would have won Mary. The very thought ate away at him and even more so today, watching them marry in the full gaze of the community. He had been working on impressing Mary for years, waiting for her to reach an appropriate age for marriage. But before he could go in for the kill, John Cozen strolls in and takes her from right under him.

"Are you happy Mary?" Jack broke the companionable silence.

"What a strange question to ask," replied Mary. "It's my wedding day. The happiest day of my life. You are funny Jack." She giggled as she tried to diffuse the tense emotion which seemed to be emanating from the man next to her.

"Well, you haven't known each other for long. I'm just worried that you are rushing into something. I wouldn't want to see you getting hurt."

Mary sighed deeply and loud enough for Jack to sense her frustration. "Oh Jack. Please just be happy for me. Would you? John loves me and I love him." She turned to face him, staring deeply into his eyes to add impact to her words. "We are happy together and as our friend, we appreciate your support."

Was there a hint of sarcasm buried in her words? If there was, Jack didn't seem to pick up on her meaning.

"Well, if you ever change your mind, you know I will be waiting," he smiled. The smile didn't reach his eyes and looked more like a grimace.

Mary shook her head at the bravado of the fellow. The arrogance of the man was outstanding. If it wasn't for John's regard for Jack, she would confront the situation as it was becoming more uncomfortable to deal with. But she wanted to avoid upsetting John and would keep her counsel.

Leaning across, she kissed Jack on the cheek. "Thank you for your good wishes, Jack. I must get back inside and see to my guests."

As she walked away, Jack placed his hand on his cheek feeling the warmth of her kiss. She is fooling herself; he knew that.

One day she would be his and he would enjoy those sweet kisses whenever he desired.

No matter what it takes.

CHAPTER TEN
APRIL 1842

Mary was trembling with nerves.

Or was it excitement? Or a combination of both?

Their guests had departed, leaving the young couple alone. Mary had rushed up the stairs before John, who was locking up. She realised her husband was giving her time to prepare herself for their first night together. His thoughtful kindness touched her soul. She smiled as she thought about the man she now called husband. She really couldn't believe her good fortune in winning the heart of this special man.

Mary had changed into her new nightgown. Her mother had spent hours embroidering an intricate pattern of lace onto the neck of the cotton shift. The fabric was soft and caressed her skin as she shivered with anticipation. Her breasts throbbed with excitement as the fabric delicately brushed her skin. Mary had let down her hair and was brushing its length, enjoying the comfort of her nightly ritual. It was calming the nerves as she waited for her husband to join her.

Husband.

What a wonderful word, she thought as she continued to brush. Her hair crackled with static, tingling through her fingers as she worked. As she finished, Mary divided her hair into three strands. The sheer weight of her hair was surprising. Her mother usually helped Mary to plait her locks before bed. Another thing that would change with her marriage. She would have to tend her own hair now. Perhaps she would cut her tendrils shorter to make the job easier.

"Leave it down Mary," whispered John as he entered the bedroom. Mary looked round, caught unawares by his voice. She smiled hesitantly as he joined her. "I want to see your hair. I want to touch it."

John came to sit beside her on the bed. His voice was calm and comforting as he coaxed Mary to relax. He knew she would be frightened of what lay ahead. She was an innocent and clearly had no experience of men. He had lost his virginity years ago with a dockside whore. She had coached him in the delights of the body for a few pennies.

It was an experience he was glad of now.

Tonight would set the tone for the future of their marriage. A success could lead to a beautiful union of their bodies in the years ahead. Get it wrong and his new wife would not understand the joys open to them. It was a huge responsibility which weighed heavily on his mind. Unknown to his new wife, he was equally nervous. He was determined to make Mary happy.

He would not fail her.

John took the brush from Mary. The horsehair bristles were soft to the touch. The body was made from ivory, a family heirloom passed down from Anne's French ancestry. A pretty pink flower pattern was inlaid into the base of the brush and the handle was made with twisted silver. He appreciated the workmanship as he turned it in his hand. Gently he started to sweep the brush down Mary's hair, enjoying the motion. He could see Mary relax with the rhythmic strokes. She reminded him of a frightened deer, who needed gentle coaxing to eat from his hand.

Once John was confident he had won her trust, he slowly undid the laces on his shirt, pulling it over his head. Mary reached out and touched his chest, fascinated by the curling hairs carpeting his front. Her fingers wove through the light-coloured pelt caressing his skin. John shivered with desire. He looked deeply into her eyes, leading her forward.

Not wanting to break the enjoyment, he wriggled his breeches over his hips, exposing himself. Mary gasped as she saw his size. Her knowledge of a man's secret was non-existent. She had seen animals in the fields but her mind could not imagine the shape of a man without his breeches. Mary could feel her cheeks redden with the thought of what lay ahead. Surely his manhood was too big for her. Her nervousness increased. Whatever her mother had told her, as reassurance, fled from her mind as she contemplated what lay ahead. Her mother had told her that the first time would hurt, and now she understood why.

Without breaking eye contact, John shuffled further onto the bed, easing his body to lie down. He encouraged his wife to join him. Mary curved her body into John's side and continued to touch the mat on his chest. Her fingers drew circles, slowly rotating downwards. She surprised herself with a confidence she didn't know she possessed.

John lay his hands on her waist, slowly drawing her nightdress upwards. She could feel the coldness of the night caressing her skin as her excitement built. His hands touched her skin sending a shiver up her spine. She quivered with anticipation. She felt his fingers reach for her breasts and heard his gasp as he felt the hardness of her nipples.

John groaned. "Oh wife. You are the most beautiful woman." A pause for maximum impact. "And all mine."

Mary smiled, looking deeply into his eyes. Any fears for what lay ahead washed away as she relaxed into his embrace.

....

The young couple lay entwined on the crumpled bed sheets.

They had made love slowly at first. The second time was faster and less painful for Mary. She was surprised at how lovely the experience had been. No-one could have described the emotions she had felt as her husband drew her forward to delight. John had been a considerate lover and guided her hands to touch him. A teacher of new delights and emotions.

Now they were spent, John rested his arm behind his head as he drew Mary into his side.

Mary sighed as she replayed the last hour in her mind. She was amazed at her lack of inhibitions. Laying there naked with John felt comfortable. The cold of the night air did not worry her. She glowed with a warmth generated by love for this man.

"I love you, John Cozen," she whispered, breaking the silence between them.

"I love you too, Mary Cozen," he smiled as he tested her new name. "And I promise you darling, I am going to spend the rest of my life loving you. And when I die, I will spend eternity loving you."

Mary shivered as if a stranger had just walked across her grave. "Oh, don't say that, John. I want us to grow old together with a brood of grandchildren sat around our hearth. So, you cannot die darling. You have to stay with me for ever."

John was deep in thought. He stroked his fingers in a circular motion across her breast. Life was tough and one never knew what lay ahead. His mother and father were young to go when they did. Sickness was an evil stalker, hovering around the periphery of life; waiting for a chance to snatch a human soul before its time. His poor brother hadn't managed to walk down the aisle with a beautiful woman. In his mind, John recognised a huge responsibility he had pledged to his brother that he would live life to the best of his ability. He would father children who would carry the blood of their Cozen heritage for his parents and lost brother.

Shaking his thoughts away from the negative, he kissed Mary heartily. "I guess we better have another go at making those babies then," he chuckled.

"Oh yes please," laughed Mary. "I can't think of a better way to spend the night."

CHAPTER ELEVEN
MAY 1842

The bar was heaving.

The noise reached a crescendo as a bawdy joke was met with a guffaw of laughter. Mary smiled as she looked out across the crowded room. Whilst the increased crowd made her job even more fraught, the sound of pennies dropping into the cash box made it all worthwhile. A night's takings could make all the difference to Mary's plans. She wanted to explore cider making and having some extra cash would help the couple invest in the required equipment.

It was Saturday night, which was traditionally the busiest of the week, but tonight was even more so. Squire Cole had made it known he would be at the inn that evening. That was a signal to a number of local farmers to join him for a few jugs of ale and some negotiation. Squire Cole was a key influencer in the local marketplace. Many a farmer would grumble that it was not fair that the richest landowner could determine their profits on almost every item sold, but there was nothing they could do about it. The sensible option was to have a few drinks with the culprit and try to influence his thinking. It was also common knowledge that Squire Cole was even more generous with his hospitality the longer the evening went on.

Jack Whiting was at the centre of the group, urging more and more ale down the Squire's throat. It was his jokes which were raising the tempo and the speed at which drink was being consumed. For once, Mary would not grumble about Jack Whiting. He was helping her profits so she would cut him some slack.

John squeezed behind her, pushing Mary up against the bar. His hands touched her buttocks as he swayed behind her and she could feel his excitement building. Leaning back into his chest, Mary looked up at her husband. He really was the most handsome man, she thought as her face cracked into a huge smile. He lowered his head slowly to kiss her plump lips.

"The honeymoon is not over yet then," called Benjamin who was sat at the other end of the bar.

The last few weeks had been bliss for the young couple. They spent every available moment together, working well as a team either behind the bar or maintaining the inn during the closed period. John had supported every change Mary had suggested to the décor of their living quarters. Because of that prompt agreement, she had been busy with needle and thread. When they were alone, she worked at her sewing, John would be whittling wood as he designed a new rocking chair for the kitchen.

In the evenings they were a formidable team in the inn. They were building a strong reputation as hosts, ensuring that everyone could enjoy the ale and feel comfortable in their surroundings. Having a woman's presence again behind the bar was a welcome addition to trade. They had separated the bar area so that women could spend some time together in the evenings without the difficulties of their drunken menfolk. So far there had been little interest in this option, but John was sure this was the future of barkeeping and was determined to keep trying new things.

At night the couple were enthralled with each other. Mary was a quick learner and soon grasped what John enjoyed. She was discovering her body and its needs, which John would pander to long into the night. Their lovemaking was something they looked forward to all day and, as soon as it was acceptable to close the bar, they would rush up the stairs, leaving the clean up until the morning. Once there, John would worship at her temple into the early hours. They would wake before dawn and often repeat their exertions before the thrust of the day ahead started.

John laughed at his father-in-law's comments. He slid back past Mary, coming to rest across the bar from Benjamin. The two men clasped hands in welcome. Benjamin was a late arrival that evening and had only really made the trip down to the inn to see his daughter and her new husband.

"I must thank you again for your daughter's hand," laughed John. "She is a jewel with no price tag, Father. She has made my life complete."

Benjamin could see that with his own eyes. The way the couple looked at each other. Their eyes would find each other across the crowd of heads and would lock together in unity. It was clear for anyone to see that there was something special between them. Benjamin was delighted. His Mary was incredibly special to him and the thought of another man in her life would always be hard for him to bear. But John Cozen was the right man for her. He clearly loved Mary and would cherish her. Letting go of his little girl was not as traumatic as Benjamin thought it would be. He had gained a wonderful son into the bargain.

Mary joined the two men as they chatted together. She had finished serving and a quick glance showed that everyone's cups were full.

"Father, how is mother feeling now?"

Anne Cooper had been laid up for the last few days with an injury to her ankle. She had fallen at the market recently and twisted her leg. Anne had been forced to take to her bed which was not something she was used to. Mary and John had ensured that their parents got a share of their own meal as Benjamin was lost without his wife in the kitchen.

"She is much better, darling." Benjamin reached across and squeezed his daughter's hand. "She can put weight on it now so she is back downstairs. We are most grateful to you both for helping us out. We couldn't have managed without you."

"Father, that's what family is for," grinned Mary. "You have been there for us so many times and it's our chance to pay you back."

Their conversation was broken by a loud cough. "Service," growled Jack. "What does it take for a man to get a beer round here?" Jack laughed loudly at his personal joke.

Mary was nearest to him so made her way down the bar.

"Another jug, Jack?"

Ever the perfect hostess, Mary smiled at Jack. Any awkwardness between them since the wedding had disappeared. Jack was a regular and it would not do for Mary to ignore her husband's friend. He spent money regularly and drank far more than he should but he was the perfect customer.

"Make it a large one," Jack slurred his words. The drink had obviously influenced him tonight. Unbeknown to Mary he had already made a visit to the privy to throw up, a present for her to be greeted with in the morn.

"Are you sure, Jack? You look a bit bleary-eyed." Mary whispered her remarks, knowing what a proud man Jack was. He would hate others to hear her ask that question.

"Just serve me, woman," he growled again. Jack reached across the bar, grabbing her arm. "And make it quick."

"Now, now Jack." John had made his way down the bar and had overheard his friend's words. "Don't insult my wife, mate. If you want another drink, be nice or go home."

Jack grimaced as he tried to fix a smile on his face. "My apologies Mrs Cozen. May I have another beer please?" The sarcasm dripped as he held himself upright at the bar.

"Let me do that for you," said John. "Mary, why don't you go and talk to your father?"

Mary did not hesitate and made her way back up the bar to Benjamin. She did not see Jack's eyes follow her swaying figure as she walked. Or the lecherous grin. Thankfully. Unfortunately, John did not see it either or he would probably have thrown his friend out.

"That Jack Whiting is an idiot," Mary sighed. "He doesn't seem to know when to stop. Good for my cash box but not very good for him."

Benjamin shook his head slowly as he watched the exchange between the two men at the other end of the bar. "Just watch him, Mary. I don't like the way he looks at you sometimes. He is a wrong 'un."

"I know, Father. He gives me the creeps but he is John's friend so I must be cautious. I don't want to get between them." Mary was pleased that her father had noticed Jack's unseemly interest in her.

"Well just play things careful, my love and if you want me to speak to John, I will." Benjamin considered speaking to John anyway as he had spotted the look Jack gave Mary earlier and the way he had gazed at her chest. It really wasn't acceptable, even if John was his friend.

"I will, Papa. Please don't worry. I don't want anything to spoil things at the moment. I am so very happy with John so let sleeping dogs lie, please."

Benjamin nodded in agreement.

Perhaps if he had spoken to John, he may have been able to stop what was ahead. But unfortunately, hindsight is a wonderful gift none of them could possess.

CHAPTER TWELVE
JUNE 1842

Mary was scrubbing the range.

Her fingers were raw from the wire brush as she pushed back and forth, trying to loosen the grease. It was her own fault. Her own slovenly fault. If only she had dealt with things immediately instead of dropping into bed at the first opportunity. Bed and the delights of John always won over getting ahead of herself for the next day.

Her mother and father had joined them for dinner the previous day. Mary and John had enjoyed their company so much and they talked late into the evening. Exhausted, Mary did not have the energy to tackle the range hob before bed. Added to that, the dry heat of the previous night had not been her friend. A film of toughen fat had congealed on the iron surface and was resisting her stoic efforts.

The sight of the fat seemed to be turning her stomach. It's jelly-like consistency stuck with globules attaching themselves to her brush. The smell of pig wafted into her nostrils adding to the agony. Oh no, why hadn't she tackled this job last night. She really didn't feel well this morning and that smell. It was too much.

A wave of nausea washed over her. She could feel the bile rising up her throat and she only just made it across the kitchen to the butler sink. Mary gripped hold of the ceramic sides as she emptied her stomach. Once she was done, she spat out the remaining taste from her mouth, wiping her lips on the towel. Running the water tap, she tried to rinse the dreadful taste. Her stomach continued to heave despite it now being empty.

Suddenly she realised she was not alone.

Unaware that she had been watched, Mary glanced over her shoulder, sensing a presence. Jack Whiting was hanging around the kitchen doorway. His eyes showed concern as she continued to freshen her mouth with sips of water.

"You are sick Mary," he stated the obvious.

Mary really couldn't understand why this man got under her skin so much. He was a good friend to her husband but all too often his company was unwelcome. He was the third person in their marriage. Frequently, he would arrive unannounced at their door. John, ever the gentleman, would be the perfect host and invite Jack to join them for a meal. She didn't resent John his friendship. But John didn't see the way Jack looked at her. She would catch his eye across the table on many an occasion. A look which shouldn't pass between them. Her father's warning resonated in her mind.

Jack's look spoke of longing. An unnatural longing. For a woman married to his best friend.

Jack didn't realise or even seem bothered that it was not right to crave his best friend's wife. His arrogance knew no boundaries. He would sit and stare at Mary across the kitchen table with no thought for his friend and whether it would make him uncomfortable. At times, he would sway back on the rear legs of his chair balancing his feet on the grate with that stupid grin on his face, as if to tempt an accident. Did he want to fall back so Mary could dress his wounds? Or was it just sheer confidence that the chair would do his bidding and keep him from harm.

Mary wished he would fall.

Nasty, to be sure, but it would wipe the smirk off his face. She didn't want to feel like this. She wasn't a bad person. Unfortunately, Jack brought out the worst in her nature. Mary couldn't understand why John didn't see what she was seeing. She just wanted it to stop happening and for John to stand up to the man.

But John did not see those looks. Whether he was just oblivious to the situation playing out right in front of him, it was hard to tell. Was he naïve to Jack's actions? Or did he see it and feel sorry for the man? John had won in the marriage stakes and was not one to brag. His natural goodness may prevent him from seeing the harm Jack's continual longing for another man's wife could bring to his door. He could not see the danger in Jack's glances, despite his wife's silent concerns.

Unfortunately for Mary, those glances were too real and she was becoming even more uncomfortable with them. She had thought to share her concerns with her mother but had stepped away from sharing her marriage secrets so early on in their relationship. Would her mother think she was exaggerating and perhaps fighting against sharing her husband's time with others? Maybe she was? She was so confused with the mixed messages.

Growing up was harder than she had expected.

Her father had seen it but did she want Benjamin getting involved? Would John be offended if his father-in-law spoke about such a personal matter? Mary was not prepared to take the risk. Her relationship with John was in the early stages and she didn't want anything to spoil their happiness. Despite being married, she remained a child in so many ways. She was naïve to the machinations of men.

Mary had a lot of growing up to do.

She would have to just put up with his interest. No matter how uncomfortable it made her feel. Jack's eyes would bore into her as if he could see her naked body. That desire in his eyes should not be aimed at a married woman. Jack was not unattractive and could have his pick of any of the young women in the parish. He didn't seem to be courting any of Mary's peer group despite her efforts to push Emily his way. He remained polite but cold to her efforts.

Drawing back to the present, Mary knew she should respond to Jack's question.

"I'm fine. Thank you, Jack. Must have eaten something which disagreed with my stomach. I feel fine now so please don't worry John."

Her husband was working in the outbuilding, checking on his latest brew. She was somewhat surprised that Jack had not seen him before he made his way into her domain, the kitchen. Or perhaps he had seen and found a way of getting her alone.

Another of his recent tactics.

Jack appeared to be figuring out some private thoughts before he laughed loudly, startling Mary. "Of course. I've worked it out. John has you with child." He slapped his thigh in an exaggerated fashion. "That's the reason for the sickness. Did you not realise girl?"

Mary gulped as the truth of his words hit home.

She really should have noticed the changes in her body before now. Her breasts had been sore for weeks now and she had put that down to their love-making. Her waistline had filled out somewhat. Again, she had thought it was contentment which had added some weight to her body. And her courses, she couldn't remember the last time they had visited.

She blushed, not wanting to have this conversation with her husband's best friend. Denial seemed to be the best approach. Whether Jack would believe her or not, she was not prepared to contemplate.

"Don't be silly, Jack. Do you think I wouldn't know if a baby was coming? And if I was with child, John would be the first to know." It was time to get rid of her secret admirer. "He's out back if you need him."

Mary turned her back, hoping that Jack would take the message and leave her alone. She waited some moments before she turned. He had left, thank the lord.

No time to rest, she decided. This range will not clean itself. Pulling herself together she returned to her chores. Turning her attention back to the greasy fat, her stomach continued to roll with a combination of nausea and excitement.

A baby.

A child made from their love.

Mary smiled as she touched her tummy. Inside lay a small being who would make their lives complete. She tenderly stroked her body, recognising the changes. Only now could she feel a small bump pushing out from her undershirts. That precious parcel she was carrying would bring them such joy.

Would it be a boy or a girl? Mary was desperate for a girl although she knew John would undoubtedly want a son. A boy to nurture. To take on the business when they became frail. But a daughter! A beautiful girl who would own the best features of her mother and father. Who would be, not only their daughter but, Mary's best friend. Mary smiled to herself as her mind jumped forward across time, delighting in the news.

She must talk to John tonight. The excitement of sharing her wonderful news with her husband made her grin even wider. He would be ecstatic. She could not wait to see his face when she told him he was to be a father. They had spent many a night sharing their hopes for the future, especially their need to bring a brood of young Cozens into the world. Now those dreams were becoming a reality.

The door crashed open, startling her from her thoughts.

"Mary. Is it true?" cried John. Her husband rushed across the room, coming to a slamming halt beside her. His face displayed shock and excitement in equal measures. "Are you with child?"

John gripped her fingers, gazing intently into her face. Mary smiled. Reaching out, she placed her fingers against his warm, ruddy cheek. A tear was squeezing its way from the corners of his deep blue eyes as she brushed it away with a fingertip.

"Yes, my darling husband."

The intensity of the moment between the young lovers was hard to watch for Jack Whiting. He had planned to steal the surprise of the news away from Mary, beating her by breaking it to his best friend. His intentions were totally selfish. He didn't want Mary to have that special moment. But now, watching the couple together, he realised his plan had backfired.

They were oblivious to his scheming.

John pulled Mary into his arms and kissed her resoundingly on the lips. He let out a yell of happiness as he picked Mary up and twirled her around the kitchen, all the time guffawing with delight. Mary giggled as she was carried away with his enthusiasm.

As he stopped and gently placed her feet back on the stone slabs, Mary caught sight of Jack lingering by the door. She sensed the distress on his face, in his role as voyeur. Always on the outskirts of their marriage. Watching but not involved. Sad man, she thought.

"Thank you, Jack, for sharing my news with my husband." Could he recognise the sarcasm in her voice?

John looked at her with confusion. It was unlike his wife to speak with spite. It was unbecoming of her. And the look on her face told of a deep dislike for their neighbour.

"Oh darling, don't blame Jack. He was just worried finding you being sick. He was only concerned for your welfare, darling."

Mary smiled at Jack although the smile did not reach her eyes. "Oh, sorry Jack. I'm sure your intentions were good. I was just disappointed I couldn't surprise my husband with our personal news. It is a special moment for a man and his wife to share." She paused to let her words have impact. "Perhaps you would give us some time alone now."

Again, she smiled as she dismissed their persistent visitor from her home.

Jack could do no more.

At least he realised his presence was no longer welcome. He would not overstay his visit any longer. Jack closed the door firmly behind him as he stalked across the yard. His face was a picture of fury and jealousy. His latest attempt to wreck their happiness had fallen flat. He would have to find a way to up his game.

Why could Mary not see that her future lay with him and not the innkeeper? Soon she would learn that life with Jack Whiting would be so much more fulfilling.

Until she did, he would watch and wait.

CHAPTER THIRTEEN
JUNE 1842
LATER THAT DAY

John held her hand as they strolled away from the village down the track, well-trodden by their customers to the inn.

They had just left Mary's parents' house after sharing their happy news. As expected, Anne and Benjamin were delighted to find that they were to be grandparents again. Benjamin had pummelled John's hand as he shook it feverishly, trying to hide the tears which were welling in his eyes. Anne had held her daughter a little bit more tightly than usual, cradling her tenderly. Mary was overwhelmed by the happiness their news had heaped on her parents.

It was nice for John and Mary to get away and have some time on their own for a change. Their life always seemed to be filled with others. Evenings were shared with the village, as the inn became packed with thirsty workers. It was only when they fell exhausted into bed that the young lovers had time for themselves. And then conversation was not on their minds. Tonight was one of those precious evenings when they could be alone and talk.

John had arranged for Will to tend the bar for the evening. Will was always keen to take on extra responsibility since John had offered him work behind the bar of the Crown and Hare. He was learning the trade with a view to making a move to Norwich in the years ahead. Work was hard to find in rural Norfolk without a trade, and second sons often had to find their own path away from the village of their birth. Will would be no exception.

The reality would be that one of John's children would take on the running of the inn so Will would need to strike his own path. In the meantime, John would provide him with the training and skills which would give him a head start in life. John understood the challenges of being a second son and could see many of his characteristics in Will. He was happy to take him under his wing and support him. When the time came, he had contacts he could use to give Will a push up the ladder.

The sun was slowly retreating for the day as the couple strolled. It kissed the horizon before bidding farewell to the day. The sticky heat of the day was cooling, causing Mary to pull her shawl around her shoulders, grateful for its protection. Grassy banks ran on both sides of the track, teaming with wildflowers, which were starting to close their petals for the night.

"You have made me so very happy, Mary," said John as he gently swung her arm in time with his own. With childlike antics, they co-ordinated their arms' and legs' strides with each other, giggling as they occasionally missed a step. "I cannot believe that I will soon be a father. All my dreams have come true."

John was an emotional man.

He was not frightened to share his feelings with his wife. Unusual for country folk where men traditionally had been brought up to be strong and powerful. Emotion was a woman's weakness. To Mary's delight, her husband was not a typical countryman. From the start, he had filled her world with love and affection. It was rare for him to raise his voice to her and if she ever upset him, it would not take long for them to dissolve into laughter. So many men in the village were renowned for laying their fists on their wife or children while in their cups. Emily was an example of that. She was accustomed to her father punching her when the mood was with him. Edith, her mother, could not protect her children from his anger. It was something the family just got used to. The older children had come to accept the cycle of domestic violence and tried to shield the littlest ones from the worst of it. Mary was fortunate that both Benjamin and now John were different. Kind men who valued their womenfolk.

"I should have known sooner. I felt different the last few weeks but never dreamt I could get with child so soon."

Mary was still puzzled as to how she had missed all the signs which had been screaming at her. She had been so overwhelmed with the wonderful changes in her life that the missed courses had not been noticed. The changes to her body had passed her by in the bliss of their lovemaking.

"Do you feel well now, Mary my love? If you need some help then I am sure we can stretch the pennies to get a girl in from the village."

Mary squeezed his fingers, grateful for the attention. "Honestly, I felt wonderful all afternoon. It was just the smell of the pig fat which turned my stomach this morning. I feel tired but I am quite well, husband."

They continued to walk, enjoying the quietness of the evening. Across their path a barn owl swooped, chasing its prey. They stopped to watch the magnificent bird flying across the fields in search of field mice. The owl's wingspan was impressive as it glided with minimal effort. Suddenly it dived into the wheat, grabbing a small rodent with its vice-like beak. With its prize won, the owl was away to enjoy the feast.

"John, there is something." Mary stopped walking and turned to face her lover. "I was really upset that I couldn't tell you my news." She paused waiting for John to realise the seriousness of her thoughts. "Jack walked in on me when I was being sick. It was only then that I realised what was happening to me. Why did he have to spoil things by telling you?"

She had said it now. And was happy that she had found the courage to do so.

"It didn't spoil anything, Mary. He was just concerned that you were ill. He didn't really tell me. I guessed when he said you were being sick."

For God's sake, John was defending the man again which frustrated Mary. Why can he not see the ulterior motive of that man? Was he truly blind to Jack's motives? Mary adored her husband but he had a weakness within him. He was too trusting. He thought every other man had the same principles and values as him. Jack Whiting took advantage of his good nature and John just could not see it. Or would not see it.

"You are a kind man John Cozen. But sometimes too kind. Jack is trouble. I wish you could see it." Mary stopped walking as she stared deeply into her husband's face, willing him to believe her.

"Oh Mary. Stop it please." John looked angry now. "Jack is my friend and he has been so good to us. I don't know why you dislike him so much."

"He is jealous of us. Why can't you see that, John?" Mary stamped her boot down heavily on the ground in frustration.

"Now you are being silly," replied John. "I won't have you bad-mouthing my best friend. He just wants to help and you are so ungrateful. It's not a becoming trait, wife."

Mary should have seen the warning signs.

John was getting redder in the face as his anger grew. She had the chance to step away from the conversation but her foolish pride wouldn't let her. She had started this discussion and was determined that John should hear her out.

"I don't like him, John. And it's not right the way he looks at me when you are not watching. It's just not proper."

John dropped her hand and turned his back as he tried to collect his thoughts. "Mary, let it rest. You don't want to turn into a scold, do you?" Those last words spat from his mouth.

Mary gasped with shock. John had never spoken to her so harshly before. Tonight, they should be celebrating their precious news not bickering like this. Jack Whiting had a lot to answer for. Coming between a man and wife on the most special day of their married life so far.

"But John."

Mary started to speak as John turned to face her again with a look of disgust. Too late. Her husband had clearly had enough. His patience had fled.

"Mary. No more. Please. I think we should forget our walk and head back to the inn."

John turned and started to walk back down the track. Mary trailed behind him, watching his strong back which appeared stiff with frustration.

It was their first ever argument and Mary felt devastated.

She had no experience of how to recover the situation. All her life she had been the apple of her father's eye and had managed to change his bad humours with a smile. But John was angry and had turned away from her. It was clear that he did not want to continue this conversation.

Moments before they had been basking in the late evening sunshine and enjoying the fruits of their happiness. And now, because of Jack Whiting, her husband was angry with her. He actually called her a scold. How dare he?

Well, if that's what he thinks I am, she thought, then perhaps that's what I will be. He can forget about an embrace in bed tonight. He can have my cold back. And if he wants friendship then at least he had Jack Whiting.

Mary was still very immature. Her simplistic mindset propelled her along a path towards conflict.

She had always been given her own way by her indulgent parents so had no experience in the art of compromise. She was livid that John had not listened to her distress and agreed to stop Jack's behaviour. She had no experience of negotiating her way through the marriage bargain. There was a time to win an argument and other times when it might be best to step away gracefully.

Tonight, was one such time.

She had spoilt their celebratory evening together by bringing Jack Whiting into an argument. She should have chosen her opportunity to talk with better judgement. They had been rejoicing in such wonderful news and now the moment was spoiled.

In her mind it was Jack's fault not hers. And John should have seen that rather than blame her.

Mary flounced back towards the inn, striding past John, ignoring his shocked face.

John sighed as he watched her go. Having never had a sister, the workings of the female mind were a mystery to him. His wife could go from pleasure to moody within seconds. Perhaps it was the changes in her body which were responsible for the mood swings. Probably best to leave her to it for now, he thought.

"I may as well go and clear up the bar then," John sighed as he headed

CHAPTER FOURTEEN
JULY 1842

The last month had been hell for Mary.

She had been suffering more and more with sickness. Traditionally, being with child could lead to a morning illness but, for Mary, she experienced nausea all day and would vomit on a regular basis. She could cope with feeling so rotten as she was doing an important task, making a new life. It was an accepted downside to the joy of bring life to their new family.

The hell was a self-inflicted kind. Mary and John were at odds. Since that night when they had argued, neither of them would back down. John was angry that Mary had tried to come between him and his oldest friend. He knew it was wrong to remain ill-tempered for long and if Mary had shown some kindness to him, it would have been long forgotten. Unfortunately, they were both stubborn and their first disagreement had festered.

Mary knew she was behaving like a spoilt child but her pride would not let her admit her fault. In her mind, John was wrong. He put his friendship with Jack Whiting above his love for his wife. She didn't expect him to choose his friend over her but she did expect that he took her complaints seriously. Her upbringing had not helped the current situation. Benjamin had spoilt her throughout her childhood, much to Anne's frustration. Normally if she sulked for long enough, others would bend to her will.

John wouldn't.

Mary did not know how to make things better with John. She had tried crying herself to sleep at night but that had been met with a cold shoulder. She didn't know that John's heart was breaking as he listened to his wife cry in the silent, dark night. He wanted to comfort her but stupid pride stopped him. Mary had tried ignoring him during the daylight hours, but that was impossible when they lived and worked together. All too often they would verbally swipe at each other.

Mary's father had noticed the struggle between his beloved daughter and her stubborn husband. He had wanted to talk to John and try to smooth a pathway to reconciliation. But his wife's counsel rang furiously in his ears. One must not get between a man and his wife. You would not be thanked for it. He held his peace and hoped that the couple would find their way back to each other.

John was hard at work in the brew house, finding solace in routine. He missed spending time with Mary and wished he knew how to stop the current strife. He was shocked to find out how spoilt Mary was but secretly he loved her even more for it. She was a feisty woman. She was far too used to getting her own way. He could not dominate her and that reality was almost seductive. But how to break this cycle of moodiness and anger?

Mary had spent the morning at the market helping Anne. She had enjoyed a morning of sunshine and good company. With conversation between her and John being stilted, it was nice to talk to her mother. She had been keen to share knowledge about childbed, which both excited and scared Mary at the same time.

Having left her mother's house, Mary was walking slowly along the lane to the inn. She was delaying her return, not wanting another afternoon of quiet and sulking behaviour. It was in her hands to do something about that but how? Deep in thought, she didn't see Jack Whiting sat astride his horse, lingering at the edge of the wheat field.

"Mary, well met."

Jack jumped down from his mare's back. An experienced horseman, Jack often rode without a saddle. His short, muscular legs were all he needed to control the old mare. He strolled over to Mary, blocking her path. His face cracked with a cheeky grin, pleased with himself to have come across Mary by chance.

"Jack," replied Mary. She avoided his glances, trying to figure how she could escape his attention.

"Are you well, Mary?" Jack had positioned himself so that she could no longer avoid his stare. "John tells me you have been suffering with the babe recently."

Mary sighed at further evidence of this man interfering in her marriage. Why was he so concerned about her welfare? It really was none of his business.

"I am faring better, thank you Jack," she replied. "And I would ask that you keep your nose out of my business. I know you and John are friends but what goes on between husband and wife is private."

"Why so bitter, Mary. You do not realise what a friend I am to you. One day you will need me so I suggest you find a more civil tongue."

Jack grinned at his own humour. It was not reciprocated. Mary's previous happy mood was turning sour.

Quickly.

"Jack, just go away. You have caused enough trouble between me and John. I honestly don't need your support. If you stayed out of our business we would get along fine."

Mary started to sidestep him, wanting to get away. His smug face was irritating her now.

"If it wasn't for me then your perfect husband would have been tupping a whore last week when we were in Norwich." Jack leered in her face. "I reminded him of his husbandly duties and how upset you would be if you found out. You can thank me for interfering in your wonderful marriage. You are obviously not satisfying your husband if he is looking at common whores."

His words were like a kick to her stomach and Mary gasped. How could John betray her like that even if he did not do the deed? Just thinking about him being unfaithful to her was beyond her imagination. Yes, they had not slept together properly since their argument but she would never think that he would hurt her deliberately.

"Liar," she spat the word at Jack. "I don't believe you. Just keep out of my marriage. You are not welcome in my home." Mary pushed past Jack and strode off down the lane.

Jack watched her go, his hands on his hips. He laughed, a nasty sound, as he delighted in causing even more strife. One day Mary would see that he had her best interests in his heart. Then she would come begging him to adore her. Until then, he would watch and wait.

Mary was shaking with distress as she rushed home. He must be lying, she thought. John would not do that. He loved her and, despite their quarrels, their marriage was strong.

Or was it?

She must not let this frostiness between her and John continue. For the first time in her life, Mary realised that her principles were not as important as her love for John. She had to fix it and quickly before the damage Jack Whiting was orchestrating bore fruit.

Forgetting her stupid pride, she decided she would make good her relationship with John. Tonight, she would make love to John. He would never again look at a whore.

Jack had done her a favour.

He may well have been trying to stir up trouble between the couple but his words had been the kick up the backside she needed to grow up. Marriage was difficult at times. Living together as man and wife needed compromise and conversation. Unfortunately, she was realising that men did not like to back down.

Her mother had actually indicated that today as they chatted. Benjamin was like John in so many ways. Kind, gentle souls with a stubborn streak. Anne had explained to Mary, earlier, that the greater good came when a woman backed down and admitted her fault, even if she didn't believe it was true. Her man would grab hold of the chance to end the conflict so in the end the woman won. She would orchestrated the end of conflict without her man being aware of her machinations.

Well Mary was capable of playing games.

If she could get what she wanted.

CHAPTER FIFTEEN
JULY 1842
LATER THAT EVENING

Mary was waiting for John to close up for the night.

It had been a busy evening in the inn. Plans for the harvest were being discussed and the noise of numerous conversations and the chink of beer bottles had given Mary a screaming headache. She had excused herself early and slipped out to the kitchen for some respite. Drawing the water from the huge saucepan resting on the range, Mary filled the tin bathtub. She had locked the back door, conscious that Jack was in the bar tonight. It would not be beyond reason to find him sneaking into the kitchen to find her undressed.

Once the bath was brimming with warm water, she pulled off her dress and underclothes and sank deep into its comforting waves. Bathing was a luxury which was reserved for special occasions. The simple act of warming enough water to make a bath worthwhile was a huge task. Tonight was a special occasion. Mary had decided that this argument with her husband had to end. She could not lose the love of this man over a petty disagreement.

Jack's words had vibrated in her head all afternoon.

Whether it was true or not was unimportant. John was unhappy enough to have talked to her sworn enemy. She was sure that Jack would have done nothing to champion her cause. If he had stopped her husband from partaking of the services of a woman of the night, then he had provided her with a timely reminder that her marriage was worth saving. And if he had lied, then he had given her the kick up the butt to realise she needed to make the first move. John was never likely to back down. His stubbornness would stop him.

Slipping down further into the tub, Mary dunked her hair under the water. With the soap she lathered her curls, tugging her fingers through the knots. Rinsing, she continued to work at the ends of her long hair, teasing it like a comb. The weight of her locks pulled her head backwards. Mary rubbed at her neck, easing the tension of the last few weeks. As she washed her body, she observed the changes. Her breasts had grown and were sore to the touch. Her nipples seemed larger than normal and hardened as she touched herself. The most noticeable change was her belly. A small mound was visible, protecting the precious baby.

Mary lay back in the tub, tipping her hair over the side to dry. The open fire was raging and giving off its heat towards her luscious locks. Her hands stroked her belly, enjoying the feel of her baby mound. Suddenly she felt a twinge. It was as if a butterfly was trapped in her belly, fluttering its wings against her fingers. The movement continued as Mary stroked. She smiled as she realised what she was feeling. The baby had quickened. A tear snaked from her eyes as she fell in love with this new human being, growing within her.

She was so engrossed that she did not hear her husband enter the kitchen. John stood at the door watching his wife. She truly was the most beautiful woman, he thought, as he watched her cupping her belly. She was confident in her body as she lay there, wallowing in the enjoyment of her bath. If only he could join her, he thought.

Mary became aware of company and smiled across at her husband.

"John, quickly give me your hand." Mary grabbed at his fingers, thrusting his palm to touch her belly. "The baby is moving. Can you feel it?"

Her face was alight with delight as she moved his palm to catch the movement. John's expression was one of wonder as he felt the fluttering of his firstborn. He locked eyes with Mary as they shared a secret moment.

"Oh Mary. I can. I can feel movement," cried John. "He is a strong boy, I can tell." John leaned over and kissed Mary resoundingly on her plump lips. "I love you, Mary Cozen, I do."

"I am sorry I upset you, John. I really don't want to argue anymore. Please?" Mary started to cry as she looked deeply into her husband's eyes. "Please can we be friends again?"

John pulled her into his arms, not caring that his shirt was getting wet from her bath. "Oh Mary. I don't want us to fall out. You are my wife and I love you so much. Come."

Gently he supported her as she stood up. He wrapped her as he would a child in the large towelling robe. Swinging her into his arms, he carried her up the stairs to their bed, laying her gently on the covers. He continued to kiss her as he rubbed her dry. The rubbing become more erotic as they both became reacquainted with each other's bodies.

Reconciliation almost made the argument worthwhile.

They had found their way back, despite the efforts of Jack Whiting.

He was forgotten as they took their pleasure.

CHAPTER SIXTEEN
MAY 1875

Spring sunshine danced across the lawn bringing twinkling warmth to the day.

Mary held court in the centre of the garden under the oak tree. She was sat in her chair surveying her adopted kingdom. The tree's leafy awning gave shade from the midday sun, resembling a regal canopy. John Greening had carried her out to the garden this morning and placed her lovingly in the wicker chair. He was a good man and an even better husband to her daughter. As he had placed her with care into the seat, she had reached out and touched his cheek. The simple action spoke far greater than words.

Her son-in-law was so like her own John. Their shared name was apt. A kind man who was made for the church. He certainly brought comfort to his flock. An unassuming man who never seemed to lose his temper. Calm and thoughtful when dealing with his flock or his growing family. Not many men would take on their tetchy mother-in-law, who could disrupt his family peace.

Despite those challenges, Mary could not remember hearing harsh words between Hannah and John. It wasn't that they were lacking in passion. Theirs was a marriage built on mutual respect and trust. Their discourse was frank at times but they would navigate a way to agreement rather than let bad temper get in the way.

Hannah had a more mature attitude to marriage than Mary had had at that age. Looking back, Mary knew that her childish nature had caused many of the early difficulties her and John had faced. She was so used to being the centre of the world and adored by those closest to her. It took her too long to grow up and put John and her children in that place instead. Those harsh lessons would also bear consequences.

Despite those early troubles in her own marriage, Mary could see similarities between her daughter's relationship with her vicar husband and her own with John Cozen. She and John did argue and at times those disagreements had the volume of a tornado touching down in the inn. But the passion they showed was just an example of their love for each other. Theirs had been a strong partnership. Without that snake, Jack, hanging around the periphery of their life, everything would have been perfect.

Over recent weeks she had spent more time in the past than the present. She kept thinking about the early days of her life with John. She drew comfort from mulling over the past and remembering that her life had been full.

Once.

The joy of discovering each other and making their family had filled their early days of marriage. She remembered the love between them which seemed to get stronger with time. How she wished they had grown old together. How different things would have been. Sarah would still be with her. Sarah would have married, had children, been happy. It all changed when she lost John. Why did he have to go and leave her alone to face the future?

"Nanna." Matthew interrupted her thoughts.

The little boy was grabbing at her skirts as he pulled himself on to her ample lap. Matthew was a confident child. At four years of age, he had grown into his first breeches. Brown worsted cloth which gathered at his kneecaps as the shorts met long woolly socks. A matching jacket was buttoned down the front and tucked firmly into his breeches. His lovely curls were squashed into a sailor's cap which was a favourite present from his Uncle Jack.

Mary smiled as she thought of her youngest son. Jack had joined the army as soon as he reached conscription age. He had wanted to travel the world even as a young boy, like an itch which had consumed him from an early age. The army had given him that opportunity. When he had come home, on leave, a year ago he had brought this cap for little Matty.

To his personal chagrin, his mother had admonished him when she found out its origins but what could she do? He was an adult now and unfortunately too like his father. The sailor's cap had been won in a late-night brawl in Gibraltar. Jack had been keen to tell his mother that he had won the fight. Something she had no doubt about. He was short and stocky like the father he was named after. Fighting came naturally to him.

The hardest part of being a mother was knowing when to let them go. Jack was the one of her brood whom she was glad to see stretch his wings and fly the nest. He had been born at the time of her worst troubles. Instead of being a comfort to her during her time of loss, Jack was a burden. He had been a sickly child and demanded attention. Mary was lost at that time and found his dependency on her overwhelming. Having banished his father from the family home, she had to take on the role of both mother and father.

It had been a difficult time and baby Jack had to make do. Perhaps that was why he had a restless nature and could not wait for the chance to leave the family home. Perhaps he realised he wasn't wanted and just served as a reminder of all that had been wrong in the Whiting family. Had he not been wanted? Mary knew the truth and felt guilt-ridden over her dislike for her last child born during her troubles. It was wrong to blame the child for the sins of the father. Another thing of which she was deeply ashamed.

Mary was surprised back to the present day as her grandchild grabbed at her finger, twisting it back. A pain shot up her arm as she gasped with surprise. Matthew meant no harm. He wanted his Nanna's attention and had found a way to get it.

"Nanna, wake up." Matthew's serious face stared deeply into her hazy gaze.

Mary smiled down at her grandchild and pulled him in for a cuddle. Her ample breast became a comfy pillow for the child to rest his curls. "I'm not sleeping child. I was just thinking about your Uncle Jack. You remember him, don't you?"

"Ummm Nanna. My cap."

Matthew pulled the cap from his hair as his curls tumbled down his cheeks. Mary decided she must talk to Hannah about cutting his locks. Now Matthew was growing rapidly, it was time to rid him of the long hair. Soon he would attend school and she would hate her favourite grandson to be bullied for his girlish curls. She tousled her fingers through the strands, enjoying the feel. She leant down and breathed in, enjoying the smell of soap.

"Yes, darling boy. Your Uncle Jack brought you the cap last time he visited, didn't he?"

Matthew looked intently at Mary as he remembered the young man who had given so much excitement during his visit. The children were delighted having someone new to play with. Jack was happy to play the fool and roll about on the floor with his niece and nephew. His leave was short but he filled the days with his family before heading back on duty. Mary had been shocked at the man he had become. He had left home as a boy and returned a strapping man, with a mouth from the sewers. Poor John Greening had grimaced with the utterances from Jack's mouth, but ever the peace-keeper, had kept his own counsel.

"Nanna, Mumma told me to bring this to you." Matthew clutched a letter in his sweaty paws. He wafted it in Mary's face.

Mary immediately recognised the writing. Her son Tom was a good correspondent and she looked forward to his missives. She ripped at the seal in eagerness.

Matthew realised all too soon that his grandmother was no longer interested in his attention. He slipped gently down the folds in her skirt landing soundly on his bottom. Using her skirts to pull himself up, he tottered off across the garden in search of his mother. Perhaps he would get more attention from her.

Mary devoured the letter from her eldest son. Tom and his wife Jane had taken charge of the inn and were making a success of it. Jane was expecting their first child hence Mary's desire to read his news. Perhaps there was good tidings to share.

"Dearest Ma, Jane has been delivered of a son this last week. He is a healthy young boy and has a hearty cry. Jane is recovering from her travail well and is delighted to be a mother. I never imagined how wonderful it would be to become a father. I didn't have the best role model in Jack Whiting as you well know. The moment I held William in my arms I knew that I would protect him with my life. We have called him William John for Jane's father and mine. I trust you will approve.

In other news, Jack is getting worse. He sleeps most of the morning and relies on Arthur to manage the farm. Not that Arthur complains. I think he likes being in charge and sees his father as a hindrance. Jack's drinking is getting unmanageable. I have tried to refuse him but he just makes such a scene that it is easier to let him drink himself into a stupor. In better news, Anne and Emma are both working hard and send their good wishes. As soon as we are able to travel, I will bring Jane and William to see you. My love to you mother, your son Tom."

Mary smiled as she imagined the joy Jane and Tom would be experiencing. Another grandchild. A blessing to the family. Mary knew her days were coming to a close but she took comfort in knowing that her children were providing a legacy for both her and her beloved John. Her blood would go on through her offspring. When she was cold in the grave, they would remember her and she would live on in their hearts.

The news about her estranged husband, Jack, was not a surprise. His mind must be troubled with the pain he had caused. It serves him right that his only respite from the pain is when he is drunk. Should she see him again before the end? That dilemma had been worrying Mary for weeks now. She had been married to the man and perhaps she should make her peace before they both met their maker. A decision would need to be made.

Soon.

But now was a time of celebration. Another child entering the world. Another grandchild to add to her brood. Her grandchild would be the legacy by which she would be judged. She was excited to share Tom and Jane's blessing with Hannah.

The wonderful news got her thinking about the past again. The happiest day in her life was the birth of her first child.

My beautiful Sarah.

Gone but not forgotten.

Sighing deeply her mind wandered.

The fog lifting to reveal the past with a clarity of mind.

CHAPTER SEVENTEEN
15TH DAY OF JANUARY 1843

Mary pushed herself up from the kitchen table.

It was a struggle now she was so huge. She was uncomfortable with her cumbersome shape, which could have filled her with revulsion, if it were not for the precious life within. Her baby was lying low in her belly, making movement slow and ponderous. The weight of the baby was lying across her bladder, which added to the challenge of sleeping. At night when Mary lay down, the cheeky mound would heave and sway as the baby tried to flex its limbs.

John loved to watch the baby's movement, staggered by the sight, and intrigued that his child would soon be born. He would place his hands on the mound, communicating with his first born with some sort of telepathic language. They had named the baby, Mound, in fun but also conscious of the risks entailed in childbed. Too many babies did not make it, so deciding on possible baby names felt a risk too far. John would stroke her belly as the baby moved under his touch. It was as if the child was reaching out to its father already.

Mary did not even want to contemplate the upcoming birth.

This beast of a child would need to be expelled from her body. The workings of childbirth were a mystery, which frightened her. Her mother would be at her side throughout the procedure, but Mary remained naïve as to what lay ahead. She struggled to understand how her private parts could stretch to allow the baby passage. Pushing those thoughts to the back of her mind had been her comfort position in the last month when the baby appeared to double in size, squeezing on all her organs and making the simplest tasks difficult.

Not long now though. Soon it would be over and she hoped to have the joy of holding her babe in her arms.

Mary waddled across to the sink clutching her cup and saucer. An early morning cup of tea seemed to be the one thing which stopped the burning acid in her throat. Drawing water from the hob she filled the sink and started to clean up from the morning meal. John was busy cleaning the bar area and she could hear him whistling a tune. She smiled as she listened to the joy in his voice as he broke into song. He was oblivious to anyone else and, no doubt, thought she couldn't hear his gravelly sound. He was enjoying the feel of his deep tenor voice as he scrubbed the floor behind the bar.

The last few months had been good.

Their reconciliation had brought them joy through the early winter months. Snow had been falling for the last week and the biting wind had kept folk within doors. Mary and John had delighted in time together as the pace of life had slowed down. The inn was not as busy at night as the community decided the cold walk to the Crown and Hare was not desirable. When the inn was quiet, John would shut the doors early and the couple would cuddle up in bed with extra blankets to fight off the chill.

On those evenings, they would talk about the future and their plans. John was a hard worker and determined to make their business a success. His own special brew was getting a reputation as a fine beer. He had orders from other establishments in the area and was looking to diversify the business. If he could supply other inns, as well as his own, then he would take a bigger share of the profits which would make life more comfortable. This expansion would safeguard any downturn in their inn's performance which, whilst John wanted to think would always be consistent, was dependent on the wealth of the village. In fallow years, the menfolk would find it difficult to spend their hard earned pennies on beer.

Life had become slow since the snow started to fall.

There was no urgency in tasks during the short daylight hours. This had suited Mary as she struggled to move with any semblance of speed since the Christmas festivities. Luckily for the young couple, Anne and Benjamin had been delighted to host the Christmas dinner. John had built a huge sledge which he had adapted with a large cushion and furs to pull his wife along the path to the village. Mary had felt like Queen Victoria herself, waving to her subjects as she was transported in style to her parents' cottage. The sound of Benjamin's laughter as he watched his daughter and son-in-law could be heard around the village.

A frown flashed across Mary's face as she felt a weird twinge in her belly. She had been used to tightening pains across her belly in the last few days but this felt different. She had back pain all night but again this felt different. She placed her hands on the mound and could feel it taut to her touch. All of a sudden, a grinding pain made its way down her back, resting at the base of her spine. That was definitely a different level of pain. Mary gasped at the immediate onslaught of discomfort. It felt like her whole body was pushing downwards and the weight between her legs became unbearable. Wetness started to dribble down her legs and Mary pulled frantically at her skirts, hoping not to see blood.

Her waters had broken. The mound was about to become a baby. Panic was her first thought. I don't want to do this now, she thought. The next pain was coming as Mary screamed. She could hear John stop singing and in moments he was at her side. The concern was written across his face.

"It's coming, John. The baby," she gasped. "Get Mother please."

John gently encouraged her across the room to the huge rocking chair. The chair he had made with love over recent months. Movement was slow as the pain washed over her body. Easing down onto the seat, she gingerly rested her swollen birth canal on an old, tattered cushion. The waters continued to flow, slopping over her skirts as she rocked in time with the contractions.

"Go John. Quickly."

Mary was struggling to speak as she watched her husband grab an overcoat and run out of the kitchen door. She knew it would take some time for Anne to arrive and for the midwife to be found. Her mother had told her that first babies take their time but this one didn't seem to be taking it slowly. The weight between her legs felt urgent. Perhaps the ache in her back last night was the start. She had felt uncomfortable then but this was overwhelming.

She could not do this alone.

Mary was frightened now. In truth she was petrified. What if John didn't get back in time? How could she bring their precious bundle into the world without help? Would she die here all alone? Taking slow, deep breaths between the pains, Mary tried really hard to stay calm. She started to count between each pain. Her mother had told her that as birth got closer, the time between the pains got smaller.

"One and two and three and four and five and six and seven and eight and nine and ten, ooh."

Mary gasped as the pain built up again in a wave. As it hit the peak and started to ease off, she blew out through her cheeks expelling the energy. The next wave was coming.

"One and two and three and four and five. Ooh no that's too soon."

Mary gripped the arms of the rocking chair. She tried to clench her buttocks together holding the baby inside her. Sweat was pouring down her face despite the chill in the air. Tears were forming at the edge of her eyes as she started to shake with fear.

The door burst open.

Her mother and Jack Whiting flew in, discharging piles of snow onto the floor. It's strange that despite being frightened at the speed of this birth, Mary could only think of the work she would need to do to clear the mess from the kitchen. The floor was swimming with the precious baby liquid and now snow was leaving footprints all over her pristine flagstones.

"Where's John?" Mary cried.

Why was Jack Whiting standing gawping at her when it was her husband's soothing face she was desperate for?

"He's coming, darling girl," replied Anne Cooper. "He's collecting Old Ma Spence. He's got the sledge so won't be long. I came across Jack on his way here so asked for his help. Now Jack, can you carry Mary up the stairs for me?"

The indignity of Jack Whiting picking her up, conscious of the wet skirts and the baby's protective liquid which was seeping around her was too much. She did not have the strength to fight it though. She was not giving birth on the kitchen floor, so if it meant Jack Whiting holding her then that was a price she had to be willing to pay.

Jack levered his hands under her back and legs, pulling her into his arms. He held her a little too close to his chest and her cheek rested against his jerkin. She could hear the sound of his heart beating loudly. It was surprisingly soothing. Mary felt ashamed that she was drawing comfort from his touch.

It was wrong.

But it felt good to be held. His manly presence eased her anxiety, almost forgetting the travails ahead.

Jack was a strong man and made short work of carrying her bulky form up the steep stairs. He kicked open the bedroom door and waited for Anne to arrive. Anne had grabbed the birthing sheet and rushed to cover the bed sheets before Jack laid Mary, with care, onto the bed. He maintained eye contact with her the whole time, as he stared deeply into her pained expression.

It was too intimate a moment.

Not appropriate at all as Mary prepared to give birth to his best friend's child. But Mary drew comfort from his gaze and sighed deeply. Jack nodded, reassuring her that everything would be fine. For a moment the pain was pushed to the back of Mary's mind as she sensed Jack's encouragement. He smiled warmly at Mary and planted a delicate kiss on her forehead. Mary felt calmer in his company. Everything would be fine, his eyes reassured the fearful woman.

The inappropriate moment was shattered by Anne.

"Now Jack, make yourself scarce. This is woman's work now. There is water on the hob. Make sure it's boiling and pour me a jug. Then when John gets back, bring Ma up here as this baby is coming now." She nodded at her daughter, confirming her fears. "And keep John away. Give him a drink and keep him occupied. I'm not looking after you men at the same time." Anne laughed to lighten the tension in the room.

Strangely, as Jack left the room, Mary felt his loss. His arms had given her comfort and his leaving bothered her more than it should. Shaking her head, she tried to clear her thoughts away from Jack Whiting.

Mary suddenly had an overwhelming need to push this baby out. She gripped her mother's hands as she pulled her legs up to her belly, feeling the baby's head bearing down. Old Ma Spence blustered into the room carrying the water jug and hissing at John who had tried to follow.

"Get away, young man," she cackled. "This baby will be born soon. Peace. You can see it in time."

The midwife was short and rotund. Her grey hair was tied up in a scarf with a few tendrils escaping to brush her cheek. A bulbous, black mole sat prominently on her right cheek with one huge, black hair protruding from its centre. Despite the pain, Mary was transfixed on the midwife's countenance. Her face may be the one of the ugliest things ever seen, but the kindness which shone out from the old midwife's visage was just what was needed to settle a first mother's nerves. Old Ma Spence was renowned for her years of experience and had been the first face each member of the community had seen for the last 40 years. The old lady remembered when she had brought Mary Cooper into this world and now, she would bring her child into it too.

Life coming around full circle.

Pushing Mary's skirts aside, the midwife took control, observing the head which was pushing its way forward. Applying goose fat to her hands, Old Ma stroked gently around the crown, easing the pathway for the new-born. The baby was making a fast entry into the world and would wait for no-one.

"Now girl, push. When the next pain starts, I want you to bear down into your bottom." Old Ma looked directly at Mary, reassuring her with a silent nod of the head. "Push with everything you have girl and we will have this babe in your arms before you know it."

The pain reached a crescendo of grinding heat. Mary screamed as she pushed with all her might. She could feel her skin start to tear as the baby made its way into the world. Her body was consumed by pain. It was her beginning, middle and end. Somewhere in her inner core she found the courage to continue to inflict this all-consuming pain.

Her head told her to give in.

Run away.

Her heart told her to continue her work.

At the point where Mary thought she could not take any more, she felt a slippery wetness expelled from her body. Mary collapsed back, taking huge gulps of air as the pain started to recede. Old Ma bent to examine the child and started to rub its feet, stimulating life. The cry of a new-born baby is a wonderful thing to hear.

The newly arrived babe screamed at the top of its lungs, clearly not enjoying the cold of this January day. Mary could not help crying now as she heard the first noises of her baby. It meant all that hard work was worthwhile. The baby was alive. Something not every mother was lucky to hear.

"A girl." Old Ma smiled at mother and grandmother. "Mary, you have a perfect baby girl. She is beautiful."

Within moments the baby was wrapped and in Mary's arms.

Mary gazed at her child in wonder.

Every mother must think it, but she really is perfect, thought Mary. Tiny rosebud lips which snuffled as the baby tried to find her mother's nipple. A fine, downy head of chestnut hair which was sticky with birth blood. Mary pulled at the towelling robe so she could examine fingers and toes. All perfect. Tiny little nails at the end of tiny wrinkly fingers.

Perfect.

The pain was forgotten.

Truly she was sore in every part of her body but it was a delightful soreness. She ignored Old Ma and Anne as they cleaned away the afterbirth and washed Mary down. Mary had eyes only for her daughter. As her companions rushed around completing the necessary traditions post birth, Mary just lay with the babe in arms and delighted in those few quiet moments before she had to share her daughter with the world.

This was love at first sight. The miracle of new life, and one so very precious.

"Oh, my darling daughter," sighed Mary. "You are so very dear to me. I am going to protect you for the rest of my life." She stroked the baby's head as she committed her life to supporting this precious bundle.

Unfortunately, she was not to know this was one promise she would break.

And Jack Whiting, who was no doubt down in the bar toasting the baby's birth with her husband, would be the reason she would break that heartfelt promise.

CHAPTER EIGHTEEN
15TH DAY OF JANUARY 1843
LATER THAT NIGHT

John looked in wonder at his beautiful wife and their darling daughter.

They were lying in bed. Mary was nestled into his shoulder. In turn, Sarah Cozen lay at her mother's breast, sleeping. Sarah was making the most delightful noises as she dreamt. Her tiny lips moved constantly as if she was talking to her parents. Little snuffly sighs burst from her lips as she dozed. The expression of concentration on her forehead showed an intensity of mind in one so young.

At that very moment, John knew with certainty that his daughter was destined for greatness.

Whilst Mary had been working hard to bring their child into this world, John had been going out of his mind with worry. The mysteries of childbirth were rightly hidden from men but John knew enough to concern him. So many women were lost during the travail and he honestly couldn't live with the idea of losing Mary. If it was a choice between Mary and the baby, he had no doubts about his decision. To his shame, he could not reveal his thoughts to his wife.

John had paced the kitchen floor.

Jack had joked he would make tracks on the stone flags with his continual movement. He couldn't have relaxed as his ears strained to catch any sounds from above. He had tried to settle his mind with a draft of rum, but even the blessed relief of alcohol could not ease his worry. He and Mary had only been married for such a short time. The thought of losing her held an irrational prominence in his mind. Despite Jack trying to play down the seriousness of the situation, John was convinced that his luck would run out soon. He had found happiness in his wife, business and home.

Was he too lucky?

Meanwhile, Jack had been sat at the kitchen table with a pint of beer, seemingly without a care in the world. Unbeknown to his friend, Jack shared his worries. His lust for Mary had never waned even though she carried his friend's child. Jack had watched Mary fill out with child and his desire for her just increased. He could not take his eyes from her impressive breasts which strained against her dresses. Despite her huge size, she remained the comeliest woman in his mind. Many a night he lay in his bed thinking of her body and taking personal relief from those desires.

When he had picked her up to take her up to the childbed, he had been overcome with desire. The sense of the woman was overpowering. He still had the scent of her in his nostrils and his body betrayed his wants. Shuffling his breeches under the wooden table, he had coughed to disguise his sudden loss of control. He could not allow John to see what he had spent so long hiding from his friend.

John was crashing up the stairs as soon as he heard the baby cries. His entry remained blocked by the women as they finished their business. He paced the landing irritated by the delay until his wife's guardians gave in. Once Mary had been made ready, he was allowed to meet his daughter for the first time.

John was not embarrassed to admit he had cried. The wonder of seeing the output of their lovemaking punched him deep in his stomach. When the baby had been passed into his arms, the fear of dropping her had him paralysed. Seeing his nervousness, his mother-in-law had placed her arms around him, coaxing his confidence. Standing with his daughter in his arms and tears tracking down his face was a sight that Mary would never forget.

Now they were alone.

Anne had left for the evening with Jack escorting both her and the midwife back to the village. The young couple could enjoy those first hours with their babe. John kissed Mary on her hair, drinking in the smell of his wife.

"She is delightful, our daughter," he sighed.

Mary glanced up at her husband, smiling. "She is beautiful. But don't get too excited. You may not think her delightful when she screams you awake in the night."

John could not imagine ever feeling anything but love for the little bundle of joy. However, the reality of a baby's needs had not entered his thinking yet. He was still in ecstasy with his child and could see no wrong.

"My only regret, my love, is that my mother and father did not get to meet Sarah. Mother would have adored her."

He squeezed Mary a little tighter as he thought about his recent loss.

"Sarah will live on in their name. I don't think I had ever thought about it that way before husband. Our children are our family legacy. They will live on after we are dust. Our memories will live on in their dreams."

"My darling, that is the most wonderful comfort. You are such a clever girl," he grinned. "Not only can you give me such an amazing present but you give me joy and comfort at the same time. I am truly the luckiest of all men."

John gently caressed his daughter's face with his little finger. She really was the most beautiful of babies. Before becoming a father, John had little interest in little 'uns. They were an inconvenience and a noise most of the time. Now he had his own daughter, the wonder of new life had captured his imagination. Staring at the precious bundle, his mind rushed ahead, thinking of the future before her. She would grow into a woman as beautiful as her mother. She would find love and happiness and produce children of her own. Mary's words resonated in his head. His daughter was the future.

He would live on in her blood, no matter what the future held for him.

John was even more determined than ever to make the business a success. The inn was the future, for the family. He would provide his wife and daughter with security and money for the nicer things in life. No doubt all new fathers experienced the same drive and determination to do the right thing but, for John, this was a promise to himself. One he would not break.

And perhaps someday soon a son.

The weight on his shoulder seemed heavier all of a sudden and he glanced at Mary. She was asleep, exhausted after the travails of the day. Baby Sarah was asleep too. Gently he withdrew his body as he took the babe into his arms. Mary naturally collapsed onto the pillows surrounding her. John could not sleep. He was too excited and relieved to rest. Holding his daughter in his arms, he went down the stairs and walked the ground floor. Silently he showed his sleeping daughter around their home, whispering his hopes and dreams for the future.

For the first time in his life, John understood the depth of responsibility which came with the birth of a child. This little bundle was dependent on him to care for her, provide for her and keep the family safe from harm. He made a solemn vow to love Sarah for ever. To protect her from evil. And to watch over her as she grew up.

In those moments the future looked promising.

John was not to know that his hopes would be dashed in the years ahead.

His aspirations for his first born would be destroyed by the man he regarded as his best friend.

CHAPTER NINETEEN
APRIL 1843

Boiling hot water splashed the sides of the laundry bucket as Mary tipped out the contents of the copper kettle.

It was a breezy spring day with fluffy clouds racing across the huge sky. The location of the Crown and Hare, surrounded by fields, allowed Mary to see the weather approaching. A huge benefit when washing needed to be done. For as far as the eye could see, the sky held a promise of warmth and wind, a perfect recipe. An opportunity which had to be grabbed with both hands, especially now there was a baby in the house.

Mary could not quite believe the amount of washing one baby created. Alongside the soiled napkins which had been soaking in another bucket, there was a selection of baby clothes and bib cloths which all smelt of drying mother's milk. Sentimentally, Mary would sniff at her daughter's cloths, absorbing the memory deep into her brain. Life was tough and children were grown before their time. Mary was determined to savour every last drop of her precious child's first months.

Sarah was sleeping in her basket, away under the oak tree, while her mother completed her chores. Washing outside was ideal as it allowed Mary to keep a watch over her sleeping child, whilst the balmy spring day added a lift to spirits. It had been hard to get Sarah outside recently and the benefits of fresh air for a small child was something Mary's mother had instilled in her. Let baby enjoy the sunshine and she will grow big and strong, Anne Cooper would preach. It had been a long, hard winter, harder than any she remembered before. The harsh winter had been both tough for the village as a whole, but rewarding for the new parents.

For many months they had been confined in the inn with very little contact with the outside world. Takings were decimated as the village hunkered down against the swirling snowstorms and icy freezes. John's foresight to build the brewing business had kept them afloat during such a challenging period. At least two of the village's elder residents had slipped into eternal sleep during this deep chill. To the distress of their families, the churchyard was frozen solid so their burials had to wait until the great thaw spread across the land.

Mary had missed the support of her parents who had been reluctant to risk the icy path to the inn. A slip could have serious consequences and, despite Mary's disappointment, she would not allow her parents to take their lives in their hands to visit their new grandchild. During the worst of the weather, John and Mary had the joy of getting to know their daughter. Never again would they have the opportunity to centre their world around this tiny human being. All too soon the business of life would get in the way.

They took full advantage of the lull in activity.

John would spend every spare moment lying on the floor with Sarah, gazing at her in awe. He loved to play with her little toes, reciting rhymes as he tickled her feet. He would tell stories of magnificent beasts and enchanting fairies, bring them to life with silly voices. Sarah could not understand but she would watch her father with her soulful eyes. He clapped with joy when she gave her first giggle, despite Mary being sure it was just wind. This was a man in love with his offspring and Mary, for one, was not going to burst his happiness bubble.

Mary had been able to heal from the trauma of birth without being hurried back to daily household chores. With no visitors, the couple were relaxed enough to let the house become untidy. Mary could spend many a daylight hour lying in bed with Sarah at her breast, enjoying the sensation. She avidly took in every aspect of her daughter's face and noticed the small, daily changes as she blossomed. Every mother believes their child is beautiful. Mary was sure hers was the comeliest ever.

Heaving the soiled bucket over to the drain, Mary tipped its putrid contents away, holding back the napkins. She tipped those into the steaming, sudsy water and started to attack them with the washing paddle. Back and forth she smacked, building up speed and trying not to slop the suds across the yard. She had soon built up a sweat as she put all her energy into making the linen spotless. She could feel the sweat dribbling down her back as she worked. Her precious daughter would always have clean napkins. No one would find her sluttish in this household chore.

Once washed, Mary passed the clothes through the wooden mangle, squeezing every last bit of liquid over the cobbles. The fabric would dry quickly upon the washing line in this clement weather.

Suddenly a heartrending wail resounded around the yard. Sarah was awake and looking for food. Mary could feel her breasts bursting with milk at the sound of her daughter's cries. The sensation was similar to a tap being opened. One cry from Sarah and the milk would flow. She knew only too well that she would need to break from her task to see to her child's needs before she was in a mess too.

Sarah lay rigid in her basket with fists punching the air as her lungs screamed in distress. How can a baby go from sleep to screaming so quickly, thought Mary as she drew her skirts around her and wedged her back against the old oak tree? Tucking her feet so she was crossed-legged, she settled her skirt in a pool between her thighs, adding this as a cushion to rest the screaming infant. Sarah clawed at her mother's breast as Mary positioned her daughter in her arms.

Breathing a sigh of relief, Mary felt the child's lips clamp onto her nipple and then there was silence. The first few pulls sent twinges of pain through Mary's chest, but once Sarah was established, her mother could lie back under the leafy branches and take a few moments of contemplation. Her eyes closed as she and the babe's breathing moved in time with each other. A snatched moment of peace, so precious as Sarah demanded more and more of her time. The long, slow days of winter seemed a distant memory now that the world was opening up to spring.

Across the yard, Jack Whiting stood silent.

John was expecting him as they had planned to shoot pigeons that afternoon. As Jack had wandered into the yard, he had spotted Mary feeding the baby. The sight was beautiful to behold. Not in a sexual way, he admitted to himself. Mary was fully exposed, with her right breast engorged in the baby's mouth. Its little fingers clasped at a tendril of Mary's hair which hung down from her serene face. It was a picture of the bond between mother and child.

The two things missing from Jack's life.

Oh yes, he could marry if he wanted. There were many girls in the village who would take him to their bed. But he wasn't interested in them. The one girl he wanted was out of reach. His desire for Mary was an itch he could not scratch. She was John's and would always be.

It didn't stop him dreaming though.

Or was it a nightmare he drove himself mad with each night. Even now, standing in the yard, he was tormenting himself with the sight of her beauty. He berated himself that he hadn't caught Mary before John returned to the village. Once her head had been turned by the handsome John Cozen, he had known his chances of winning Mary had gone. His lack of confidence at winning his heart's desire was a source of continued disappointment.

Or was it just bad timing?

John was his best friend and he enjoyed his company. They regularly shot together, enjoying time out in the fields keeping down the pest numbers. John would help Jack on the farm, as was the way in rural life, and clearly seemed to enjoy the work. Jack decided that if John hadn't owned the inn, he would have made an excellent farmer. Not that a swop in livelihoods would work for the two mates. Jack would be the first to admit that he would drink the profits of the inn and no mistake.

Despite their friendship, there were times when Jack hated John. He hated the fact that John could lie in bed with Mary every night. He could hold her in his arms and love her. The closest Jack had got to holding Mary was the night Sarah was born. Even in the midst of childbed, the woman he loved was driving him mad with desire. The smell of her in his arms made him forget she was about to give birth to another man's child.

He hated John for that.

John didn't even appreciate what a jewel he had. When they were alone together, he would moan about Mary's little ways. Her habits, which irritated her husband, were well known to Jack. Jack vowed that if he ever won the hand of Mary, he would forgive her anything. He would cherish her for ever.

He could be a better husband to Mary than that fool who was married to her.

The jealous thoughts whirled around his brain as he watched Mary.

She was oblivious to his presence. Mary was delighting in a precious moment of peace. If she had noticed Jack watching, she would have been angry with him. She always seemed to be angry with him. He knew that and accepted the risk.

But he couldn't leave.

He couldn't move.

He just stood and stared.

And fantasised that one day she would be his.

He had no idea how, but he was convinced it would happen.

One day.

CHAPTER TWENTY
SUMMER 1848

John eased back in his chair with a satisfying groan, as he filled his pipe with tobacco.

"That was a lovely meal, Mary. Thank you." He smiled across the oak table at his wife.

Mary was busily wiping the mess from Sarah's face before she allowed her wriggling daughter to escape from her chair. Sarah was five years old now and growing into a very determined young girl. She was the apple of her father's eye and, in his opinion, couldn't do anything wrong. Mary felt she was always the nasty one for driving discipline into her first born. It frustrated Mary that teaching her daughter essential manners was a duty falling heavily on her shoulders alone.

It was a case of history repeating itself.

Mary had always known how to wind Benjamin around her little finger. It fell to Anne Cooper to try and manage her daughter's behaviour. As a small child, Mary had disliked her mother intensely at times when she saw her as the spoiler of all fun. Rolling forward through the years, it was now Mary who scolded her daughter for wrongdoings and John was seen as the saviour of all Sarah's troubles. Mary resented John for letting that fall on her shoulders. Was it really resentment or just pure jealousy? She had thought that having a daughter would have resulted in a bond of friendship with a mini version of herself. The reality was oh so different.

But she couldn't stay angry with John for very long. He only had to look at her with love and she would forgive him anything. She loved watching the relationship between father and daughter. It was a joy to behold, even if she could admit to being a little bit jealous. The couple had been married for six years now and were still very much in love. The little touches and gentle smiles were a feature of every day spent together. Of course, they had down days when they bickered, but nothing is ever perfect.

It had been a shock that another child had not followed as night follows day. It was not through want of trying. John had never blamed her for her failure to quicken. To their distress, Mary had miscarried twice in the last few years, both happening before the baby had moved in her belly. Each miscarriage had sent Mary into a period of real desolation. It took her months to perk up again, despite John's valiant efforts. Once the worst of Mary's despair was over, they would try again.

Finally, they were blessed with the arrival of a son, Tom.

Now three months old, Tom was the perfect baby. So different to his big sister. He slept through the night within a few weeks, to the delight of his parents. He cried only when hungry and once he had had his fill, would sleep again. Mary was not even sure they had seen the colour of his eyes in the first few weeks of life as he slept, ate, and slept again. But she would never complain. He was a precious gift after the pain of loss. She had given up hope of building their family. In the early days, Mary and John had planned a huge family. The reality of losing a baby before life had fully become, created a deep hurt for the young couple.

Sarah adored her baby brother.

She would follow her mother around the kitchen as Mary nursed Tom, watching her mother's every move. She was his protector, checking his mother did not drop the precious cargo. Mary would smile as she watched the concern on Sarah's little face as she changed his napkin. The little girl's detailed examination of Mary's actions was a result of Sarah's care for her new brother. This would continue as Tom grew. His big sister was the first person Tom walked for and, once he was able, he would follow Sarah everywhere. She would have a huge amount of patience with her little brother and would never seem to be bothered if he irritated her with his incessant questions.

Because of her fascination with Tom, Sarah had baulked at starting school so soon after the baby was born. She was reluctant to be parted from her brother. The schoolmaster had agreed to take the eldest Cozen child as soon as the Easter festivities were over. It was a blessing for Mary who would have the mornings to herself and her new baby, without the usual raft of inquisitive questions from Sarah. The cost of a penny a week for her education would be a penny well spent.

Her daughter was ripe for school.

She had an active imagination and a mind which was keen to learn information and facts. On her return from school each dinnertime, she would regale her mother with stories learnt at the knee of her much-admired teacher. She would chatter non-stop until her mother's head ached. Sarah wanted to know the answer to everything, with her favourite question being 'Why?'.

Mary lacked book learning. She had done what she needed to as she completed her studies when a child, but her flighty nature had not been conducive to retaining knowledge gained. She left the inn's books to John who was good with his numbers. Her daughter's endless questions were a real challenge for Mary. She felt her daughter would soon surpass her mother's ability to answer the questions posed.

Sarah finally managed to escape Mary's handkerchief and launched herself into her father's generous lap. She squirmed around like a squirrel in its nest until she had found the most comfortable position and then stuck her thumb into her mouth. Sucking away, she twirled her fingers around her hair, quickly creating a knot. John recognised the motion, knowing she would soon drift off after the exertions of the morning. He stroked her hair as she snuggled into his chest. John had been busy all morning so his daughter's cuddling gave him an excuse to rest awhile.

Business was booming for John.

His brewing operation was in demand which had allowed him to formally take on a couple of apprentices from the village, Will and Harry, who helped with the bottling and preparing the inn for evening opening. Will had been on hand to help out in the past so it felt good to have him on the payroll. It was a bonus to have a couple of young lads around the inn, meaning that John could spend the time he wanted planning for the future. Harry was too young to work the bar at night but that was not a problem. Will could be called upon to help on the busiest nights. Mary and John worked well together and had found a way of balancing the children and the demands of the bar. Having the chance to sit quietly together during the day was recompense for the demands of the evening service.

Once the children were in bed, the couple made a great team, serving beer and building an atmosphere of welcoming conversation which was valued far and wide around the countryside. The Crown and Hare had a reputation for good, tasty beer at a reasonable price. The landlord and his wife were known to keep a firm rein on behaviour. John would not stand for fighting when men were in their cups. He was an imposing figure and customers were sure not to get on his wrong side.

Suddenly the kitchen door burst open, banging against the wall. Sarah woke with a start and the baby started to wail. Emily, Mary's childhood friend, gasped as she tried to get her breath. She had obviously run from the village. Why the haste?

"Mary, come quick," she cried. "It's your father. There's been a terrible accident."

Shock was the first reaction as both adults tried to make sense of Emily's garbled narrative. It appeared that Benjamin had been kicked by an angry horse whilst shoeing it. Her father had suffered severe injuries. His life was in danger and, in her desperation, Anne had sent for her daughter. Grabbing her cloak, Mary looked across at John who was consoling their daughter. Sarah was crying loudly. Sarah adored her grandpa and was old enough to understand something dreadful had happened.

"Go Mary," said John. "I will watch the babies."

Without a backward glance, Mary ran at speed to the village. Emily struggled to keep up as their clogs sparked on the path as they ran. Mary's heart was racing. It felt like it would simply burst from her chest. Her father was an expert with the horses he worked with and never underestimated the power of the animals, especially when they were distressed. She could not believe the nightmare which was happening.

Before long, they arrived at the Cooper's home. A small crowd was hanging around the front door and murmurs of consolation greeted Mary as she pushed her way through. Conscious of their good wishes, Mary attempted to smile despite a sickness settling heavily in her stomach. She was dreading what lay ahead.

Her father was lying on the settle in the front room with her mother knelt beside him. The colour had drained from his face. He was ashen and lines of pain were fixed on his brow. As Mary stood at the open doorway watching her father draw in breath, she was shocked to hear the gasp at each attempt. He was struggling to do the most basic task required for life.

Doctor Green hustled in from the kitchen with a bowl of steaming water and gently moved Anne Cooper to one side. The doctor carefully peeled away Benjamin's shirt. Both women cried out at the sight. A huge bruise was forming across his chest. The skin around it was broken in places and faint dribbles of blood navigated their way down his sides. The shape of the horseshoe was clearly visible. The horse had connected with his chest around the centre of his ribcage.

Doctor Green continued his examination, listening to Benjamin's lungs and gently feeling his way around the site of impact. At each touch, the patient cried out with pain. His head thrashed from side to side as he became more distressed. The doctor tried his hardest to keep him still as it was clear that movement was making the pain worse.

Once he had made his initial assessment, Doctor Green pulled Anne to her feet and ushered her and Mary into the kitchen. The news did not look good, judging by the expression on the kindly doctor's face.

"Anne, you need to prepare yourself," he started. "Benjamin's injuries are severe. He has cracked a number of ribs and one of them has probably punctured his lung. That's why he is struggling to breathe."

"Is he going to be alright?" gasped Mary. Her mother was obviously struggling to comprehend the doctor's words.

Doctor Green slowly shook his head and his whole body seemed to have slumped inwards. "I'm so sorry, Mary. There is nothing more I can do other than to make your father comfortable. I will give him something for the pain. It will make him sleepy and hopefully ease his suffering."

Anne started to sob and fell into her daughter's arms. Mary gently rubbed her mother's back as she tried to take in what the physician was telling her. Her wonderful father was going to lose his fight for life. They were going to lose him far too soon. She was not ready to let him go.

"How long?" she whispered.

"I don't think he will see the morning, Mary. You need to say your farewells while you can."

Doctor Green had been friends with Benjamin since Mary was a baby. His knowledge of the Cooper family made delivering such bad news so incredibly difficult. He would make Benjamin's last hours as pain free as possible, but he could not take the pain away from the two women in front of him.

"I am going to give Benjamin a dose of sedative now so if you want to come and sit with him? He may not wake again so perhaps now is the time to say farewell."

Anne and Mary sat beside Benjamin for his final hours.

He did not wake and the only evidence of life was the gasping breath in and the rattle as it was expelled. His body spasmed with pain on occasions although he remained unconscious. Sweat pooled from his face and Mary moped his brow gently throughout the night.

Anne could not accept what was happening. How could her husband be dying? Only this morning he was full of energy and optimism. He had left the house with the usual spring in his step, kissing her on the cheek as he left. How could a man so full of life in the morning be dying later that day? Anne was powerless to stop it. All she could do was sit at his side and wait for the inevitable to happen.

Her face spoke of her distress, although the words would not be spoken. Both mother and daughter realised that Benjamin could maybe hear them and did not want to distress him any further. They decided that if he was listening, then they would make sure he was listening to words of comfort and love. Both women talked to the dying man, reminding how loved he was.

It gave Anne and Mary an element of comfort, remembering the good times. Often, they would fall silent and just watch Benjamin breathe. They were checking he was still with them. Once they could see and hear his lungs struggle to take in breath, they would hold each other's hands, clinging to each other.

As the evening lengthened, John arrived, having left Emily to watch over the children. John slipped into the room silently, putting a comforting arm on Anne's shoulder. She reached out and clutched his hand, squeezing it to acknowledge his support. Mary got to her feet and pulled John into the kitchen. Once they were alone, she fell into his arms, sobbing with distress. For hours, she had tried to keep a brave face for her mother. Now with her husband's loving arms around her, she could allow the grief to flow. No words were spoken. John knew how important a role Benjamin played in his wife's life and, having lost his own parents, he could understand her impending loss.

Once Mary had composed herself, they returned to the front room to rejoin Anne. The desolate group sat around Benjamin's bed, enveloping him with their love and sharing happy stories about his life and his importance to the wider family. Each played a part in trying to hide their sadness so that Benjamin would not be frightened of the darkness which approached.

As dawn flickered across the horizon, the time came.

For hours now, Benjamin's breath had slowed. His face appeared to be getting greyer as the lightness of morning started to drive out the gloom in the shadows of the room. Benjamin's hand was being held by Anne. She felt a slight movement and looked up, trying to see a change in his demeanour. A faint smile passed over his face and Anne was certain he squeezed her fingers.

She looked around the room, catching Mary's eye, willing her to see the improvement in her husband's health. Mary shook her head slowly. This was not a positive change in his situation, it was an awareness of the end coming.

Benjamin gasped.

A long breath in and then silence.

He was at peace.

CHAPTER TWENTY-ONE
MAY 1875

Mary woke with a start.

She had been dreaming again. These days she spent more time in the past than the present. She had been remembering her father's death. The dreadful sense of loss hit her again in a fresh wave of grief. That awful day had been a nightmare. The pain and suffering her father had experienced in his final hours was fresh in her mind. It had been a blessing when his soul had departed. She remembered vividly her mother holding his hand as he passed, watching the life ebb from his sorrowful eyes.

Her father.

The first man she had loved in her life. Her heart broke that night as her father left for a higher plain. She had always been his favourite and the feelings were reciprocated. She could not imagine life without her gentle Pa. He would never see his grandchildren grow. They could not play at his feet, a pleasure she enjoyed with her grandchildren, Matthew, and Gwen.

It had been such a hard time, those first weeks after Benjamin had passed. Anne had collapsed with grief, leaning heavily on her daughter, who was struggling with her own pain. It had been days before her sister, Victoria, made it home to take over the burden of her mother's loss. Victoria was hard-faced in attitude, something Mary could never understand. She had the ability to shut away her grief and pick up the reins of caring for their mother. It was this fortitude which helped Mary to step back and care for herself and her children. Selfish it may be, but the emotional pull from her mother was just making it impossible for Mary to cope daily.

Fortunately, John was a blessing.

He took control of the formalities, including arranging the funeral. Benjamin had not expected to go so soon and little provision had been made. John had paid for the burial, unknown to Anne. It was his way of recognising the man he called father. It was also his way of making up for not being there for his own parents' funerals.

The church had been packed with both villagers and Benjamin's customers from across the county. He had been a popular man. His friendly manner and his hard-working approach helped him build a reputation for quality horsemanship. It was ironic that it was one of the beasts he loved would bring an end to his life. The funeral was a beautiful service and one that would be talked about for many years.

John had delivered the eulogy with passion and consideration. Mary had been extremely proud, watching her husband at the lectern speaking of her father with love and respect. Both children had behaved throughout the ceremony, which was unusual, but perhaps a testament to the respect held for Benjamin Cooper by all that met him. Sarah was desolated by the death of her grandfather. She didn't really understand what had happened but could see he was no longer there. John had tried to explain to his daughter, but she just didn't want to hear and had run away to hide. The funeral was something new to her too and added to her confusion. All those people talking about her grandfather but he was not there.

Mary's mind had been in a turmoil in the days after the funeral. Victoria was insistent that Anne should come to live with her. It was clear that their mother could no longer cope on her own. Her world had fallen apart and she seemed to lack any drive to continue her normal life. On one hand, Mary was relieved that the burden of caring for her mother was being lifted from her shoulders, but on the other hand, the thought of Anne moving away, perhaps for good, hurt. Victoria was better equipped to take on the responsibility, but it didn't stop Mary feeling guilty. Was she letting her father down by allowing her mother to go? And selfishly, could she cope without her mother's support? Anne was always on hand to help when the challenge of managing the house, children and the business got too much for the young couple.

Victoria's husband, Michael, had arrived at the funeral with horse and cart. Anne's belongings and precious furniture were loaded high on the cart. The house was emptied, with the keys handed over to Squire Cole who owned most of the village homes. With a hasty speed, her mother was packed and shipped off to live with her big sister, leaving Mary to mourn alone for her beloved father.

In the weeks which followed her departure, Mary had struggled. John tried hard to console his wife but she fell into a deep depression. Mary waded through each day as if she was dragging a boulder behind her. The children could not shake her out of her grief and even added to her pain, as they were constant reminders that her father was no longer with her, seeing her babies grow.

The door opened quietly and in tiptoed Hannah, holding Gwen in her arms.

"Oh, you are awake," she sighed as she noticed her mother's eyes open. "I wasn't sure whether to disturb you."

Hannah pulled over a chair and wedged her bottom onto the seat. Shuffling Gwen into a more comfortable position, she started to feed the child. Gwen was almost two years old but still had the breast before bedtime. It was a perfect way to get the child off to sleep and usually guaranteed that she went through the night. Most evenings, Hannah would sit and talk to her mother as she fed the babe.

It was one of Mary's favourite times of the day. Hannah was usually so busy and Mary really didn't want to slow her down with her own needs. In the evening, they used this time for Hannah to share stories of her day, especially reflecting on the children's antics. Matthew was probably now sat on his father's knee, having a story book read to him.

"How are you feeling this evening, Mother? You seemed to have been dozing most of the afternoon. Are you sure you feel quite well?" The worry was evident on Hannah's face.

"Peace, my darling girl. Don't you worry yourself about me." Mary smiled encouragingly at her daughter. She knew she was a worry to Hannah. She tried her hardest to hide her pain but her daughter was very intuitive. She picked up on the slightest wince. "I seem to be so tired at the moment. It must just be the passage of time. I seem to be dreaming a lot now. I was at it again just now."

Hannah loved to hear stories of her father and this had been the subject of many of their nightly conversations recently. "Oh, were you dreaming of my father?"

Mary smiled. "I was thinking of my father, Benjamin. I was so sorry that you didn't get to meet him. He died when Tom was a baby."

"Wasn't that a dreadful accident?" asked Hannah. "I'm sure I remember a story that he was kicked by a horse."

"I remember it clearly. It's strange how I can forget what you told me last night but, in my sleep, I can see the events of the past as clear as the day it happened. That particular night was dreadful. It was so hard to watch your grandfather gasping for air." A tear started to trickle from the corner of her eye. "I lost both my parents that fateful night. Your grandmother was never the same after that. She went to live with my older sister but she wasted away."

"She couldn't live without her husband?" asked Hannah.

"I think so. She didn't eat enough and within a year she just slipped away in her sleep. It was a fairy story of love, my parents. I think I was aware of that from as early as when I was a child. They loved each other deeply. Their relationship was the example for your father and I to aspire to."

"I wish I had met them," sighed Hannah. "I wish I remember father. It would be lovely to talk to him. I used to be jealous of Sarah as she remembered him. Silly, isn't it?"

"Oh, sweet girl, it's not silly. Your father would be so proud of the woman you have become. He wanted the best for his children. When we were first married, we would lie in bed at night and talk about all the plans we had for the future." Mary took Hannah's hand and stroked it gently, seeing the emotion flying across her face. "He would have made the inn a success. Everything was going so well until he got sick. Anyway, less of the reminiscing. That baby is fast asleep, so why don't you go and put her down and spend some time with your husband, darling?"

Hannah didn't need to be told twice. She pulled herself up, trying not to wake Gwen with too sudden a movement. Bending down she kissed Mary on the cheek. "Be back later to help you into bed Mumma dearest."

After she had gone, Mary shifted in her chair, noticing the continued aches and pains of old age. She was slowing down gradually. It was an effort to move around her room. Even picking her grandchildren up for a cuddle took more effort that she could cope with.

She did love the time she could spend with Hannah, John, and the little ones. But was that enough? Was she really living or just waiting for her time to come?

Soon she would be reunited with those who had gone before. She was sure time was against her.

Now was time to put her affairs in order. Her mind had been thinking for some time about the plans she needed to put in place before she left this world. Time was no longer on her side.

Soon she would have to face the ghosts of the past.

CHAPTER TWENTY-TWO
WINTER 1848

"Sarah, will you sit down and shut up," screamed Mary at the top of her voice.

The little girl fell to the floor in a heap, throwing her head into her hands. Loud gulping sobs broke out as Sarah raged against her mother. Mary always seemed to be angry at the moment. Sarah couldn't do a thing right. She was constantly in trouble for mistakes she didn't see coming. She was not an especially naughty child, but now she seemed to push all the wrong buttons as far as her mother was concerned.

Mary glared at her eldest child, who now lay kicking her feet against the kitchen table. Mary was trying desperately to finish Tom's feed and change his napkin before she started on dinner preparation. Her daughter's latest tantrum was certainly not what she needed right now. Just in time, Tom spat her nipple out of his mouth and gurgled with delight at his full belly. Hoisting him upright to rest his head on her shoulder, Mary rubbed his back forcibly to bring his wind up. She had to control her built up frustration as she held Tom. It was not fair to inflict pain on her youngest because his big sister was playing the brat.

Sarah continued to kick at the table leg with an annoying rhythm. The child was craving attention rather than trying to provoke her mother, but unfortunately it was not seen that way. In utter frustration, Mary reached down to slap her daughter's leg. The volume of sobs reached a horrifying crescendo. Tom decided it was time for him to join in and wailed his disgust at his wet cloths. He did not want to be outsmarted by his big sister and cranked the volume up a notch. Both children seemed to compete with each other in the noise stakes as screaming filled the room.

Mary wanted to cry.

But instead, she screamed at both children. "Will you just stop it now! I have had enough of you both."

She slapped Sarah's leg again and put Tom down on the rug by the fire, rather too hard. A shiver of guilt travelled up her spine as she realised she had shocked the baby into silence. Turning her back on them, she held onto the table, trying to control her anger. She was trembling with a pent up volcano of emotion. Deep within, she knew that screaming at the children was not helping. It was just stoking the rage they were all experiencing. It was her job as mother to set the example, calm things down and be rational.

Except right now she wasn't feeling very rational.

With slow, deliberate movements, she took off her apron and made her way across to the kitchen door. Throwing it open, she walked out into the yard and breathed in deeply the fresh mid-morning air. The chickens pecked at seeds on the floor and surrounded her feet as she stood there. Glancing towards the sky, she watched the rain clouds dance across the horizon, threatening a change in weather. It had been mild for November over recent days, but the country girl in her knew that a storm was brewing. And not just the storm currently playing out in the kitchen.

Mary settled her skirts around her as she sat on the bench under the kitchen window. She let the chickens gather around her skirts, a welcome distraction. Life was so much easier for her feathered friends, she contemplated. They seemed oblivious to the stress within the household as they continued their task of eating as much meal as they could. Of course, their journey would end in said kitchen when their egg laying days were over. In the meantime, they didn't have a care in the world.

Mary rested her weary head against the wall, not even noticing the cold chill creeping from the bench and into her bones. It was so nice to have a few precious moments of peace. Her life had changed immeasurably over recent weeks. If she was honest with her thoughts, Mary did not like her life right now. She really wasn't coping and John seemed unaware of her personal struggles.

It had been three months since Benjamin had died.

Three long months of grief, which didn't seem to get any easier. Being a mother, Mary had so little time to herself. During the daylight hours there was always some pull on her time and energy. She sleepwalked her way through the day, trying to meet the demands of house and children and craving the darkness of night. At night, in the gloom of their bedroom, the grief would become monstrous. Harsh cries would engulf her as she let the feelings flow from her.

If John was awake, he would hold her tight as she let the pain flow. But often he was exhausted from the day's travails and would sleep through her sobs. Those nights were the hardest for Mary. She felt so alone and didn't know how to explain her pain to her husband. Mary could sense a distance growing between her and John. They seemed to be quick to an argument and slow to make up. Their lovemaking had all but stopped, as exhaustion and the demands of both business and children challenged their previous idyllic relationship.

Mary was falling into a dark place where her thoughts and feelings were becoming increasingly sad. She struggled to see the joy in anything. The children were just annoying and she took so little pleasure from all the things she had enjoyed before Benjamin's untimely death. Even her love, John, seemed to frustrate her. He couldn't do anything right and just seemed to say the wrong thing at the wrong time. Everyone else knew that this was grief dragging Mary down. Mary was the only one who thought that everyone she loved was dragging her down.

Mary took some comfort from the regular letters Victoria sent. Her mother appeared to be improving slightly. Anne had settled in well with her eldest daughter and was keeping herself busy supporting Victoria and her family. The only concern, which Victoria had raised, was her mother's lack of appetite. She was an excellent cook, but over recent weeks had pushed the food around her plate rather than enjoy the output of her efforts.

Mary missed her mother. Mary needed her mother.

Before Benjamin's dreadful accident, Anne would often help Mary with the children. Today was an example of Mary's inability to cope with two demanding children. Before her father's loss their tantrums would wash over her, but the dark cloud which had settled above her head seemed to suck the energy from her body. If Anne were here, she would knock Mary out of this downward spiral.

Shrugging her shoulders, Mary eased her body upwards. She knew it was time to return to the children. There appeared to be a quietness coming from the room as she gently opened the door. Sarah had collapsed under the kitchen table and was frantically sucking her thumb. Her body gently heaved with silent sobs as she drew comfort from that digit. Tom was asleep. Lying on his back on the floor, his arms thrust outwards like a crucifix. A tear track had made its way across his cheek which, mixed with dried milk, left a visible trail.

Mary was overcome with guilt.

This was her doing. She had allowed her unhappiness to spill over this morning. The children had thrown their tantrums, picking up on their mother's stress. It was not their fault but hers. And now she was left with two distressed children, a kitchen which bore the evidence of the earlier chaos, and a dinner to prepare for her husband.

As if he could read her thoughts, John chose that moment to enter the room. He stopped at the door and took in the scene of destruction facing him. He spotted the children in their state of disarray and his wife seemingly ignoring their plight. He stared at Mary who had dragged a chair from beside the table to rest herself for a moment.

"Mary, what the hell has happened?" shouted John.

At his raised voice, Tom woke suddenly and started to wail again. Sarah wriggled out from under the table and wrapped herself around her father's leg, clinging on as he strode across the room. The momentary silence was well and truly broken.

Mary gasped as she saw the look of anger on her husband's face. Why did he straight away assume that she was at fault? She glared back at him with the full force of her frustration. If he wanted a fight, he had certainly picked the wrong time.

"Mary, are you going to answer me?" The tone of John's voice became more challenging.

"Your children. That is what has happened here, husband." Mary shouted back.

Both the accused watched as their parents drew battle lines. Sarah sucked more frantically on her thumb as her concerned face followed first John, then Mary as the argument escalated. Tom hiccupped sobs as he waited for the situation to calm.

"Mary, the kitchen is a mess and there is no sign of the mid-day meal. I honestly don't think you can blame your housekeeping tardiness on the children, can you?"

Mary wanted to cry. How could her husband get it so wrong? How could he not see the distress she was in?

"John, can you not see the mess your children have inflicted on me today? I have not had a moment to myself all morning. Sarah has been a horror, demanding every minute of my time when I have been trying to complete my chores."

She slumped further into her seat as she fixed her stare on John's face. She could tell he was angry but her own distress at the unfairness of the situation was her overriding emotion at this point. She did not know how to reach her husband. He was not an unreasonable man but recently he had been swiping at her failings. He didn't seem to understand that she was trying her hardest. But her hardest was simply not good enough.

"Mary, you really need to get a grip. The children need discipline. Once you have a grip on that your life will be easier. You are too soft on Sarah. She must learn how to behave if she is ever going to grow up into a good child."

John's attitude was the taper which lit the fire smouldering in Mary's belly.

"You bastard," she screamed. "How dare you speak to me like that? I have had enough of your arrogance. If you think you can bring up our children better than their own mother, then you can have a go at it."

Mary got to her feet and grappled with the knot on her apron. Her fingers struggled to function as she ripped at the fabric, trying to free herself from its constraints. She threw the apron on the kitchen table and flounced towards the door without a backward glance. If she had, she would have seen the look of horror on John's face. He had never witnessed such behaviour before from his wife. She was normally controlled and sensible. Where had this whirling dervish appeared from?

Mary was at the door when she looked back. "You can get your own dinner and feed the children. I will be back later. Much later."

She turned her back on her family as they watched, shocked at this display of motherly anger. With immense satisfaction she threw the door open, grabbing its swing to bring it back to close with an enormous slam.

As the door crashed closed, Sarah started to cry. Not the cries of an unhappy young girl but the loud gut-wrenching screams of a daughter scared. Her mother was leaving them behind. Sarah was distraught. She clung harder to her father as she screamed.

Tom picked up on his sister's distress. He was far too young to understand the magnitude of what was happening but old enough to understand that something was upsetting Sarah. He screamed as he made his father aware of his need for comfort.

John collapsed on the rocking chair, trying to lever his daughter away from his legs. Reaching down, he picked up his son, nestling him against his chest whilst pulling Sarah on to the remaining space on his lap. With soothing noises, he comforted the children, gradually bringing their cries under control.

As he rocked, his mind focused on Mary.

Never before had he seen his wife so angry. He was shocked at the passion in her reaction. He knew she had been struggling over recent weeks but never had he imagined that she could explode in the way she had. Perhaps he shouldn't have said what he had. His frustration after a busy morning of work had overtaken his thinking. He should have been more moderate in his reaction but he had not expected Mary to speak as she had. The venom in her words shocked him.

Had he taken her for granted recently? Should he have seen the signs of her frustration? He understood that she missed her father, but the grief seemed to have taken over her being and made her almost mad with the pain. He really didn't know how to help her.

John missed Benjamin too.

It felt like he had lost his own father. Over the years, they had developed a bond of mutual respect. Benjamin was the person John could go to for advice and guidance. He missed both Benjamin's and Anne's support. Anne would be with them most mornings, supporting her daughter with the children. She had revelled in her grandchildren, keeping Sarah's attention fixed as Mary fed Tom. The absence of Mary's parents in their life had left a big hole. A hole which, John was now realising, may not be filled.

"Now children, hush." He spoke softly as he rocked. "Mumma just needs a little time to herself. When she gets back from her walk, we will be ever so good and quiet for her."

Two little faces gazed back at their father, trusting in his faith.

CHAPTER TWENTY-THREE
WINTER 1848
LATER THAT DAY

It had started to rain.

A fine drizzle which penetrated her clothes, chilling her to the core. Mary regretted her impetuous nature, which had meant her leaving the house without a sturdy cloak. Her day dress was getting damper by the minute. Her hair hung in wet braids and she pushed it away from her face in frustration. Her pride had put her in this situation but there was no going back.

There was no way she would contemplate returning home for dry clothes.

She was making an assertive gesture and she could not sneak back with her tail between her legs. John needed to see she was serious. Mary grinned, thinking how her husband would be struggling with the children in her absence. That at least gave her some satisfaction. Tom would not need another feed for a few hours, so her need to assert her authority in the household would not have serious consequences. She had no desire to hurt her child. She needed John to realise her role in the family and perhaps think before criticising her in the future.

As she stomped on in the rain, Mary did not stop to think about her own behaviour. Her mother was not there to chastise her and remind her that John was the best of husbands. He was kind and gentle and never raised a hand to her. Mary knew the value of her man but she wanted his respect as well as his care. Perhaps if he saw the work she had to do, bringing up his children, he may appreciate her more.

In her rush to make a statement, Mary had not considered where she was heading. She had charged out of the yard and set off across the fields. She had no desire to meet any neighbours so had subconsciously headed away from the village. The rain was picking up its pace now. Her hair was soaked and the skirt of her dress flapped its weight against her ankles as she strode forward. Her clogs squelched as the muddy path grabbed hold of her feet.

Each footstep was an effort. Dragging the material of her dress, heavy with rainwater, made Mary realise she probably had made a mistake. It was all well and good making a stand, but why not do it when the weather was a bit more clement?

Deep in thought, she didn't see Jack Whiting approaching. Jack was riding his work horse, which was trudging along the track, head down, ears back, as the wind bit into its face. The horse was keen to get back to its warm stable and bag of hay after a long journey from market.

Unlike the horse, who was weary from its hard morning in the rain, Jack was in high spirits after making a few good deals. His purse was heavy and his heart was light. A hearty breakfast in the White Hart inn had been washed down with a few jugs of beer to further enhance his good mood. He wasn't drunk but the beer had taken the edge off the frightful weather.

His good mood reached a peak as he spotted Mary.

Jack's groin ached as he stared at her. She hadn't seen him yet so he took his time watching her body move. Her dress was soaked and clung to her body. Her full breasts strained against the fabric. He could see the contour of her paps and he licked his lips in anticipation. The skirt clung to her buttocks and legs, leaving little to his already overactive imagination. Jack's desire for this woman knew no boundaries. Seeing her wet and exposed drove him mad with lust. He pushed at his trousers trying to disguise his excitement.

Drawing alongside Mary, he coughed to catch her attention. "Well met, Mary. What the hell are you doing out here in this rain? Is something wrong?"

Mary shook her head, tossing her braids over her shoulder. The last person she needed right now was Jack Whiting. Suddenly, the need to return home and eat humble pie was appealing. She couldn't be rude to Jack though. That would just result in yet another argument with her husband.

"I just needed to get out for a while," she cried, her voice fading into the distance as the wind whipped up.

"Come." Jack lent down to grasp her arm. "Up you get. Let's go back to the farmhouse and get you dried. You will catch your death of cold in this rain. You're soaked."

Without thinking of the consequences, Mary grabbed hold of his outstretched arm and vaulted up before him. Settling her skirts around her for modesty's sake, she grabbed hold of the horse's mane for support. Jack encircled her in his arms. Was it just her imagination or was he holding her a little bit too closely?

"Gee up horse," Jack shouted as he kicked his heels against the mare's flank. "Let's get you inside into the warm."

The horse seemed to know it was nearly home as it increased its pace to a trot despite the additional load. Before long, its hoofs struck the stone paved yard of Wood Farm. Jack dismounted and held his arms out to catch Mary as she swung her leg over the horse's withers, trying not to reveal her underclothes to the man. Jack led her into the kitchen where a fire was smouldering in the hearth. With a practised efficiency, Jack threw a few more logs on the flames as he grabbed a large blanket, thrusting it towards Mary.

"Look, I need to go and unsaddle the horse. Get out of that dress before you catch your death. Here, use this blanket and drape your wet stuff over there," indicating a wooden clotheshorse positioned near the fire. "Be back soon."

Mary didn't hesitate. As soon as he had left the kitchen, she struggled out of the wet dress and her woollen tights, hanging them in front of the fire. The heat from its flames would not take long to dry her clothes and then she could make her way home. She only had a flimsy petticoat and knickers on, so Mary pulled the blanket around her shoulders as she settled into the rocking chair.

Before too long, Jack was back.

He had the forethought to prepare for the storm when he left for market that morning, donning a heavy overcoat which now dripped onto the flagstones. His brimmed hat was hung on the back of the door as he kicked his boots into the corner. His eyes avoided Mary at first. He knew that if he looked, he would be lost. But how could he avoid seeing her in such a state of undress?

Turning slowly, he looked towards the fire. A vision presented itself. Mary looked like a faerie queen. Her hair had escaped its braids and was tumbled down her back. Her cheeks were red as the warmth returned to her body. He could only imagine the delights which lay under the blanket. Oh no, he mustn't torment his body with such thoughts.

"Where is your mother, Jack?" Mary broke the silence.

Jack's father had died some years ago and he had taken over the running of the farm when he was still just a youth. Harriet Whiting had never remarried and lived with her only child. She wasn't often seen in public as she suffered with ill health. Jack was very understanding of his mother's lack of activity, which was surprising to Mary, given her usual low opinion of him. She struggled to acknowledge anything good about him. Jack was definitely his father's son. His health was always good. He was fit, strong and ruddy of character. If had not been for an argument with a scythe Jack's father would have lived to a ripe old age.

"She will be abed by now, Mary. Unfortunately, Mother doesn't spend much time on housework these days. I think I may have to pay for some help soon as I don't have time for women's work too."

Mary grimaced, thinking about the earlier argument with her husband.

Jack noticed the pot hanging from the range and lifted the lid, taking in the smell. "Good, at least Mother has made a stew. I bet you haven't eaten yet, Mary. Hungry?"

Mary nodded as the smell of the stew hit her senses. Her stomach grumbled in expectation. "Please, Jack. That would be lovely if you can spare some."

Jack busied himself grabbing bowls and spoons, trying his hardest not to look at Mary. The close proximity to her was driving him to distraction. He could smell her scent, which was overpowering. He kept his distance as he heaped a generous spoonful of stew into a chipped bowl, passing it across. Jack took a seat opposite Mary and they ate.

The stew was hearty, filled with root vegetables and a whiff of chicken. Jack ripped a chuck of bread from the loaf and passed it across to Mary. Once she started to eat, all animosity went. She even managed a smile. Mary devoured the bread and stew as if she hadn't eaten for weeks. It was delicious and its warming qualities were just what she needed.

With the food and the warming fire, her body was at last returning to normal. A tingling started in her toes and gradually worked its way up her legs. Twinges of pain shot through her fingers and toes as her body reached normal temperature. A nice pain, as it told her she was going to be alright. Her impetuous behaviour could have had serious consequences. What would her children have done if they had lost their mother so young? What the hell was she thinking of?

Mary noticed Jack had finished his stew and was watching her.

Intently.

Embarrassment washed over Mary as she suddenly realised she was in the presence of another man unclothed. She pulled the blanket a bit tighter around her shoulders and lowered her eyes to the table. Just because she couldn't see him, didn't mean he wasn't still watching her.

Jack was mesmerised by Mary.

She had never looked more beautiful. Her hair was loose and tumbling around her shoulders in waves. As it started to dry, it curled into ringlets which framed her face. Her cheeks were flushed and her rosy lips pouted, slightly open as she breathed in and out. Jack could see a hint of flesh within the folds of the blanket. Enticing images of the wonders he had been imagining for years. The beauty which was Mary Cozen both excited him and tormented him in equal measure.

All thoughts of allegiance to his best friend were banished.

Mary rose, picking up the bowls with one hand as the other held the blanket close around her shoulders. The sudden movement was enough to make the cloth slip through her fingers. The blanket fell to the floor. Mary dropped the bowls as she crossed her arms across her ample breasts. She gasped as she watched Jack get up from his seat. He reached down to pick up the woollen cover and slowly rose. As he unfurled, his eyes travelled up her body, from her delicate toes, up her long, elegant legs. His eyes rested for too long at her special place where the fabric of her petticoat had gathered in a haphazard mess. Her breasts strained against the cotton slip. He could see her dark pink areolas which were hardening under his stare.

Jack was beside himself.

Passion flooded through his body as he held Mary in his gaze. She did not move. She did not attempt to cover herself with the proffered blanket. Her lips parted as small gasps emitted. Slowly Jack moved closer. Mary still did not move. She continued to be locked by his eyes. Her heart was racing and beads of sweat formed across her top lip.

Jack touched her arms and she flinched as if his touch was hot. He stroked his fingers up and down her arms reassuringly. Meanwhile his eyes never left her face. Gradually his lips moved towards her mouth. Gently he laid his lips on hers, placing butterfly kisses across her mouth.

The dam broke.

The kiss became deeper and stronger. His tongue pushed its way into her mouth, exploring her taste. His hands held her head as they drank their fill of each other. Passion built as she wrapped her arms around his shoulders, pulling him closer. She could feel his hunger as his crotch pushed against her.

Jack pulled back from the kiss and slowly undid the buttons at the front of her petticoat. Her breast fell out of the fabric into his hands and he groaned as he felt it harden with desire. His mouth dropped to her swollen nipple, sucking deeply. As her desire grew, he nibbled on her areola. Mary cried out as he pushed her onto the table, grabbing at her skirts. His fingers found her desire as she gasped again.

Before she could change her mind or even understand what they were doing, he had his breeches down, his enlarged member ready. Jack could not stop things now, even if he wanted to. He had to have her. Right here. Right now, on the kitchen table.

As they reached a crescendo, Mary cried out, Jack shuddered.

All was quiet.

Jack looked at the woman of his dreams and knew his patience had been worth the wait. It was the most satisfying lovemaking of his life, and he had been with some very experienced whores. There was an innocence about Mary which added to the passion. His fantasies of Mary could not compare with the reality of what had just happened. The baseness of their coupling had turned him on in a way he could not have imagined.

Mary looked at Jack and died a bit inside.

What the hell had she done? She had allowed Jack to tup her. And she had been willing. How could she face her beloved husband after this?

"Jack, we shouldn't have done that." Mary shook her head slowly from side to side as she extracted herself from his arms. She raced over to the raging fire, grabbing her dress, and hastily throwing it over her head. Pulling the fabric downwards, she reached for her stockings.

"Mary, I don't regret a thing. It was wonderful. I love you," he whispered.

"You can't love me, Jack. I am married. To your best friend." Mary was crying now as the enormity of her mistake hit her full on. "You have got to promise me, Jack. You must never speak of this again. And John must never know."

Jack sat down hard on the table as he watched the distress on her face. He would not be the one to tell John Cozen. He had waited for Mary for years. Having her was better than he had ever expected. He could wait a bit longer. Now he had tasted the future, there was no way he would be waiting too long.

Mary would be his. No matter how.

He reached out and touched her hand. "Mary, our secret is safe with me. John need never know. I will be here for you whenever you need me. Just remember that." He squeezed her fingers as if to seal the deal. "You may not love me yet, Mary darling. But you will. In time."

It was all Mary could do to bite her tongue at his last remarks. She had to get out of here. Grabbing her wet cloak, she pushed her feet into her muddy clogs.

"I must get home," she cried, as she made her way to the door.

Jack watched her go without trying to stop her. He knew she would be back. One taste of him and she was hooked. His arrogance could not imagine her feeling guilt. Loyalty was not a feeling to which he aspired. He wanted the woman and he had had her.

And he would again.

And again.

CHAPTER TWENTY-FOUR
WINTER 1848
THE SAME DAY

Mary was frantic.

She made her way back across the fields, dragging the weight of her guilt behind her. What in God's name had she done? Jack had been after her for years and she had walked right into the lion's den without any persuasion. Was she crazy or simply foolish? Of course, she had imagined that Mrs Whiting would have been there and would have provided the necessary chaperon.

Once she realised she would be alone with the man who secretly lusted after her, what did she do? Took off her dress and invited even more attention. How could she blame Jack for his actions? She had thrust her sexuality in his face. Could she have expected him to behave any differently in the circumstances?

And was she a willing participant?

Mary was most troubled about her own behaviour. Jack's desires were one thing, but Mary was the one in the wrong. She was married. To the man she loved with all her heart. The man she had just betrayed, with his best friend. How could she have done it? She honestly didn't know herself at this moment.

For years she had been moaning at John about Jack's involvement in their marriage. It had caused so many arguments between them. She must have known the outcome of today's chance encounter. But she still went back to his farm. Her stubborn pride had driven her from her home and into the arms of her arch enemy.

But. It was good.

The sex.

She couldn't call it lovemaking.

There was no love involved. Well not on her part.

Mary was ashamed of herself, but at the same time she knew their sex was amazing. To be admired in the way Jack worshipped her. He had taken her with a ferocity of passion unknown to her before. Her lovemaking with John was tender and true. Jack was a monster who had driven her to heights unimaginable.

Slapping herself in the face, Mary pulled up suddenly. "Stop!" she shouted out loud. This fantasy had to stop right now. She had made a huge mistake but that was it. A mistake. She would never tell John about her idiotic misdemeanour. It would be her secret to the grave.

And Jack's.

Would he keep the secret? Surely he wouldn't risk his friendship with John by telling him. Her heart was racing as she worried about Jack's loose tongue. She would have to talk to him again. Make him realise that he must keep the secret too. If he found out John would probably kill him, or her.

Oh Lord, what a mess.

The inn was in sight. She had to get home and make things up with her husband. Before she did, she found a small coppice and removed her knickers, burying them under some large stones. She washed herself from a puddle of water to hide the smell of her sin.

If only her guilt could be washed away quite as easily.

Her feet dragged as she approached the kitchen door. All sounded quiet from within. Mary stood outside for a few moments, trying to compose herself. She opened the door gently and saw a sight which broke her heart even further.

John was asleep, sat on the rocking chair. Tom was cradled in his arms with Sarah nestled in his lap. If the guilt could get any more painful, Mary could not imagine the circumstances. Watching her beautiful family reminded her of everything which was so precious to her. How could she have done anything to hurt these three innocent souls?

Mary tiptoed across the kitchen floor in her stocking feet, watching her family intently. She didn't really want to wake them but she knew if she didn't apologise to John immediately, then her courage would fail. As she approached the chair, John opened his eyes and smiled.

She was lost once more.

"Mary, you're home," he whispered in an attempt to avoid waking the children.

Mary reached out to stroke her husband's arm. "John, I am so sorry for my behaviour. It was inexcusable." Her words spoke volumes in her mind. Not only was she apologising for her tantrum of earlier but her terrible actions of afterwards.

As she spoke, Tom awoke. Perhaps it was simply hearing his mother's voice which started him off or perhaps he was genuinely hungry. No matter which, he screamed himself awake, reaching out with his arms for Mary. A smile passed between the parents as John passed over the screaming child and comforted Sarah as she started to wake from her nap.

Within moments, Mary had the child settled at her breast and was sat opposite John at the hearth. John managed to rock Sarah back to sleep which gave the couple a chance to talk quietly without interruption.

John broke the silence. "I'm sorry for what I said Mary. I know it has been tough on you recently with your mother not being here to help. I should have been more understanding."

"Your criticism was fair, darling. It all got too much for me this morning. I lost my temper with the children." Mary shook her head as her husband tried to jump in. "No John. I behaved like a child myself. I screamed at Sarah and just made the whole situation worse."

"Look, Mary, the inn is doing alright now so we could afford a girl to help you in the mornings. I will ask in the bar tonight. At least if you have some help, it may take some of the strain off your shoulders. And with Sarah at school, that will help too."

John had been thinking of employing some additional help for a few days now and wished he had suggested it sooner. Why did he have to wait until his wife reached breaking point before he acted?

"Husband, that is good of you and more than I probably deserve." Mary's guilt piled higher.

Sarah wriggled in her father's lap as she gradually woke from her nap. In her initial confusion, the time between sleeping and waking, she glanced around the room. Seeing Mary, she threw herself from John's lap and ran to her mother. She grabbed hold of Mary's skirts and buried her head in her lap, nudging her brother off her mother's breast.

"Mumma, home," Sarah cried as her little arms rose in demand.

Mary reached down and picked her daughter up, making room for her. "Sarah, my sweet girl. Mummy is sorry she was angry earlier."

No further explanation was needed. Sarah was both relieved and delighted in the return of her mother. She had been so scared when she had stormed out and the look on Daddy's face had worried her even more. He had looked frightened. Was Mummy leaving them for good? Her little world had shifted as she panicked. Having so recently lost her precious grandfather, the shock to her world seemed to be growing. Her father had tried to reassure her but it had been emotional exhaustion which had driven her to sleep, rather than comfort.

Mary had been surveying the kitchen, only to realise that her family had not eaten yet. As Tom was satisfied, she gently laid him in his cradle.

"I best get some food ready. Are you hungry, John, Sarah?" Mary was on her feet, pulling together some cold cuts which would have to do for now.

"Starving," smiled John. "I'm no good at these domestic duties, wife. Thank God you came back when you did as we cannot cope without you."

Mary had her back to John as he spoke. The tears were rolling down her cheeks. She felt rotten inside. She really did not deserve John's forgiveness. She felt his arms under hers as he wrapped her in an embrace. Gently he kissed her neck, small gentle kisses, filled with care and love. The tears flowed stronger as she turned to face him. John touched her tears with his fingers, wiping them away. He kissed her eyes, her cheeks and came to rest on her plump lips.

"I love you, Mary darling," he whispered between kisses. "Always."

Her heart broke at those words.

How could she have behaved in that way when all she ever wanted in life was right here? John and the children were her life and she would do all in her power to ensure it remained that way.

CHAPTER TWENTY-FIVE
MAY 1875

The horse and trap pulled to a halt outside the vicarage.

Hannah threw the front door open, excited to get the first glimpse of her brother and his family. Tom jumped down from the carriage seat, grabbing his sister and enveloping her in a huge hug. It had been some years since they had seen each other and the joy of reunion was clear on their faces. As children they had been inseparable, and the closeness in ages often had them mistaken for twins.

"Hannah dearest. It warms my heart to see you looking so well." Tom was like a wind, swirling with excitement as he proceeded to help Jane and the baby down from the high seat.

"Jane, Tom, welcome." Hannah's husband, John, arrived to greet his guests, pumping Tom's hand and kissing his sister-in-law on both cheeks. "Oh, what a fine son you have there. Welcome William."

"We are so very honoured that you agreed to christen William for us this weekend, John. It is so very kind of you."

Tom had been delighted with the offer from his brother-in-law. Of course, William could have been welcomed into the church at Little Yaxley, but having a vicar in the family made for special treatment. Hannah was going to stand as godmother and the couple would spend the night with the Greening family before travelling back. It was also a good chance for Tom to see his mother. Hannah had written to him to keep him advised of Mary's slow decline. This might be his last opportunity to visit his mother before her death.

Hannah was quick to relieve Jane of the baby as she guided her brother into the kitchen. With Mary occupying the front room, life in the vicarage existed in the huge kitchen. Hannah had managed to organise the room to separate the cooking area from a living space, which made it easier to keep the children from under her feet as she cooked. Fortunately, John had a small study where he could work on his parish duties and write his sermons, although most of his work took place either in the church next door or within the homes of his congregation.

Matthew and Gwen could not sit still as they watched the adults settle into chairs. They had been nervously awaiting the arrival of their visitors, intrigued to see their new cousin. Both children were used to waiting for questions to be directed to them before they spoke, so could only use their wriggling movements to display their excitement. Hannah had shot them a warning glance already but the children were not for sitting still.

Once Jane was comfortably seated in the parlour area, Hannah set to making tea. As expected, Tom and Jane were gasping for refreshment. It had been an early start for the couple. The distance between the two families was normally an impediment to meeting up except for important family occasions, such as the christening tomorrow. For Tom, leaving the inn overnight was not something he liked to do. He had a barman whom he could rely on for support, but Tom worried about his step-father's behaviour. If Jack Whiting knew the innkeeper was away, he would no doubt take advantage.

It was rare for Tom to leave the inn in the hands of another, and Jane realised her husband would have little rest until he was back watching over his business. It was a double-edged sword; the need to see his family balanced against the risk to the business in lost profit. Closing down for the weekend was not an option, so Tom would have to put his trust in others, something he had struggled with for years. His lack of trust of others was a gift from Jack Whiting. A gift he could have done without.

Over a cup of tea, Hannah and Tom could catch up. The obvious topic of conversation was going to be their mother. Both Jane and John remained silent as the brother and sister chatted. They observed the two siblings familiarising themselves with each other's news. The subject soon moved onto their parents.

"Hannah, tell me about mother. How is she faring?"

"She is fading slowly, I'm afraid," answered Hannah. "She sleeps more and more every day. She was asleep when I just checked up on her. And I am worried about her mind."

"I suppose age has a bad impact on the mind. Is there anything particular that concerns you, sister?"

The last time Tom had seen his mother she had been full of conversation. Although he remembered her confusion over the oak tree in the yard at the inn. Perhaps that was a warning of what was to come? She had seemed obsessed with missing the chance to sit beneath its canopy. The willow in Hannah's garden just would not do. It was surprising to both Tom and his sister. They could not remember their mother ever having a fascination with trees. She never had the time to sit at leisure, especially after she banned her husband from the house. Mary had taken over the running of the inn after Sarah's death. Holding down a successful business, alongside caring for baby Jack, did not allow much time for sitting around in the orchard.

"It is hard to say, Tom. She spends most of her time in the past. Recently she has been speaking about our father more and more. Sometimes she speaks as if he were still alive. It feels like she is stuck in time before Jack was her husband. She never asks after Anne and Emma and how they are doing in service."

Hannah's sisters were both in service at Squire Cole's. Anne was handfasted with one of the footmen and was planning to wed this summer. Emma was sixteen, five years younger than her sister, and had settled well into life below stairs at the manor. Arthur, who was nineteen, lived with Jack Whiting at Wood Farm. He would inherit the farm and, because his father was all too often in his cups, was responsible for the day-to-day running of the business.

Tom and Arthur were close friends as well as brothers and supported each other in a similar way to how John and Jack had all those years ago, before tragedy had struck. Tom would drop everything if there was a problem at the farm so that he could help his brother out. Arthur had inherited his mother's skill with cider making. He seemed to have the art of feeding the apple juice to get the right level of alcohol content, so his services were essential to the Crown and Hare Inn.

The youngest of the Cozen brood was Jack, who had been born some weeks before his oldest sister, Sarah, had died. He had escaped the home as soon as he could, enlisting in the army. All his young life, Jack junior had felt the black sheep of the family. His mother didn't want him; his father hardly remembered he existed. He had found a new family within the army, a tough life but his new fellows did not know his family's chequered past and accepted him for himself.

"I can certainly understand why Mother would want to forget about Jack and their marriage. It is just sad that her children with him seem to be forgotten too. It is not their fault. Any of it. It doesn't feel fair. I know Arthur misses her desperately, although he does his best not to show it."

Tom shook his head sadly, thinking how different the relationship was between the elder children and their mother and that of the Whiting children and Mary. How different would life have been if Mary had not married Jack Whiting? If their father had been around until they were adults, the tragedy of Sarah's death would not have happened. The family no longer held the same names even. Both Tom and Hannah had reverted to Cozen once Sarah died.

"How is that rat, Jack Whiting?" Hannah asked.

She would never forgive him for the pain he had inflicted on her beloved sister. She stopped calling him father the day she found out.

"Crazy. That is the best way to describe him. He drinks far too much and sleeps all morning. Without Arthur to run the farm, that place would have gone to ruin years ago. He tries to throw his weight around but Arthur has the measure of him. If I'm honest, we don't see much of him," Tom smiled at Jane. "He hasn't been to see William since he was born, although I haven't encouraged it either."

"Thinking of your beautiful baby, shall I see if Mother is awake?" asked Hannah. "I am sure she will be delighted to meet her newest grandchild."

Tom nodded as Hannah made her way to the front room. Within moments, she returned with Mary on her arm. The old lady shuffled slowly to a seat by the fire. Tom grimaced, seeing the pain etched on her face, the reality of his mother's decline evident. Jane gently held the new-born on her mother-in-law's lap so that Mary could view William. She was reluctant to hand over her precious bundle to this frail lady.

Mary seemed fully alert as she watched her family together. As Hannah had indicated, her mind appeared to have discounted her later children. In her new world, her family was here surrounding her. Mary didn't get involved in the conversation. She observed. The conversation flowed around her as she enjoyed being in the bosom of her family. Mary was proud of Tom and the man he had become. He was a credit to his father and she could tell the similarities between the two men. She approved of Jane. He had found a good wife there.

She listened intently as Tom gave her an update on the finances of the inn. Even though she had made it clear that the Crown and Hare was Tom's, he insisted on sending a share of the profits to Mary. For years after John had died the inn lost money, mainly due to Jack's mismanagement and not helped by the fact that Jack had drunk most of the profits. Tom and his mother had turned things around after Sarah's death. Tom had restarted the brewing side of the business and had gradually regained the reputation so quickly destroyed by Jack.

Both Tom and Hannah were settled and doing well. Mary knew they no longer needed her. Soon she could depart and, whilst she may be missed, her family would manage very well without her. It was a sad reality but one she accepted. She knew she would not see young William grow to be a man, nor dear Matthew and Gwen. Just like her own parents, the luxury of seeing their legacy grow would be robbed.

She was not bitter.

Her time was approaching and she needed to make peace with the past. Hannah may worry about her mother's mind but Mary could see the past clearly. Over recent weeks, her memories of the past served a purpose. She could reflect on what had happened and understand her wrongs. Remembering how she had been unfaithful to her beloved John had laid heavy on her heart. It was her shame which she had to shoulder. She had spent most of her later years blaming Jack for his fault in Sarah's death. Now that a reckoning was coming, she had to face the fact that she had made some devastating mistakes too. She was not without fault. Thinking back on the twists and turns of her life was helping her to make a decision.

She needed to speak with Tom alone.

Soon.

....

It was the following morning when Mary had the chance to talk to her son alone.

William had been christened at the morning service in the presence of his parents, Hannah and her family and his grandmother Mary. John had been surprised that Mary had managed the short trip to the church, as she often missed the weekly Sunday service. John, the attentive son-in-law, would usually save communion bread and wine to administer to Mary after the service.

The day was warm and, after church, Mary had found her seat under the willow tree in the garden, leaving the family to their chores. Tom had brought her a cup of tea and pulled a chair up next to her. They had sat in companionable silence for a while before Mary decided the time had come to share her decision.

"Tom, I want to come back to the inn for my final days."

Tom gasped in surprised. He had not expected that. He had always imagined his mother would end her days at Hannah's side. His immediate feeling was fear on how he would break this news to Jane. She was a good woman but would she really want his grumpy mother living with them? Following swiftly on from that thought was a feeling of shame that his first reaction was to reject his mother's request. What sort of son did that make him?

Conscious of the silence between then, Tom finally spoke. "Mother, I thought you were happy here with Hannah?"

"I am happy, my son. Hannah and John have been so good to me. But I know I need to come back to Little Yaxley before I die. I need to be close to your father and Sarah. I need to be buried in the same earth as they are."

"Mother, this is such a sad topic of conversation. You are not going anywhere for years. Let's not talk about it yet."

He knew he was lying. It had become more apparent to him that his mother was failing fast. But was he prepared to manage those last few months of her life? Caring for his mother was a burden Hannah had shouldered for these last few years. Now it was his turn even if it was not something he wanted. It would be a difficult conversation with Jane and one to which he would not look forward. She was a good woman but would she be able to stomach caring for her mother-in-law?

"I want you to talk to Jane and make arrangements with Hannah and John. I will not get in your way for long but I want to come home." Mary grasped Tom's hand and squeezed it hard. "Do this one last thing for me, son."

"Of course, Mother." Tom squeezed her hand in response. If this was what Mary wanted, he could not stand in her way. He would have to deal with Jane's displeasure.

Tom gazed into the distance, alone with his thoughts. What would Jack do if Mary came back to Little Yaxley. Having the couple living far apart had helped the family to live in peace and harmony. Even though Jack had moved out of the inn after Sarah's death, the atmosphere between them had been dreadful. Jack was a regular at the inn and Mary could not refuse to serve him. But it didn't stop the two parents swiping at each other verbally whenever the opportunity arose.

The last few years had been easier on all the family. Jack was tolerated and, as long as he got enough beer, was pleasant enough. Putting the two of them together in the same parish was a recipe for disaster. Mary was insistent, so as her son, he had to make it happen.

It was a problem that would have to be faced.

CHAPTER TWENTY-SIX
SPRING 1849

Mary smiled at her neighbours as the villagers mingled outside the church porch.

The sun was beaming down, a blessing after the recent wet winter that Norfolk had experienced. It had rained every day during January and February without any respite. The track into the village had been waterlogged for months. Carts had been stuck in mud tracks, making the movement of goods difficult. A trip to the market in Watton was fraught with problems, which had caused many in the village to dig into their dry stores rather than buy fresh. Pale faces and thinner bodies were a feature of the congregation as they met up with friends and family.

With the welcoming sun returning, despite the chilly breeze, Mary looked forward to getting the children outside in the yard. They had been under her feet for too long but, after her temporary loss of patience, which had led to that awful row with John, Mary had controlled her temper. Even when Sarah pushed her to the limits, she took a deep breath and stepped back from confrontation. School had been shut during the worst of the weather and that had led to a number of tantrums from their eldest child. Thankfully she was back in her routine of morning learning, which allowed Mary to cope with Tom. He was developing fast and could crawl at speed around the kitchen, whilst Mary worked on her chores. He was a good-natured little boy who always seemed to have a smile on his face.

Life had been better recently for Mary.

John had quickly forgotten their argument and had been paying her more attention than usual. Their lovemaking had returned after the fallow months, with greater tenderness. Mary had tried hard to keep the peace. She had avoided scolding when she was frustrated with John for dropping his dirty boots on her clean floor. The effort was difficult but it was the least she could do after her fall from grace.

John had not suspected anything untoward after that fateful afternoon.

Clearly Jack was true to his word and had not spoken about it to his friend. Fortunately, they had not seen much of Jack over recent weeks. His mother, Harriet, had been seriously unwell. She was not in the best of spirits since she lost her husband. From what John had told Mary, her son had taken his responsibilities seriously and had forgone his daily pint to stay at home with Mrs Whiting. The sickly woman had passed away two weeks past.

As Mary stood in the churchyard, enjoying the warmth on her face, Sarah played with her skipping rope. She jumped at all the wrong times, meaning the rope would get tangled between her legs. Mary suppressed a laugh as she watched the concentration on her daughter's forehead. It was progress that Sarah tried again rather than throw a paddy. Perhaps her daughter was finally learning how to control her impulsive behaviour, thought Mary. John was away across the yard, picking up with the new blacksmith. Their horse had lost a shoe earlier in the week and John was determined not to let her go lame. He had taken Tom with him. John was so proud of his bouncy young boy that he always took any opportunity open to him to show off his son and heir.

Mary groaned as she saw Jack approaching. Why hadn't she started a conversation with one of the other matrons rather than stand by herself. Now she could not avoid him.

"Mary, good to see you looking so well."

Jack grinned as he perched his bottom on the nearest gravestone. It was an outstandingly disrespectful action. No regard for the dead. He was totally oblivious to the views of anyone else in the congregation who might see his action and be offended. The utter arrogance was astounding at times.

"Jack." Mary nodded.

She made no attempt to continue the conversation. They stood in silence for some minutes, an awkward silence which appeared to stretch for ever. Sarah soon got bored and started to run around the path attempting to jump in time with her rope swings. Mary did not have the heart to call her back.

"I haven't seen you in ages, Mary. Are you avoiding me?"

"I saw you last week at your mother's funeral. I am sorry for your loss, Jack." Bringing up his mother's loss was a low tactic, but Mary wanted to keep the conversation away from dangerous subjects.

The funeral had been a small affair with just a few villagers in attendance. Jack did not have any other family so had looked to his friend John to support him in carrying the coffin into church. Mrs Whiting was a small, wizened lady so between the two men, the task had been easy. Mary had sat quietly towards the end of a pew so that she could make her way out of the service quickly. There was no need to speak to Jack, and she used the excuse of the children's needs to avoid any contact after the burial.

"Thank you, Mary." Jack lowered his voice to a whisper. "I meant we haven't managed any time alone. I have missed your company." He winked at Mary has he rocked back and forth on the gravestone.

"Jack, it was a mistake and you know that. We agreed to forget about it," Mary hissed at him, as her cheeks started to blush.

She had tried hard to forget about the betrayal of her husband. At night, when John was snoring beside her, she would remember how Jack made her feel. Sometimes she would touch herself and remember those lustful desires. Her feelings confused her. She hated the man but the things he had done to her had driven her to distraction. She had been taken to heights she had never known with John. It was this realisation which tormented her. John was the best husband and she loved him with all her heart.

But she desired Jack.

There was nothing kind about the man. He would make a dreadful husband. He was so selfish and aggressive but the lovemaking, it would be magical. Why was she even thinking of Jack as a husband? The cocky man smirking at her was nothing to her. Just a dreadful mistake she would never make again.

"Jack, well met," shouted John, as he smacked his friend on the shoulders.

Mary had not seen her husband returning and was filled with relief to see him. She walked over to his side and took Tom from his arms.

"Come for dinner, Jack," offered John as he glanced at Mary. He didn't ask for permission and the look itself ensured that she didn't question her husband's hospitality.

"Thank you, John. I would be delighted to join you. Mary's cooking is mouth-watering." He looked across at Mary with a hidden double meaning.

"Sarah, come here now," Mary raised her voice.

Grabbing her eldest by the hand, she headed back towards the inn. The thought of sitting across from Jack all afternoon was turning her stomach. Why did John have to go and invite him? She stomped towards the church gate with a determination to get this done.

………………………….

Jack slumped back in his seat, rubbing his rotund stomach. "That was wonderful, Mary. Thank you. You know, friend, you have the most talented wife."

He addressed that last comment to John with a huge grin. The true meaning was obvious to Mary. She winced.

"True love is a full belly," laughed John.

Her husband was oblivious to the underlying atmosphere between Mary and Jack. Mary had remained quiet during dinner, allowing the men to share their news. She was happy to supervise Sarah, who had made an adequate attempt to behave for their guest. Tom was playing quietly on the floor with a wooden horse. Despite his early years, Tom had fallen in love with horses. He would squeal with delight if John hoisted him up in front of him on the saddle. Whilst Mary would cry out with fear as her precious son sat astride the huge mare, she trusted her husband to keep him safe. It didn't stop her nerves, but she realised her son would face numerous challenges in his life and she could not protect him from them all.

"We didn't get time to talk much at the funeral last week, but is there anything Mary or I can do to help you out? I know your mother was ill for some time so I guess you are used to faring for yourself." John became serious as the two men discussed Jack's recent bereavement.

Jack nodded slowly, watching Mary's face before he answered. "I am thinking of getting some help in from the village. The farm is getting very busy now that planting is underway." Jack glanced Mary's way once more. She was intentionally looking the other way, pretending to play with Tom.

"What you need is a wife, Mr Whiting," laughed John. "Surely it is time you settled down and found yourself a good woman."

"She's taken, my fellow," sighed Jack, raising is hand to his forehead in a histrionic fashion. "You got there first. Mary Cooper was the woman everyone in Little Yaxley wanted and you came back and stole her from under our noses."

The two men guffawed as they chinked beer mugs in toast.

Mary dropped her gaze to the table and worked at a knot in the wood with her finger. This conversation had an underbelly of truth which John really wasn't picking up on. How many times had she nagged at her husband about his friend's over-familiarity? Could he not see what was going on? Could he not see Jack's ulterior motive? The fact that Jack was happy to joke about it was even more disconcerting. Was he doing it to punish her further? Lord knows she was punishing herself and didn't need Jack adding his two penn'orth.

Before she knew it, the conversation took an unexpected turn. Her husband was offering up her services without even consulting with her. John found it acceptable to suggest that Mary came to help sort through Harriet Whiting's clothing, to see what could be sold or offered up to the poorhouse in Watton. If either of the men had decided to look at her, they would have witnessed the horror on her face.

John continued, "Mary would be happy to take this difficult task off your plate, Jack. It's women's work and will bring too many memories crashing down on you. Let us help."

Let us help.

Her husband was an imbecile sometimes.

Offering her services when he clearly knew she was struggling with managing the household chores. It was only months since their huge argument and, whilst she had been trying hard to make things good between them, the problem remained. Despite John's promise of help from the village, none had been forthcoming. It was difficult to find girls willing to take on the work. Most parents were keen to get their youngsters into service on a permanent basis, or needed their labour for their own farms and businesses.

Jack would struggle to find the help he needed unless he decided to take a wife. Now that her husband had decided she could sort out Hannah Whiting's old clothes, how long would it be before he offered her up to clean and cook for Jack? She would have to deal with this when they were alone. This simply was too much. She would do as her husband wished on this occasion but no more.

The two men continued to talk as Mary picked up her knitting. She had not uttered a word during the discussion and John clearly did not realise how upset she felt about his presumption. She seethed inside but portrayed a smiling countenance for the men to see.

Little did John know that he would face her wrath later that night. He would face a night with her cold back turned to him. He would shrug with frustration at his wife's childish behaviour and expect all to go back to normal the following morning.

Whilst John discounted Mary's sulking behaviour, his wife would feel sad that her husband lacked the intuition to see what was happening right under his eyes. She adored John but he really was stupid when it came to the machinations of others. He was just too trusting. Not only was he playing into Jack's hands but he was pushing her into unnecessary temptations.

Would that be his downfall?

CHAPTER TWENTY-SEVEN
SPRING 1849

Mary dragged her feet as she approached the yard to Wood Farm.

She was in no hurry to face her nemesis. Several days had passed since John had agreed for her to help Jack and she could put the task off no longer. Sarah was at school this morning so Mary only had to manage her young son, who was content as she strapped him to her front with a woollen shawl. He was sleeping and would no doubt stay like that for the next few hours. His belly was full of milk as he burped and dribbled milky stains down the front of Mary's day dress.

As she clattered across the flagstones, the kitchen door flung open. Jack stood on the threshold in his breeches, sucking on his pipe. Mary's first thought was not very Christian. He certainly didn't look like he was so busy that he needed her help, she contemplated. Her second thought was how magnificent his chest looked, devoid of a shirt. She could feel the excitement building in her gut as she looked at his barrel shaped torso, muscular and covered in a light brown, tawny pelt.

He was so different to John, in so many ways.

And she appreciated that difference.

Jack smiled. A grin full of confidence and desire. He was sure she would bend to his will this morning. He could see the lust in her eyes. Just a little time alone and he would make her his again. Jack had been up early, before light, so that he could prepare the groundwork for his second attempt at seduction. It was effort he had no intention of wasting.

"Good timing, Mary. I have just made a pot of tea. Shall ye have a cup before we start?" Jack retreated into the kitchen, expecting her to follow.

Mary was the proverbial lamb to the slaughter as she wandered behind him. Her body language screamed resigned defeat, as if what was about to come was inevitable. Fate was something over which she had no control. Her body led the way whilst her mind tried to fight against her instincts. An internal struggle over what was right and wrong. It was wrong to feel this way about her husband's best friend. Today, her duty was to provide neighbourly support, not to lust over a semi-clad man.

Mary was also somewhat intrigued by his words. Before we start? Was he planning to help her? What was the point of her being press-ganged into the job if he was about to join in? Or was it all about spending time alone with her?

Sadly her gut knew the answer to that question.

A huge steaming cup of tea was placed on the wooden table. The smell hit her taste buds and she licked her lips in anticipation. Gently she untied the shawl and rested Tom in her arms. He wriggled in his sleep, as she adjusted her position to drink. No words were exchanged. The two of them just glanced sideways at each other, like warriors in a dance of avoidance. It would be amusing if it wasn't that the stakes involved in this dance were so high.

They tiptoed around the precipice of their deceit.

Once she had finished her cup, Mary leapt to her feet and started towards the stairs. A door hid the stairway from the kitchen. It allowed the heat from the range to be retained in the kitchen. Families spent most of the winter months in the kitchen for warmth. There was rarely a need for a fire in the upper floors of houses, a luxury for the landed and rich.

Jack followed as they ascended the rickety staircase.

Harriet Whiting had used the back bedroom. A huge bed dominated the room along with a wooden closet. It was the bed Jack's parents would have shared. The bed Jack would have been conceived in and born onto. Despite being troubled by that thought, Mary gently laid Tom in the centre of the bed, wedging floppy pillows around him for safety. Jack began to show her the contents of the wardrobe as she perched cautiously on the edge of the bed. Within moments he had gone. Back down to the kitchen.

Now that confused Mary.

He had seemed to imply that they were to do the task together and for a moment she was excited at the prospect. She should not feel like that, but could not stop the wave of feelings crashing over her confused body. But he had retreated, leaving her bereft of his company.

Jack was well aware of his approach. He had seen the weariness in her eyes alongside the lust in her stance. He would give her some time alone to build up a frenzy of want. He was playing the long game. Keep her wanting more so that her guilt about her husband would be easily forgotten. It was premeditated, his plan to make Mary his again.

The last time was delicious and he was determined to drink from her sweet cup again.

Shrugging in resignation, Mary started on the task. The clothes smelt musty and dank. Their owner was long past but a whiff of her former personal perfume lingered on. Most of the garments were well worn and only good for the poorhouse. They were normal, country fare, heavy duty cotton and woollen dresses which had withstood endless grime and washing. Many of them looked like a wash would be the end of the fabric, being heavily worn. There was one dress which Harriet must have used for the most special occasions. It looked very dated and, whilst it was patched around the hem, would possibly earn a few pennies.

As Mary piled the clothes onto the corner of the bed, she checked pockets and folds. In one day dress she found a couple of wooden pegs, a reminder of chores completed. In the best dress, Mary came across a necklace which appeared to be better made than the normal tin ornaments people of their station aspired to own. She held it up to the light, seeing the early morning sunshine glint through the coral disc which hung from a silver coloured chain.

It was beautiful, delicate, and not something Mary could ever imagine Harriet Whiting wearing. The times she had met Jack's mother were few as she was a very private woman, especially since she lost her husband. Harriet had been a dumpy woman with a solid waistline, who would instantly fade into the background in a social environment. What was this unprepossessing woman doing with such a delicate piece of jewellery?

She must show it to Jack.

As if he read her thoughts, Jack was there, behind her. Standing at the entrance of the room, he lent against the door, smiling at her. She blushed. Suddenly, she felt like a girl again, embarrassed by the attention of a young stud. To hide her embarrassment, she held out the find to Jack.

"Isn't this the most attractive thing ever?" Mary blushed again as she was caught in the light of his eyes.

"It's yours, Mary." Jack saw that she was about to refuse so interrupted her thoughts. "Take it. I have no need for it. Call it a gift for your help."

Why is he being so nice to me, she pondered?

Jack reached out his hand and took hers, encouraging her with a firm force out of the room. Mary looked back to check on Tom, who continued to sleep soundly in the midst of the lumpy mattress. She followed Jack's lead across the landing area to another door. He kicked it open with his foot. Mary could see a further bed, much smaller than his mother's. It was a large cot covered with a patchwork blanket, unusually colourful.

Jack turned to face Mary and raised his hand to stroke her face. She quivered under his touch, feeling the excitement build in her belly. His face moved closer and she could smell his breath. Stale beer and onions were not the most romantic of whiffs but she was too far gone to be judgemental. He kissed her. A deep kiss as his tongue explored her further. Mary was lost. She clung to the man, who was not her husband, as his hands pulled at her clothes.

Jack pushed Mary back onto the cot, pulling her legs apart as he buried himself between them. Mary cried out as he entered her, quickly and forcefully. His body pumped against her as they rode a wave of passion.

The baby's cry broke through their passion as Jack reached his heights. Tom wailed as he found himself alone and in strange surroundings. The noise was one that could not be ignored, even when all other thoughts of propriety were lost to Mary.

Struggling from under Jack, Mary pushed him away as she pulled her skirts down. She ran to her child, trying not to think about what had just happened. Tom was thrashing around on the bed, fighting with the covers which had fallen over his face. His panic increased as his little arms pulled the covers further over his head. The guilt hit Mary full force.

If this was not a reminder of her deceit, then what was?

Pushing the blanket aside, she held her son in her arms, cooing in his ears. A soft musical song to comfort his distress. Tom hiccupped as his crying stopped and he nestled into her chest, seeking the breast. The last thing Mary wanted was to uncover herself with Jack entering the room behind her. She turned her back to him and made a cover with her shawl so that her son could lie in her arms securely, drinking deeply from her milky breasts, whilst any modesty she could now grab hold of was maintained.

"I must get home, Jack." Mary barely turned her head as she spoke. "Sarah will be back soon and I have dinner to get."

"Shall I walk you back?"

As he spoke, Jack took the necklace and placed it gently around her neck, doing up the delicate clasp with his chunky, fat fingers. He took his time as he enjoyed the sight of her neck, which he yearned to kiss.

"No. I will be fine." Mary sighed. "I am sorry, Jack. That should not have happened. I promised myself I would not disgrace my husband again and I have failed him."

A tear started to well at the side of her eye. With a tenderness unrecognisable in Jack, he touched the pool of wetness. He then placed his finger into his mouth, sucking in her sadness.

"Do not blame yourself, Mary my love. We have a passion for each other which cannot be ignored."

"But it is wrong. We know it. It is not fair on John. It will break his heart and I cannot do that to him." Mary paused then whispered, "I will not. No more."

Jack stroked her hair as her head slumped into her chest with the grief of her actions. Jack felt no guilt. He loved this woman. And one day she would feel for him the same passion she now felt for her husband.

He would make her his wife. Come what may.

As if making a bond with himself, he placed his hand on her head in a gesture of ownership. He would find a way to fulfil his ambition and nothing or no one would get in his way.

He would let her go now, knowing that she would be back. She may feign guilt for her actions but he knew deep down that he was getting under her skin. She could not do without him in her life and he would do everything he could to remind her of that fact.

All thought for his best friend had flown. He did not see the moral dilemma with which Mary struggled. In his mind it was all so simple. He wanted Mary Cozen and she wanted him.

John was the one in the way.

CHAPTER TWENTY-EIGHT
MAY 1875

The necklace glistened as the sun hit the precious metal surround. Pink coral shimmered in the fingers of the old lady.

Mary was sat in the garden, alone with her thoughts. Hannah was busy in the kitchen, watching over the children as she worked. John was out seeing to his flock. The solitude was a chance for Mary to think about the tainted necklace in her hands. Mary let the chain roll through her fingers, feeling the quality and intricacy of the links. It was the most beautiful necklace but held far too many dark memories from the past which were not welcome.

She had dreamt of it last night.

As soon as dawn lightened the shadows, she sought out her box of keepsakes. She had so little of importance or value, but the box held mementos of time gone by. Her most precious item was a lock of Sarah's hair, tied with ribbon. When she held it to her nose, she could smell her daughter's scent. Logically that was impossible but just holding it in her fingers, Sarah came back to life in her memory. Sarah had been dead for over fourteen summers now, but smelling her hair sent Mary back to those days.

Also in the box was her wedding band. A plain copper ring which John had placed on her finger that special spring day in 1842. She placed her lips to the cold band as she laid it gently back in its resting place. Her wedding band from Jack remained on her finger. It wasn't there for sentimental reasons. Her finger had swollen over the years as her body had changed. It was a simple, practical issue. She could not shift it over her knuckle.

Hidden at the bottom of the box was the coral necklace which had been owned by Jack's mother. Now, as she sat alone with her thoughts, she played with the necklace. The metal chain was delicate, suggesting a value far greater than one which Mary was accustomed. The coral was dark pink and shaped into a tear drop. It truly was a beautiful piece of jewellery but one that symbolised a deceitful time in her life.

For so long Mary had blamed Jack for the hurt he had inflicted on her family after John's death. He was hated for the damage he had brought to her door and the havoc he had created when he abused her precious daughter. Jack had done so much wrong in his life and it was easy for Mary to keep that story at the forefront of her memories of the time. It helped her to avoid examining her own part in the disasters which befell her family. It was so much easier to blame Jack for all that went wrong.

But was that entirely fair?

Should she examine her own behaviour? And if she did, would she find herself wanting?

This beautiful necklace was a reminder that she was not without blame. She had laid with Jack when she was John's wife. It was not a mistake she made once. It was a mistake she repeated a number of times that summer of 1849. Jack became an obsession from which she could not walk away. They coupled whenever they found themselves alone. Their deception was made easier by the friendship between the two men. John did not question his wife spending time in Jack's company. In fact, he had given them a ready excuse when he pushed Mary into helping after Jack's mother's death.

How could she be blaming John for putting her in temptation's path?

She knew it was wrong. But she kept going back for more. She did not love Jack. In fact, most of the time she hated him. He had a way of getting under her skin. He was an itch she couldn't help scratching. Their coupling was fast and furious with no real affection. It was exciting and forbidden. Perhaps that was why she was so addicted to the man. He offered her something John could not.

Danger.

The risk of being found out made their brief encounters exciting. They did not see each other's bodies completely naked until they married. Their frantic copulating involved moving clothing to one side so they could take their passions quickly. It was so different to her lovemaking with John. She behaved like a wanton whenever she was alone with Jack. It wasn't only him seeking her out. She was as much at fault as he was. More so, perhaps. She knew what she was doing and the risk she was taking, and yet still continued to do so.

Jack was not the only person to blame.

Mary had done much which was wrong. She betrayed her wonderful husband and she had to live with that shame for the rest of her days. When her time came, would John shun her for her deceit? Would Sarah blame her for not protecting her? She had many sins for which she needed to atone. Her younger children had no idea of the sins which troubled her conscience. She could not confess to her son-in-law out of fear. The thought of watching John Greening's disgust when he knew what a wicked woman she was, would be more than she could bear.

The punishment for her wrongs was that she would carry too many dreadful secrets to her grave. Her soul would be unshriven. In truth, she may not have to face John or Sarah beyond the grave. They would surely be in a better place than that for which she was destined. That thought alone troubled her hugely. It was fundamental to her core beliefs, and the fear of hell kept her awake in the small hours of the morning.

The thorny issue of Jack Whiting continued to trouble her as she moved her body in the chair. Her bones ached for sitting for too long. She realised she needed to face Jack one more time. She knew that now. Her need to return to Little Yaxley to see out her last days had a further purpose. She did want to slip off into eternal sleep in the bed she had slept in for most of her life, in the bedroom of the inn.

But she also needed to see Jack.

Did she want to make her peace with him? Did she have questions for him, to understand where everything went so wrong? Did she want to forgive him?

Possibly all of those needs were driving her decision. She needed to understand the paths they had chosen and the consequences of their actions.

Mary could not change the past.

But she could accept it.

And she could seek forgiveness for the part she played in others' pain.

CHAPTER TWENTY-NINE
WINTER 1849

Snow was falling heavily, spreading a white blanket over the fields. Its freshness gave the early dawn a surreal look, brighter than normal. The air was freezing cold and a chill wind whistled through the windowpanes, finding every crack to aid its creeping dance into the bedchamber.

Daylight peeped through the cracks in the curtain as Mary rolled onto her side. She pulled the blanket with her as the coldness attacked her shoulders. John was still asleep, snoring softly. His breath wafted into her face as she watched him. He was a handsome man, his features chiselled, his beard neatly groomed.

Mary knew she was a lucky woman to have such a wonderful life partner. A fresh wave of guilt flushed over her. Perhaps it was part of her punishment that every morning the shame was the first thing to come to her mind. Many a night, sleep evaded her as she worried about the path she had started on.

Fortunately, both children were still asleep in the back bedroom, meaning Mary could be grateful for some peace before the business of the day ahead. Once they woke, she would face the daily battle of dressing two impatient children and getting them to break their fast. Mary would then walk Sarah to school with Tom strapped to her chest before she could start her chores.

In the still child-free quietness, Mary could not resist the temptation of touching her husband. She traced his facial features with her finger, starting at his hairline. His blond hair had a curl to it and his locks surrounded his cherub-like face. Asleep he looked so much younger, like a boy rather than a strapping man. Her fingers moved between his closed eyelids and worked their way down his perfectly formed nose. As she reached his lips, Mary gasped as John nibbled her finger. She giggled as he came awake and pulled her into his arms. Kissing her, with passion, on the lips, he embraced her soundly.

"Morning, wife," he whispered.

"Morning, husband." Mary grinned.

It was not often that the couple had time alone in the early mornings. John was usually up as soon as dawn had broken and the birds called their morning chorus. His waking would normally rouse the children and the family home would resonate to the cries and laughter of her children. Now that Tom was walking, he and his sister often found their way into the parents' room before they were properly awake. Mary loved to cuddle her daughter in her arms as she stroked her bed curls. Tom would naturally find his father to jump on his belly which usually led to a tickle fight.

John must have decided to adopt his young son's morning routine. He pulled himself up to crouch over Mary's prone body. He pulled her arms above her head as he used his bristles to work his way around her chin and down her neck to rest on her breasts. Mary groaned in anticipation.

Suddenly the noise of Sarah opening the door distracted them.

"Mamma." A sleepy voice broke their moment of passion.

Sarah pulled herself up onto the bed, reaching her arms out for Mary. As Mary sat up to lift her daughter, a wave of nausea hit her. She only just managed to grab the empty chamber pot before she was sick. Dry heaving continued for some moments as Mary had little within her to bring up. Her throat stung with the acid.

Mary was oblivious to the look of concern shared by both her daughter and husband. She realised instantly what was happening. She was with child again. She groaned, thinking of what was to come. Tom was still so young and she had hoped that she would have more time before the next one came along. It had taken so long after Sarah was born for her to quicken with Tom and foolishly, she had discounted a pregnancy happening any time soon.

"Sarah darling, go and wake your brother up." John was keen to get a moment alone with his wife before the day fully started. He suspected Mary was about to share some news. "Mary, what's wrong?" He held her hair back from her cheeks as she dry heaved again.

Mary wiped her mouth on the hem of her nightgown as her stomach started to settle. "John, I think we are expecting another member of the household," sighed Mary.

John cupped her stomach in his arms and gently rotated his fingers down her sides. He dropped his head to her shoulder as he planted butterfly kisses on her neck. "That is wonderful news. Another little Cozen come the summer."

Mary did not share his excitement just yet. She realised the winter would be spent with morning sickness and evening exhaustion, far worse than her normal tiredness. A new baby would arrive before Tom reached two years of age, so her hands would be full for the coming years. A baby was a welcome blessing, especially after the years between Sarah and Tom when she thought it would not happen. But it was only when the realisation of a baby nestling in her womb hit that Mary remembered the fear of childbed.

Each time a woman was brought to bed, there was a real fear for her life. Anything could go wrong during the birthing process. A mother could die from bleeding after the birth, or fever. Her dear friend Emily had died last year after giving birth to her first child, a stillborn son. She had bled so badly and had wasted away within a few hours. The shock of Emily's passing had sent ripples through the young women in the village. Emily had only been married less than a year and had been so excited to have a baby welcomed into her home. Coming from a huge family where everyone had to fight for attention, Emily was looking forward to having something of her own.

Mary had been lucky that both of her births had been without problem. Her mother, along with the midwife, had been with her throughout. This time it would be different. Her mother was no longer with them. The midwife had recently passed away leaving her duties to a less experienced woman. Emily's demise was evidence of the lack of experience in the community, especially when it came to a difficult birth. It had all happened so quickly. Mary had been distressed that she had lost her best friend without being able to say farewell.

The realisation that very soon Mary would have to risk childbed again was a worry. She had hoped to have more time between Tom and the next sibling. Some time to enjoy her babies growing without being chained to the breast. Tom was weaned now and she was enjoying having her body back as a thing of sexual pleasure rather than as a milk cow.

Shrugging off her sad thoughts, Mary dressed and prepared to face the day. The children would not wait for their mother to recover.

Their demands would continue so she had better pull herself together.

....

It was later when Mary could sit in quiet and think about the months ahead.

Sarah was safely at school. She had bombarded her mother with questions about the nature of her sickness. She had lied, putting her sickness down to illness. Sarah was old enough to understand the basics of babies so needed to be put off the scent. Mary was not ready to share the news with her daughter just yet. Sarah would never keep the news a secret and Mary was not ready for the village to know.

Or, if she was honest with herself, for Jack to know.

The last thing she needed right now was Jack's involvement. He would put her under an emotional pressure she was not able to deal with yet. The longer it took for him to be aware, the better.

Mary was sat at the kitchen table nursing a pot of tea, as Tom dozed on the rug by the fire. Her mind was churning with unwelcome thoughts. Her courses last visited nearly two months ago and she was racking her brains to think when she and John last laid together. Their life had been so busy over recent weeks that most nights they fell into an exhausted slumber as soon as they slipped into bed. She could not remember and that was frightening her. Would her husband remember or was that just something women are aware of? John was not accustomed to discussing her courses, thankfully. Having not grown up with sisters, the monthly cycle of a woman's body, in John's opinion, was just an inconvenience rather than a marking of time.

She had been alone with Jack just a month ago.

She was ashamed to remember it. They had come across each other in the barn at the far reaches of Wood Farm. She was supposed to be gathering apples from the orchard while John had been watching the children. Her footsteps had dragged her away from her tasks and into Jack's embrace.

Mary liked to pick the windfalls each day and, once she had a suitable stack, she would make cider. John had been impressed with her home brew, which they only used for their own consumption. He was considering extending the orchard so that he could diversify into the cider business. Mary's skills in brewing had been noticed by others in the village and he had been asked by a number of his customers when cider might be included at the inn. He was particularly proud of his wife's determination to support their business expansion.

If he had realised her ulterior motive, John would not have been as forthcoming with his praise.

Jack had become practised in following Mary when she left the inn. Somehow his behaviour was intuitive. He seemed to know where she was going and would seemingly engineer the opportunity to meet up with her, by chance. As if chance was so precise. Every time this happened, Mary would tell herself it could never happen again.

And every time it happened again.

She was weak and foolish when she was alone with Jack. The excitement of their coupling sent all thoughts of propriety and loyalty out of her head. She was lost in his hands. Not that Jack would treat her tenderly and with love. He would take what he wanted and then be done. There was little exchange of conversation. Once he had departed, she would be filled with remorse and a resolution to stop this foolishness.

That resolution would be fierce until it happened again.

If John were to catch them together, it would be a disaster. She could not bear the thought of hurting her husband. But for some reason, she could not stop seeing Jack. That was the thing that disgusted Mary the most about her behaviour. She knew full well what she was doing. She knew that she risked being found out. She knew she risked her husband's love and her children's future. But she couldn't stop.

John, meanwhile, had no suspicions. He never questioned her movements and never seemed to notice if she returned home flustered, with her hair in disarray. He never questioned her continued moans about Jack Whiting. If anything, she believed he had become used to her nagging about his friend. Her complaints about his best friend had continued, despite her true feelings.

What were her true feelings?

She really was not sure.

Jack irritated her more than ever. He spent more time than ever in their home, sharing meals and drinking late into the night with John. His arrogance astounded her. He had little regard for their privacy and would arrive unannounced whenever he wanted company. There were three adults in this marriage. Unbeknown to John, there literally were three people in their relationship.

John had tried to pair Jack off on a number of occasions, but Jack was persistent in his rejection of any offers coming his way. At one stage, Mary had thought that Emily and Jack would marry but her best friend soon got weary of his persistent rejection and found herself another bedfellow.

Mary suspected Jack was waiting for her.

Jack had his feet firmly under her table and was watching for any cracks in her relationship with John. If anything went wrong, he would be there to pick up the pieces. Marriages did not end unless by death. Divorce was something with which only the landed or rich could play at. Not that Mary would ever walk away from her marriage. Despite her foolishness with Jack, she adored her husband. Her family was the most important part of her life.

Even if she was playing with fire.

And those who play with fire, eventually get burnt.

And now she was with child.

What if the child was Jack's? Would it look different from Sarah and Tom? Would her husband notice the difference? Sarah and Tom had been so similar in looks as babies and even as they grew. They were a perfect mixture of Mary and John, a beautiful combination of the best parts of their parents. Their characters were very different, with Sarah being very determined and wilful, whereas Tom was quiet and accommodating. But visually, they were almost identical.

She could not continue to let her mind explore this very real problem. The baby was John's and would be a brother or sister to their lovely children. She was sure of it. Why now would she be punished for her foolishness?

No, the child was John's.

She was sure.

As if all doubt had flown out of her mind, Mary decided that was that. Her simplistic mindset neatly packaged up the problem of the baby's parentage and stored it away, never to be looked at again.

She picked up her teacup and continued with her chores. All thought of the future baby had disappeared.

Conveniently.

CHAPTER THIRTY
SUMMER 1850

Mary sat outside the kitchen door, enjoying the sun warming her face.

She had a bucket of juicy plums before her. The task of removing the stones was a tedious and messy one. Swiftly she scored the skin, digging her paring knife into the plump, juicy flesh. Cutting around the central core, she pulled out the stone, leaving as much of the flesh intact as possible. The stone was thrown into a pile at her feet, with the flesh dropping into the bowl on her lap.

Plum jam was a new addition to Mary's pantry. She had taken a cutting from one of her mother's trees some years ago, before her mother had gone to live with Victoria. With care she had nurtured the small tree as it developed and grew. Once she had coaxed it to lay down roots, Mary had planted it within the orchard so that it could befriend the apple trees. Its new friends were expert fruit producers. The proximity would prove to be the right decision. It was as if the apple trees had directed their pupil to flourish under their guidance. This summer, the newest tree had been bountiful with rich plums.

Mary was very excited to be making jam. Her mother had been the finest jam maker in the village. Her sweet preserve had been sold at the local market throughout Mary's childhood. The thought of making a few pots was bringing back some wonderful memories for Mary. As she sat working, she was remembering her mother.

Sadly, Anne had died a year ago when Tom was a baby. Anne had never fully recovered from the loss of her beloved Benjamin. Victoria had cared for her mother to the end, sparing her sister from that dreadful task. Because of the distance between them, it had been impossible for Mary to travel to her mother's funeral. She had only recently been brought to bed with Tom and the journey to her sister's home would have been far too difficult. In an attempt to atone, Mary had sat quietly in the village church on the day of the funeral, alone with her thoughts.

Mary had not fallen apart with despair when her mother had passed. She had felt very differently to the mess she had become after losing her father. Her relationship with Benjamin had been unusual. Mary had been the apple of his eye, his spoilt little girl. The idea of living without him had been too much for her to bear.

The relationship with Anne was markedly different. Her mother had been more distant. She had always been the correctional influence in Mary's life and they hadn't shared the same deep love as daughter had with father. She missed her mother but was not desolate. She missed her help and the support she had given, especially when Sarah was a baby. But the reality was that she had lost her mother when her father passed. When Anne had gone to live with Victoria, Mary had had to cope alone. That distance had helped to lessen the blow of her loss. And at least her mother was now at peace, with her father.

However, the job of dissecting the plums was affecting Mary in a way she had not expected. A tear seeped from her eye as she remembered her childhood. Sat at her mother's knee, she had helped pulled the juicy flesh from the stone. Her fingers remembered the feeling, her nose remembered the smell. It was amazing that smells and mundane tasks could bring the past back in a rush of memories, both good and bad.

Life was so simple as a child. Mary had been wrapped up with love and guidance from her parents. How she wished for some of that guidance now, as she struggled with her conscience.

As if to jog her out of her thoughts, the baby kicked hard.

Oh, this one is a fighter, thought Mary. She was heavy with the child, which lay deep in her body. Whenever Mary sat down, the little terror had a way of knowing. There would be no time for rest when the latest addition to the family arrived. Both the births of Sarah and Tom had been straightforward. She had missed the calming presence of her mother when Tom was birthed but old Ma Spence had been by her side.

The house behind her was quiet.

John had taken the cart into Watton. He had a meeting with the owner of the Windmill Inn who was keen to purchase some of the Cozen own brew.

John had agreed to take Tom with him. Their son loved being outdoors and had an affinity with horses. He would squeal with delight as he sat astride the mare's back, safely held by his father. Despite the importance of the meeting, John was happy to take his young son along. Tom would sit quietly next to John as he negotiated the deal. As an aside, John felt having his young son with him may even help seal the deal. A family man was seen as trustworthy in John's experience.

Sarah was attending school, which had allowed Mary to settle down to the task of tackling the plums. Sitting on the bench outside the door meant that she could keep a watchful eye over the hens as they pecked at their meal. She smiled to herself as she enjoyed the peace and quiet so rare in her life. The bustle of dealing with two children, a busy inn and her hungry husband normally kept her on her feet all day.

Mary stretched her feet out in front of her, kicking off her clogs. She sighed as the blood rushed to her toes. She was sorely tempted to remove her woollen stockings and let the sun warm her toes. If it wasn't for the sticky mess on her fingers, she may well have done so.

The side gate of the yard swung open.

Jack Whiting strolled into the yard as if he owned the place. It was that arrogance which drove Mary wild. It irritated her and excited her at the same time. Jack spotted Mary immediately and grinned. Of course, he must have known she was alone.

He always seemed to know.

"Mary, don't you look glamorous."

Was he taunting her?

Without being invited, Jack settled his backside on the bench next to her. Slightly indignant, Mary shuffled along to make some room between them. She continued to peel the plums, trying her best to ignore his presence. His distinctive smell of horse, mud and grain was pronounced; mixed with the sweat of hard labour, it had a heady smell. It overpowered the sweet whiff of plum juice which had filled the atmosphere before his arrival.

"Are you quite well, Mary? Is the baby tiring you too much?"

"I am well, Jack. Thank you for asking. It is kind of you." Mary smiled at him.

She was feeling generous with her courtesy. Because of the baby growing heavy within her, they had not laid together. Jack did not desire her, large and cumbersome. She had decided it was time to end their furtive fumbling anyway. She had come close to being found out by her husband and was not prepared to risk hurting him. John had not questioned her pregnancy. Why would he? He never doubted her loyalty. It was this unwavering trust in his wife which had shamed Mary into controlling her baser desires.

The atmosphere seemed to change rapidly as an icy cloud surrounded their bodies. "Tell me. Is the child mine?" Jack stared deeply into Mary's eyes as he uttered the words.

"No."

Mary convinced herself with the lie.

In truth, she did not know for sure. She would not give doubt a window into her soul. She had decided the baby was John's and it would be John's. There would not be a single part of Jack Whiting in her child. If it carried any of his features, she would ignore them. It was a determination which was naïve in the extreme, but had been the only way Mary could cope with the shame she felt.

"Are you certain?" he continued.

"Forget it, Jack," Mary raised her voice in frustration at his persistence. "The child is John's. My husband's. We made a silly mistake which will not be repeated."

Mary fixed a determined stare at Jack as if she wanted to burn her words into his skull. She needed him to believe her. His pursuit of her always led to her capitulation. She was weak and he knew it. He played on her weakness as a cat torments a mouse, before it snaps its head with its jaws.

"I do hope the child looks like John, in that case," grinned Jack. "But if it doesn't, you know I will look after you. When John finds out you are just a common whore, then I will be there to help you out. You can come and live with me at the farm."

Mary slapped his face with a force she did not know she possessed. "You bastard. How dare you?"

Jack looked shocked at her reaction.

He loved to play with her emotions. It was part of his nature, to bully those he saw as weaker than him. Whilst part of his attraction to Mary was her strong will and determination, he wanted to dominate the woman. He liked her fearing him and the threat he could hold over her head. At any time he could spoil everything and tell John about their deceit.

Although if Jack were truly honest, he would never tell John. He was not stupid. John was a gentle giant, respected by his customers and the wider community. But if Jack told his friend he had dipped his wick in his wife's candle, there would be hell to pay. He did not fancy his chances in a fist fight with John Cozen. He may like to bully Mary but he was a coward when it came to her husband.

Mary's anger had a surprising effect on him. He was aroused. Grabbing her sticky hand, he thrust it towards his breeches, where his passion was obvious. Mary reacted as if burnt, pulling her hand away, scratching his palm as it pulled away.

"Ouch, you bitch." Jack rubbed at his hand, watching the red weal form on his skin.

"Get lost, Jack. And do me a favour. Leave me alone." Mary shouted the last words as she lost her patience with his presence.

Jack loved it. Within a few moments he had her all hot and bothered. She may well try and convince herself that she was done with him. How stupid of her. He would decide when she was done with him. But her fiery nature had its benefits.

The woman had spirit, he loved that about her. He wanted a woman with spirit.

And this one would soon be his.

He had a plan and soon it would be time to put it into play.

In the meantime, let her have her husband.

He could wait.

The best things in life were worth waiting for.

Rubbing his hands together, he scuttled out of the yard without a backward glance. He had done what he wanted today. Just remind Mary Cozen who was boss in this relationship. Keep her wanting him so that when the time came, it would seem natural for her to fall under his power and protection.

If he had looked back, he would have seen the confusion on Mary's face. She could not understand why he had visited that day. Did he just come around to annoy her? To add to the stress she was already feeling about the upcoming birth. That man has an evil streak, she thought.

Mary hated Jack with a passion.

But it was that passion which had been her downfall.

CHAPTER THIRTY-ONE
AUTUMN 1850

The squeals of her older children penetrated Mary's thoughts.

The family was enjoying an afternoon of rest in the late summer sunshine. The inn was closed until evening time and to celebrate a few hours together, John had suggested a walk alongside the riverbank. The heat of the day had beckoned the family towards the cooling delights of the stream. Mary had packed a basket of bread and cheeses with a flagon of ale, whilst John had carried a blanket. The children had been full of enthusiasm as they ran ahead of their parents, keen to play.

It was on that rug that Mary now lay. She had stretched out her body in the sunshine, placing her straw hat over her face, protection from the strong rays. She had pulled off her stockings in anticipation of a chance to wade in the cool stream later. Mary could feel the heat warming her body, sharing its healing powers to ease the recent pains of childbirth.

John was in the water with Sarah and Tom.

It was their excited squeals which had woken Mary. She could not believe she had slipped into a doze, especially as baby Hannah was asleep on the rug beside her. What if she had rolled over onto the child? As an experienced mother now, Mary knew that she had to take rest when she could. The endless sleepless nights took their toll and looking after a baby, as well as two enthusiastic children, was hard labour at times.

Mary shifted to lie on her side and examine the features of her newest baby. Hannah was a couple of months old now and was already developing her own characteristics. She was so very similar to how Sarah had been as a baby. She had the same urgency for life and demanding nature as her big sister. Tom had been so much more subdued and gentler, whereas both his sisters were taking life at full pelt. Hannah had the same dark hair as Sarah and Mary. Her nose and profile again were similar to the older sibling.

She was John's child.

Mary had no doubt.

The relief when she compared the two girls was the reassurance she needed that her past misdemeanours were not her undoing. John would suspect nothing. Nor would anyone else, more importantly. She was not frightened of her husband having suspicions, as his nature would never allow such thoughts.

It was that man, Jack Whiting, she feared.

Shaking her thoughts away from her previous sins, Mary sat up and looked for her family. They were playing together in the stream right opposite where she lay, giving her a good view of their antics. It was a sight to warm her heart. John was stripped to his breeches, with his glorious downy chest glowing in the sunlight. He was on his knees in the stream, tickling fish. Sarah, dressed only in her petticoat, was by her father's side, trying to copy his actions. She shrieked every time a tiddler passed by her fingers, making it almost impossible for her to catch any. Tom, meanwhile, stood the other side of his father, laughing as he watched their efforts. He was desperate to take part but fearful of failure. He would be content to watch his older sister lead the way. Again, this was a feature of her son, never confident unless he had his sister to guide the way for him.

It was a picture of domestic bliss.

Her family, so precious to Mary, enjoying play together.

She smiled as she watched John wrap his fingers around a small fish and launch it onto the bank. The sprat flipped its tail as it struggled to find water. All too soon, it fell still as life was expelled. Within moments, it was joined by a further fish and the same death dance took place. Tom charged out of the water and climbed the slippery bank. His fingers gently stroked the slimy fish and the smile on his face showed the excitement of seeing nature in action. He picked the fish up one by one and placed them in the bucket John had brought with him.

It didn't take too long for a small feast to be captured. Mary would make a fine meal later tonight with their winnings. John climbed out of the river, pulling Sarah up the bank in his arms. He grinned at Mary as she sat watching him. She had recovered quickly from the latest birth. Her breasts were full but her waist was trim, pulled in with stays. Her cheeks were rosy again as her strength returned. Her glory, which was her hair, had been released from the normal plaits and fell in waves around her shoulders.

She really was a beautiful woman, thought John. He was the luckiest of men.

John fell onto the rug, dragging Sarah and Tom with him. Within moments the pair were giggling as John tickled their torsos. He had a stubbly beard which he rubbed with his hand. Sarah instantly knew the sign and she screeched with faked fear. John pulled Sarah's little arms above her head and rubbed his stubble under each armpit. The girl giggled and then laughed, with full force, as she delighted in the game. She wriggled beneath her father as Tom jumped on his shoulders, tickling behind John's ears.

Mary smiled as she watched her husband with his children.

Sarah and Tom adored their father. It was a special relationship, very like her childhood memories with her own father, Benjamin. As history repeats itself, Mary knew that she had become the more correctional of the parents now. Initially John had been the disciplinarian with Sarah, but it didn't take long for her to exert her girlish powers over her father. They were inseparable whenever John was not working or Sarah at school. In fact, most afternoons, their eldest daughter would be found in the brew house, watching her father working and trying to help. She was already becoming proficient at tasks needed in the inn, cleaning tankards and washing floors to support her beloved father.

It didn't take long for the play to come to an abrupt end.

Sarah was hiccupping as she gasped for breath. Tom had wriggled off his father's shoulders and managed to worm his way onto his father's lap. John sighed as he held both children in his ample arm hold, kissing them lightly on their heads. He looked across at Mary who reached out and touched his cheek, red from his exertions. She tenderly stroked his face as she gazed at him with an intense stare, as if she were imprinting his features in her mind. There was an urgency in her stare.

A need to remember his face and commit it to memory.

Hannah chose that moment to break the blissful silence as she announced her hunger to the world. With a sigh, Mary was quick to pick the baby up and nestle her to the breast. To complete this perfect picture of a family in harmony, John placed his arm around Mary's waist, drawing her head to his shoulder.

If anyone was to walk past at that moment, they would witness a delightful picture of love. A man and his woman who cared for each other, more than words could say. Two beautiful human beings who fitted together like peas nestled in a pod. The product of their love, their children, were delightful to look at and would grow into strong, determined adults.

It was a perfect picture of family harmony.

How different it could have been if fate had not played them a cruel hand.

If history could be rewritten, John would grow old with his family surrounding him.

Why did things have to turn so sour?

Why do dreams not come true?

Mary would not know it then, but this was their last truly happy day. If she had known, would she have done more to capture every moment in her mind, cherishing those memories to keep her company in the dark days ahead?

And there were stormy days ahead.

CHAPTER THIRTY-TWO
JUNE 1875

Tom pulled the horse to a halt, applying the brake to the cart. It groaned under the strain as the timbers creaked to a stop.

Mary sighed in relief as she felt the wooden slats relax under her from the strain of motion. The journey from Suffolk had been hard on her bones. She did not have the padding of youth to protect her old body from the battering of a rattly cart. Tom had kindly made what seemed like a mountain of blankets for her to perch on. It had lessened some of the bombardment to her weaken bones, but she still felt exhausted.

Hannah and John had not been overly supportive of her determination to go home. They were worried about the impact the journey would have on her health. Mary could understand their genuine concern and was thankful for it as an expression of their love, but she was not worried about her health. She knew she didn't have long left and something was pulling her back to Little Yaxley. Her home. Where she had lived during the best of times and, unfortunately, the worst of times too.

It was a mission she understood she must complete before the light faded in her eyes.

Her daughter had finally accepted her decision and had worked with Tom to make her wishes come to fruition. It was a tearful goodbye shared with Hannah, John, and the children. Mary knew this was the last time she would see her favourite child, whom she had lent on for the last few years. She was sad that Hannah would not be by her side at her passing, but Mary had a purpose and that had to be the priority rather than her own wellbeing.

Hannah held her mother's hand a little tighter than normal as they parted. Hannah felt this parting was more than goodbye. She respected her mother's wishes, even if she disagreed with the sentiments behind it. Why her mother was so obsessed in seeing her husband before it was too late was beyond Hannah. Under the guidance of her vicar husband, Hannah held her counsel, making her mother's departure easier on all the family.

What point would there be to rage against the inevitable? She had to see her mother off with love and the good wishes of the family.

Tom was not best pleased to have his mother home. He could do without the added distraction, even if it would not be for long. He and Jane had made the Crown and Hare inn their home since Mary had moved to live with her daughter, Hannah. He was building a strong reputation with the inn, picking up the mantle laid down when his father had died. It was taking time, but Tom was turning around the business which had nearly been destroyed by Jack Whiting.

Jane had not shared her kitchen with her mother-in-law before and was nervous that having Mary living with them would lead to arguments. Jane was still nursing young William and was jealous of sharing those family moments with another woman. Little did she know that Mary was incapable of interfering in the couple's domestic life. She would spend her last days sat by the fire, or asleep in the cot they would make up for her in the kitchen.

With the help of Tom and her daughter-in-law, Mary slowly made her way into the house she had called home for so many years. She made a mental note of the small changes Tom had made over the last few years, appreciating his decisions. All signs of Jack had been discarded. The inn felt new and alive with the young family now in situ.

But some things were still the same.

Within the kitchen sat her old wooden rocking chair, covered now in plump cushions. This was the chair she sat on to feed her numerous children; it was the chair she sank into when mourning her beloved John; it was the chair she cowered in against Jack's temper; it was the chair she had sat in as she said farewell to her daughter Sarah. The chair held myriad memories, some good and far too many, bad.

Tom led her to the rocker and she sank gratefully into its arms. Gently he removed her shoes and rubbed her feet, bringing the warmth back. It was a sunny, warm day but Mary rarely felt warm anymore. Perhaps it was the passage of time or just her lack of a fleshy blanket to protect her body temperature.

"Cup of tea, Mother?" asked Jane as she bustled around the range, arranging cups and saucers.

Mary recognised the tea set which was originally her mother Anne's. It was good to see it being cherished still. She nodded to Jane as she watched the woman preparing a beverage for them all. It seemed strange to watch another in her place. The range, which Mary had spent many hours scrubbing, the wooden table which held the remains of a meal along with a pile of clean baby napkins. Mary welcomed the sight of family chaos rather than the pristine order which Jack had beaten her into maintaining.

The kitchen felt like a home again.

This house needed a young family again. It enfolded Tom and his wife into its arms, as it had cherished Mary and John. The memories of the happy times she had lived with her first love filled her with cheer. Her son was watching her and noticed the warm smile on her face. It had been so long since he had seen his mother show any sign of happiness. Perhaps bringing her home was the right thing to do.

Jane and Tom sat at the kitchen table as tea was served. Mary gasped as the drink hit her throat. She had such a thirst on her and the wetness and flavour of the tea was welcome. Tea was both a healer of worries along with the most delightful drink.

"Son, will you bring Jack to me in the morn?"

Mary folded her hands in her lap in an authoritative manner. She was resolved to deal with the matter before her courage fled. Once her mind had been made up, she was certain that a conversation had to be had. Neither party would probably welcome it but the air needed to be cleared. Once and for all.

Tom remained silent for a few moments as he looked at his mother. He had not welcomed Jack Whiting into his house since he took over the running of the business from Mary. He stomached Jack in the bar as he paid good pennies to drink himself into a stupor. But that was business and Tom had a level head when it came to making money.

Tom would never forgive his step-father for the wrong he did Sarah. He was only a young lad when Sarah died. He had been sick to his stomach when his mother told him what Jack had done. The evil man had taken his sister when she was just a girl. He had got her with child and let her take the shame for his evil ways. Thankfully the product of his evil died as his sister struggled to birth the baby. That birth would go on to kill his sister.

Tom could remember that night, when their world turned upside down, with a clarity he wished he did not own. The hate which had swirled around this kitchen as Mary confronted Jack. The disgust Tom had felt knowing his beloved sister lay dead in the bar, awaiting burial. He had come close to hitting Jack and was relieved his mother stopped him. The anger he had felt would have made it impossible to stop once he had started hitting that bastard.

And his mother had decided she wanted to see the evil man again. Who was he to stand in her way?

"If that is what you wish, Mother." Tom leant across and took his mother's hands in his. "I do not profess to understand why but I will bring him. I will be here throughout so he cannot harm you."

"No, Tom. I wish to see Jack alone. We have things to talk about that you know nothing about. There are secrets between me and Jack which need to be spoken of." Mary squeezed her son's fingers, willing him to understand.

"But Mother, should you be alone with the man? He is evil. I do not trust him."

Mary did not want to share her shame with her son. "He is evil, yes. But he was my husband for many years so I know the man. The real man. I am not without sin either, son. There are things you know nothing of. And it will remain that way."

It was clear the conversation was over. Silence descended on the room as both of them were lost in their own thoughts. Tom was intrigued by his mother's remarks. What could his mother have done that seriously compared to the evil of Jack Whiting? Perhaps it was for the best that he did not know. His mother had been the steadfast person in his youth. He had such respect for the way she had coped after Sarah's death and Jack's departure. She had managed the business expertly, handing over her knowledge to Tom. She had given the children stability and love, despite the sadness in her own heart. Tom adored his mother and had no intention of digging into the past.

Let it lie.

Mary had no intention of sharing her plan with Tom. She wanted her beloved son to remember her for the good things she had done. Selfishly it suited her purpose for Jack to be the evil one.

Thinking of the conversation to come, Mary had to prepare herself to challenge Jack about his actions. She needed to make her peace with the man who had brought her shame and sin. He had been the one everyone blamed for Sarah's death, but Mary knew that she had a part to play in every wrong in her life. She had made some big mistakes which had had consequences. Those consequences had changed the course of her life and brought her family pain and distress. She could not go to her grave blaming Jack for all that had gone wrong.

She had to know the truth about John's death. Her mind had been mulling over the events of that day for weeks now. Something didn't feel right and she must know the truth. Even if the truth was painful.

And at the same time, Jack needed to explain his involvement in her family's troubles. She needed to understand what drove the man to rape her daughter. What made him take a happy family and destroy it, for his own personal gratification?

She must know.

CHAPTER THIRTY-THREE
SPRING 1851

It was late morning.

Mary had been on her hands and knees for the last hour, scrubbing the stone flags surrounding the kitchen fire. It was a chore she had been putting off for weeks. Sparks from the fire, which burnt continuously, warming the whole house, left their residue on the hearthstones. As she scrubbed, the blackened colour of the slabs was washed away, revealing the grey stone. Its former glory was restored. Her bucket of water was a testament to her work, full to the brim with black liquid.

Mary rested back on her heels, stretching her back out. She raised her arms skywards, pulling the knots which had formed across her shoulders. Mary was not afraid of hard work, in fact she thrived on it. There was nothing more satisfying that surveying your work and taking pride in a clean kitchen. John would probably not notice it on his return, but Mary knew this was a job well done which would not need doing again for some months.

As she struggled to her feet, she hoisted the bucket, taking care not to slop the contents on her pristine floor. She shuffled across the room, trying to avoid any sudden movement, and emptied the dirty contents down the drain outside. As Mary poured, she surveyed the yard, taking in the scene. Tom was playing with his ball, kicking it against the privy wall. Suddenly he stumbled as he stood on the ball by mistake. Swiftly Mary was at his side, steadying her son. She received a beaming smile in return.

Tom was such a happy child, full of smiles and with a nature which appealed to both his parents and all those who met him. It would be a trait which would stand him in good stead throughout his life. Meanwhile, baby Hannah was asleep in a basket placed next to the kitchen door so that Mary could check on her at regular intervals. Hannah was more similar to her older sister. Both girls seemed to be in a rush to grow. They were determined of character and keen to learn about the wonders of the world.

John was over at Wood Farm this morning. Jack was calling in a favour and had asked her husband to help. As usual, John dropped everything and rushed at his friend's bidding. Jack had a small flock of sheep which grazed on the common ground around the village. As it was lambing season, Jack had herded the ladies back onto his land. His decision was two-fold. Firstly, it was not unknown for lambs to be taken by thieves and secondly, he had lost many an ewe during lambing. A good shepherd needed to be available to help if a lamb got itself stuck on its journey into the world.

Today, several of Jack's ladies were pushing out their babies, and he had called in his friend to work with him to watch over the sheep. Between them, the friends had been up most of the night and into the early morning with their arms covered in blood and birth sacks as they helped the lambs' birth. Without their work, a number would have been lost. Turning a baby lamb's legs was a skill John had acquired over many years of lambing. Should it attempt to enter the world the wrong way around, it could have terrible consequences for both mother and baby.

Earlier, Mary had walked over to the farm with fresh bread and cheese for the workers. The exhaustion was apparent on John's and Jack's faces as they slumped to the floor and devoured the food. Unusually, Jack had supplied the ale which was resting beside them. Mary was surprised to see the two small jugs of ale. Jack was notorious for his lack of hospitality when it came to beer. He hardly ever shared his small supply of home brew, even with John, despite him working half the night for his friend.

Conversely, John was generous with his labour. Working for the good of others was something most farmers and villagers would do for each other. Life in the countryside was tough, and the support of a neighbour was offered whenever the farming calendar reached its peaks. It was this community attitude which ensured the harvest was completed before the rains ruined its yield. The whole village would step in and work hard, enjoying the benefits in kind.

John had helped Jack with the lambing for many years now. In return, Jack would save a lamb for him when the annual slaughter took place. Mary licked her lips thinking about a fresh lamb roast, which was a treat for the whole family. The normal meat for most country families was mutton, which had to be roasted slowly to avoid it tasting like old boot leather.

Lamb was for the rich and not a staple in Mary's diet. When Jack arrived with the yearling lamb, the children would scream with delight at the precious creature.

The children would be hastened away while the animal was despatched. There was plenty of time for them to understand the harshness of nature. Mary had no qualms about slicing its throat open. She was a country girl and knew the importance of making death quick for those creatures they were going to eat. She would drain the blood and use it in black pudding over the months ahead. This blood pudding could be a staple diet during leaner times. Every part of the lamb was precious, and Mary would ensure that the animal fed the family for weeks.

Mary dropped to the bench outside the kitchen door as she continued to watch Tom play. Dinner needed cooking but she was determined to take a few moments of peace before the next chore. She tipped her head back and let the sun's weak spring rays warm her face. Clouds rushed across the vast sky as a strong northerly wind blew. The smell of approaching rain twitched her nostrils. All too soon outdoor play would be restricted.

The yard gate creaked as it swung open.

John was home, dragging his feet with the look of an exhausted man. Mary jumped to her feet and was beside him within moments. She raised his arm and positioned herself under his shoulder, trying to take his weight.

Something was wrong.

This was not just the weariness of a long night's work. John appeared sick. His face was a strange colour, almost green. There was a smell lingering around his shirt which was not normal. Mary's face puckered into a grimace from the exertion and the unusual smell. She had to get John inside quickly.

John groaned suddenly and gestured towards the privy. "Help me," he croaked.

Within seconds of reaching the privy, John was violently sick. His body trembled as he emptied his stomach. His embarrassment was complete as his bowels lost all control. What seemed like an age passed before the explosions eased up. He was shaking with shame. His body was a trembling mess over which he had no control.

Mary held her husband as he cried. She was frightened. Never had she seen her husband ill. And this wasn't just ill. This was something different. He shared her fear as if he knew something serious was happening. His hair stuck to his head as the sweat poured from his body. She held his shoulders as his body continued to flux. She wiped the hair from his eyes and rubbed his back as the vomit continued to rise.

Once the worst was over, Mary gently encouraged her husband to his feet. With all her strength, she managed to help him upstairs and dragged his filthy breeches from his body. Gently lowering him onto the bed, she wrapped him in blankets to try and stop the trembling. John was shaking and shivering despite the sweat pouring down his face. She wiped his forehead, trying to clear the damp hair from his eyes.

"John, I am just going to leave you for a moment. I will be back as soon as I can. I need to get help."

Mary squeezed his fingers. She must find someone. She couldn't do this on her own. She was alone with two small children in her charge. The look of panic on John's face was gut-wrenching.

"Don't leave me, Mary. I'm scared. Please," he groaned, as a fresh wave of pain rolled over him.

John seemed to know instinctively that if his wife left him now, he would die alone. He was sure this was something life-threatening and that no doctor could help him now. The pain in his stomach was unlike anything he had felt before. It felt like his gut was on fire. He was losing consciousness as wave upon wave of pain buffeted his body.

Mary was shaking with fear. She needed help but she could not leave John alone. She was conscious that Tom and Hannah were alone downstairs, but they would have to shift for themselves for now. Her whole world was dissolving in front of her. John was slipping away. She could sense it.

Whatever this illness was, it was fast-acting. His body was being hit with spasms. His forehead was burning with heat although his body shivered with cold. John was no longer aware of his bodily motions as his bowels continued to expel as he doubled over with pain. With every last bit of strength remaining, John gripped hold of Mary's hand. He was trying to anchor himself to her, to absorb her energy to keep him with her.

"Mary, please don't leave me," he whispered.

Darkness was surrounding John as he clung to his wife's hand. The shadows seemed to have a life of their own, pulling him towards the gloom.

"I will stay, John. Try to rest, my love." Mary stroked his head as she spoke.

"I'm sorry," he groaned.

"Why are you sorry, my love?"

Mary was growing increasingly worried now. John was failing fast. What was this mystery illness which could be taking her beloved husband so quickly?

"I don't think I'm going to get better," John cried. A tear started to make its way down his cheek as his body convulsed again.

"Hold on tight to me, John. I will make you well."

Mary lay on the bed beside her husband, using her body as a pillow for his racked torso. His breath was now laboured as he struggled to get air into his lungs. Mary was crying now, silent sobs. She wanted to breathe life back into her husband. She would give her lifeblood to save him from the dreaded moments ahead.

John gripped even harder to her hand as he fought to stay with her. One more gasp of air and he felt the room darken. He felt he was rushing away from his body. He was looking down on the bed. He could see Mary laying on the bed, holding his body. But he wasn't there anymore.

He could not feel her.

He could not touch her.

He was going.

Mary felt his body shudder.

The death rattle sounded.

He was gone.

CHAPTER THIRTY-FOUR
SPRING 1851

A fine, misty rain dripped down the back of Mary's neck. It was the type of rain which lingers, coating her hair, penetrating her clothes, and making the ground soggy and mud-riddled. Mary did not notice the wetness.

The rain represented her sorrow.

Aptly.

Mary stood at the graveside; her eyes fixated on the shroud being slowly lowered into the ground. His body had been washed with love, his hair combed and tied back. She had wrapped him in pristine cloths, tied at head and feet. Her husband would go to his maker wrapped with loving care. The body, which had gone through utter torment the day before, was now at rest.

His pain was over.

Hers was just beginning.

Despite her desolation, Mary could not cry.

Her heart was broken in two pieces and one part was being buried in the muddy, sodden ground. She willed it to be a mistake; for John to get up and walk out of the grave, like Lazarus. How could she manage without her rock, her husband?

She had never been alone in her life.

Mary had been surrounded by love since birth. Her father and mother had nurtured her as a child, spoiling her with their loving attention. They had handed that responsibility on to John, who had cared for her, loved her and again, spoilt her. She had been cosseted all her life which made this loss even more unbearable. She could not imagine a life alone with three young children to care for. If it wasn't for the needs of her children, Mary would have happily crawled into the dark hole to join her husband.

She was lost.

Cut adrift on a storm of grief, so huge that she had no idea how to function.

Last night she had held her children in her arms as they cried for their father. Sarah was devastated. John had been her daughter's world. The similarities with Mary's adoration of her father Benjamin were strong. Sarah's heart cracked as her mother uttered those dreadful words. "Your father is dead." It sounded so final.

It was.

Tom and Hannah were too young to understand what was happening. But they saw their mother droop with the burden placed on her shoulders. Their older sister understood. Sarah was initially shocked at the quickness of her father's death, then filled with despair and finally, as night came, anger set in. Sarah flung herself against the bedroom wall, trying to find a way to take the pain out of her heart and on to her body. Mary was concerned for her daughter as she held her trembling body, kissing her hair. She held her tight until the anger eased and the tears flowed again.

Earlier, Tom and Hannah had been aware of their father's distress as he lived his last moments in this world. It was a blessing that Sarah did not return from school until later. She would have been old enough to carry those memories all her life. Mary did not want her daughter to witness her father's embarrassment as his body lost all control. It would have damaged her even more than the simple loss of her beloved father.

For the younger children who had heard the noises coming from their parent's room as they cowered downstairs, Tom might remember the pain and distress but, with the comfort of extreme youth, he would forget soon. Hannah, the baby of the family, was simply unsettled as her mother left her alone in her wet napkin and with a hungry belly. She had screamed with disgust until the effort of crying wore her out and sleep settled her.

For Mary, help had arrived last night at the hands of the vicar's wife. She had taken charge of the children, without needing to be asked. She slipped into the house, once word reached the rectory, and quietly picked up the reins of normality amidst the storm of tragedy. After feeding the family, she had put Tom and Hannah to bed and sat with them as they cried themselves to sleep.

Mary could not eat, despite the kindness. She pushed food around her plate. The only sustenance she took was a tot of brandy, which burned her throat as it slipped down to warm her body. She felt like a sleepwalker, waiting for the nightmare to be over. Perhaps she would awake soon and her John would walk through the door, full of life.

Once the children had been cared for, the two women had the painful task of preparing John's body for burial. Mary was glad of the support. She could not imagine bearing that burden alone. When the time came, she could not cover him. Pushing the cloth back to take one more glance at his peaceful face, as he slept the eternal sleep. How could he be dead, so young? The pain had been washed from his face, his torment over. He remained her perfect husband, her beautiful soulmate.

And now he was being lowered into the ground.

The ground where his beautiful face will provide food for the worms. Mary gasped in horror as the realisation hit her. If it were not for the many souls stood around the graveside, she would have thrown herself into the void to heave his body back out.

Beside her, Sarah clutched at her skirts, burying her weeping tears into the fabric. Her body was racked with sobs as her tiny heart broke. Tom held the vicar's wife's hand as she cradled Hannah in her arms. Mary stood slightly away from the rest, alone in her grief, away from the rest of the villagers who had gathered to share her pain. None of her friends knew how to face the young widow, who stood invincibly at the side of the hole. Mary looked strong and determined, to those who had not seen her distress the day before. How impressions can be deceptive. Mary was holding herself rigid knowing that if she broke, she could never put herself back together again.

Across the grave mouth stood Jack Whiting. His eyes followed Mary. He watched the emotions play across her face. Better than most observers, he understood how much of a display Mary was perfecting. He knew the woman. He knew how much she adored her husband, even if he hated that.

Her pain oozed from her pores, directed at him. Her devastation troubled him. He felt responsible. Would Mary blame him? It was working with him which had led to John's death.

Jack could not look at his friend's body. He could not bear to do so. He shared Mary's grief. Jack and John had been inseparable in life and only death could part them. Jack had found out the news much later last night when he had sauntered down to the inn for a pint. Finding the door firmly closed, he had entered the kitchen uninvited. He had been met by the vicar's wife who had broken the sad news. Mary had taken to her bed by this time so he had been unable to comfort her. He had sat at the kitchen table with a tot of brandy as he listened to the woman's words, describing the sudden nature of John's illness and demise.

The vicar came to the end of his short sermon and with a finality which set a look of panic on Mary's face, he picked up a clod of earth and dropped it onto the shroud, uttering the words, "Earth to earth, ashes to ashes."

Mary started to cry then. It began as slow channels of tears wending their way down her cheeks. Her body started to shake and then convulse as huge sobs emitted from her throat.

Suddenly she collapsed to her knees beside the graveside. Her body slumped as her hands sunk into the sodden ground. The wail which came from her body was frightening. Sarah clutched at her mother's arm, scared of her mother's grief. Sarah could not remember seeing her mother cry before, let alone wail with pain. Sarah clung to her mother in an attempt to stop this dreadful noise. Meanwhile, Tom was crying as he watched his mother, confused by her behaviour.

Mary was past caring what others thought. She could not let them bury her John. Her hands scrabbled in front of her, trying to find purchase. She was so close to the edge of the hole that one wrong movement and she would fall. Two strong arms grabbed hold and pulled her back. Slowly she was raised to her feet. She tried to struggle but the hands were strong and firm. Looking up, she stared into Jack's eyes.

"Don't let them do it, Jack," she cried.

"Peace Mary."

Forgetting that others were watching them, Jack stroked her face, pushing the damp tendrils of hair which had stuck to her cheeks.

"He will be scared all alone. Stop them, Jack. Don't let them cover him. Please."

Mary was becoming hysterical. She was oblivious to the distress she was causing her children. Both Sarah and Tom were shaking with fear, confused by what was happening. She was oblivious to the concerned stares of her friends and neighbours. In her world, the only thing that mattered now was to prevent those huge clumps of soil landing on her beloved's body.

"Come away," Jack whispered in her ear. "You are distressing the children now. Come. Let me take you home and let the men do their work."

It was as if Mary had been punched in the stomach.

She deflated as all the fight left her. Like a child, she allowed Jack to lead her away from the graveside. Head bent, Mary walked away with Jack by her side. Sarah still clutched to her skirts and Tom ran over to her to hold her hand. Those standing around the grave, watched as the young widow lent heavily on her husband's friend's arm as they walked with dignity back towards the inn.

Clearly Mary would not be alone for long.

A woman running her own business was not acceptable. She needed a husband to provide for her and her family. Today was not the day for those observations, but the watching villagers could see the support being given by Jack Whiting to the grieving widow. Some would remark that the young widow could not do much better than the local farmer, who was young, strong and had a thriving business of his own. They were obviously friends so it would be natural for her to lean on him for support.

No one would be surprised at what happened next.

But that was for another day. Today, Mary was burying her beloved husband, father of her children. Today, Mary could not imagine how she would get through the next day, let alone the rest of her life. She would take one step in front of the other towards her destiny.

But each step would be filled with sadness.

CHAPTER THIRTY-FIVE
SUMMER 1852

Church bells rang out in celebration.

Mary and Jack left the church just as the sun peeped out from behind clouds. Mary smiled as she looked across at her new husband, pleased with his look. Jack had made a huge effort for their special day. His best trousers and shirt had been cleaned and pressed. His hair, which usually had a mind of its own, was slicked back with oil, and his beard had been neatly trimmed. Jack had found his best boots, under the bed. They hadn't been used for years and, to his surprise, he had found a mouse nesting in one of the black leather footwear.

Mary had treated herself to a new dress. Nothing as elaborate as her first wedding dress. A simple cotton dress in a bright blue fabric, which fitted neatly around her much thinner body. The extra weight she had added to her frame over the years of childbearing had fallen from her bones as she grieved for John. At one stage, Jack had been concerned that she would do herself damage. She had not eaten properly for months during those dreadful days after John's death.

Gradually Mary had come back to life.

She had three young children who depended on her. The passage of time healed most wounds. Mary would always carry the scar across her heart, but she learned to manage the pain. Eventually she could smile again. She could remember John with happiness rather than grief. She could walk into the bar without looking for him. She could watch his children grow and develop without a heavy sadness engulfing her.

Jack was beside her throughout.

He visited every day once the funeral was over. It was he who opened the inn, making sure there was an income coming in. He found a worker to take on the running of the inn when the challenges of Wood Farm had his attention. He didn't get involved with the children initially. They were a necessary distraction in the healing process for Mary but, for Jack, they held little interest. John's bairns were the only downside of his quest to have Mary. It was a necessary evil he would have to put up with.

From the start, Jack knew he would marry Mary. For once, he used his brain to manage his approach. He treated her as a frightened deer, gently coaxing her forward. Making himself available whenever she needed someone. He was by her side whenever she needed help so that eventually she came to rely on him for most of the tasks John would have been responsible for during their marriage. Gradually, Mary became dependent on Jack until it seemed natural to the woman that marriage to Jack was a good idea. Jack had put in the hard work for months and when he came to ask Mary for her hand, she did not hesitate.

Mary didn't love Jack.

She would never love another man like she had John. But she needed company. Mary was not made for struggling alone. She had been cared for all her life so it was necessary for her to find a mate. Jack seemed the obvious option. He was useful. He had independent means and she felt she could trust him with the children's future security. Between them, the couple could combine the businesses of both farm and inn. Their combined businesses would make them one of the leading families in the village which would enhance their future prosperity.

And of course, there was the thorny issue of bedding. Mary had been consumed with passion for Jack when they were at the height of their lustful affair. She was deeply ashamed of her behaviour but at least John had never suspected a thing. She knew that her shame was a cross she must bear, but a cross she was prepared to carry. Sex with Jack was exciting. He drove her to heights she could never have imagined. There was an absence of love in their lovemaking but perhaps that was why it was so exciting.

If she had to share her bed with another, then Jack was a good option. She did not have to love him. If she cared for him, gave him more children, and made his life comfortable, then they could probably live well together. Mary believed Jack was in love with her and was prepared to let him. As long as he didn't ask for that love to be reciprocated then life could be pleasant.

The one fly in the ointment was Sarah. She was old enough to understand what was happening. She saw Jack getting his feet under her father's table. Jack was nothing like Sarah's father and the young girl was reluctant to bow to his authority. Mary would catch her daughter making faces behind Jack's back. Her attitude changed as soon as he entered the room. Sarah was far too open in her dislike of the man. Her naturally rebellious nature was not appreciated by Jack.

Mary could see trouble ahead.

Tom and Hannah were young enough to accept the change without any complaint. Tom needed the presence of a man in his life. It wasn't right to grow up without a father figure. Jack was already taking Tom under his wing, encouraging him to enjoy the outdoor world. Jack was the master of his farm and until another son came along, Tom was the nearest he had to a son and heir.

The marriage ceremony had been a quiet affair. Most of the village could see that Mary was making a strategic decision to align herself with another business owner, and especially one who was so close to her first husband. It was a marriage of convenience in the eyes of their fellow villagers. That was clearly apparent by the look of resignation on Mary's face as she spoke her vows. Conversely, those watching Jack's face as their vows were made would clearly see his devotion to his new wife. There was also an air of triumph that he had landed his prize.

After the ceremony, Jack led Mary back to the inn.

They had decided to live in the inn rather than the farm for convenience, especially as the Crown and Hare had bigger family accommodation. Jack was going to rent out the farmhouse to a local couple, who would also work for him on the farm. Mary had mixed feelings about this decision. She was struggling with the idea of sleeping with her new husband in the bed she had shared with John. But she understood it would be easier for the children not to be uprooted after all the upset they had already suffered in their short lives.

Opening the kitchen door, Jack entered first. It was symbolic. He was now the owner of the inn. Mary may think she was joining forces in business, but Jack was determined that she knew her place. Oh yes, John Cozen had some fancy ideas about his relationship with Mary being a partnership. That was not Jack's style. He had married Mary and a huge benefit of that arrangement was ownership of the inn. As long as Mary kept the house and provided him with a brood of whelps, then they would rub along nicely.

But any ideas of a partnership would be knocked out of her very early on, he thought to himself.

....

The children were asleep as Mary dragged her feet up the stairs. That motion was at odds with her first wedding night. Then she had been full of excitement and bubbling with anticipation for what awaited her. She was bubbling with anticipation. Now she dragged her feet. Her body edged its way forward, totally lacking enthusiasm or desire.

It was a chore which needed facing.

True she had slept with Jack before so she was no innocent virgin. In fact, over recent weeks, Jack had insisted on taking her at regular intervals. Why wait, was his mantra. Mary had insisted that for propriety's sake he did not stay over. They had grabbed moments alone together, but actually spending a whole night with him beside her would be something new.

Once supper had been cleared away, she had sat opposite Jack by the fire, supping on a small flagon of ale. The look on her husband's face had told her the time had come. He was excited about the thought of having Mary in his bed and available whenever he wanted. No more grabbed moments, waiting for the children to interrupt. No longer worrying about being found out. It was now official and he could not wait to own her fully.

Mary was an experienced lover and no longer a nervous bride. The blushing virgin on her wedding night with John Cozen had grown up. She had loved, born children and lost the man she adored. The thought of sharing her bed with Jack held a different range of emotions. They had never held each other like she used to with John. They didn't have the deep discussions about their future together. Jack seemed to accept whatever life threw at him and never spoke to Mary about his hopes and aspirations.

Mary accepted that her life had changed beyond all recognition.

She needed the protection of a man and it may as well be Jack rather than anyone else. He had been a presence in her life for so long that marriage to him would be accepting the inevitable. She did not love Jack, but she didn't want love. She had lost the love of her life and Jack could never replace him. Jack would be her partner, her security, and the man who would help her raise her children. His influence would help her children obtain the best start in life.

That was all she needed now.

So different from her first husband, Jack could not be described as a deep character. Some would even say that he was a base fellow. Shallow in his desires. He had needs and Mary would satisfy those needs. But did he really know the woman he had married? Was he seeking true love or was Mary just the woman he had chased all his adult life? Forbidden fruit which he could now possess. Did he just want to own her rather than desire her? Or love her?

Jack had wanted Mary for ever.

He had chased her down as a hunter seeks out a fleeing hare. Cornering her and giving her no chance of escape. Mary had been trapped in his snare and all too soon would be devoured.

He had desired her, and those snatched moments they had grabbed when John was still alive were exciting. He had no trouble with his conscience. The fact that he had betrayed his best friend did not concern him. The fact that Mary had betrayed the husband she adored did not trouble his mind. He did not have the emotional fear that she would stray again. That idea did not come into his head. Was it arrogance or indifference?

He had the woman he wanted.

Finally.

She was his property now. Mary had not disappointed him before, and he was confident she would not disappoint him in the marriage bed. She had a beautiful body with a magnificent chest, and he looked forward to nestling his head in their comfort whenever he wanted. No more snatched moments. He could tup her whenever the desire hit him.

Love did not enter his head.

Jack was not familiar with that emotion. He had watched John fall deeply for Mary and saw his friend's behaviour as a weakness. Women were not equal to men, in Jack's mind. Mary would keep house for him. That she brought a thriving business into the marriage was an added gift. Mary would provide him with children. Again, that was not something he had thought about in the past. Children did not hold his interest. They were a distraction which he would have to learn to live with. But if he was to bring up John Cozen's whelps, then he may as well have some of his own.

Mary was abed as Jack strode into the bedchamber.

The blankets were pulled up to her chin, hiding her magnificent body from sight. She looked like a frightened dormouse, he thought. It was a bit late for modesty, he chuckled as he pulled his braces over his shoulders. Pulling his shirt over his head, he quickly dropped his trousers to the floor, kicking them into the corner.

That would be the next surprise for Mary to deal with. John had been meticulous in his ablutions. He would never dream of coming to bed without washing his body clean from the sweat of a day's work. This would be another change for Mary to stomach.

Jack was not concerned about cleanliness. His clothes would be worn all week despite the sweat marks growing down his sleeves. He would bathe once a month if he was inclined. The smell of labour constantly oozed from his body, an earthy smell. Washing of his underclothes would be a chore Mary would come to detest.

But that was for tomorrow.

The bed creaked as Jack's weight sunk into the mattress stuffed with hay. Mary had freshened up the stuffing, but this was not noticed by Jack in his eagerness to have his wife.

"Come here girl," he groaned, as he lay flat on his back. As Mary rolled towards him, his face turned. "What the hell are you wearing?"

Mary shook her head with confusion. "'Tis my best nightdress, Jack."

"And what's it doing on you?"

Jack pulled at the fabric with his fat, sweaty fingers. Grabbing the neckline, he ripped the lace as the fabric fell apart. Mary gasped. The lace was her mother's which had been lovingly saved and sewn onto her newest nightdress. She had sought to impress him with it but, in his need to have her, he had not even noticed its beauty.

Quickly he pulled the remaining cloth from her body leaving her naked and vulnerable. His eyes travelled up and down her body, delighting in her discomfort. He licked his lips in anticipation.

Mary lay still, watching the man she now called husband. There was something primeval and visceral about his demeanour. There was no gentleness. His hands pawed at her flesh, kneading it like a loaf of bread. This was not lovemaking, in any sense of the word. Jack had no regard to her enjoyment. It was purely about sating his needs.

Their secret lovemaking had been exciting, unlike this. It had been part of the attraction she had for Jack. Forbidden fruit which always tasted sweeter than the reality. Her reality tonight was one of disappointment. This was all she would get going forward.

Soon it was over.

Jack eased himself off her and lay flat on his back. His arm casually draped across her breasts. Before too long, Mary could hear low snores emanating from his form. Mary rolled onto her side and stared into the darkness. Jack had clearly enjoyed his release and was happy to roll off to sleep. He did not seem concerned about whether Mary's needs had been met.

How different a wedding night from her first. She remembered her night with John. They had made love throughout the night, interspersed with silly conversations as they planned their future together.

But if she was honest with herself, the disappointment was of her own making. Jack was no different with her than he had ever been. In her head, she had made him something he was not. He would never be her lover in the way she had wanted. It was the excitement of forbidden passion which had made Jack seem exciting before.

But this was her life now. She had made her bed. She had chosen the man to share it with.

It would be the biggest mistake of her life.

Time would prove that.

CHAPTER THIRTY-SIX
JUNE 1875

Mary sat alone beside the fire.

Tom and Jane had reluctantly agreed to leave her alone to speak with Jack. The couple were walking the baby across the fields to enjoy the early summer sunshine. Tom had not been at all keen with Mary's proposal, but had finally agreed to respect her wishes. Mary had no desire for her eldest son to bear witness to the conversation she was about to have. Despite all her wrongdoings, Mary wanted her children to remember her with love and affection when she was gone. With a vanity she probably didn't deserve, she wanted Tom to see her as a good woman. If he heard the things she intended to confront Jack with, his opinion would be altered for ever.

As she sat there awaiting Jack's arrival, she thought back over the years she had been married to him.

Life together had started in an agreeable fashion but things had changed far too quickly. Jack became angrier and would use his fists to get his own way or to just assert his authority. He struggled to affirm his place as master of the house using words alone. Cuffing Mary or one of the children became a daily occurrence. His drinking had got worse. His reputation as a lush was known far and wide, which attracted the wrong type of clientele to the inn, lowering the previous high standards of hospitality. Many regulars had found excuses to avoid the Crown and Hare, even travelling into Watton for an ale.

Mary had become more sullen over the years. She had produced more babies and each one had sapped her strength a little bit more. She had tried to protect John's children from the worst of Jack's anger but she had little success. Her youthful comely looks faded quickly, something Jack had been quick to curse her for.

Life had been so very different with Jack Whiting.

She was nervous to see her husband again. Too much had happened between them in the past. They had been apart for a long time, but the feel of his fists could still strike a fear into her heart.

Now the moment was upon her, the thought of confronting Jack scared her. Oh, she had nothing to lose right now. What more could he do to hurt her? She was old and weak. Her days were numbered. But the man she had spent so many distressing years with was a monster. He knew how to hurt her, both emotionally and physically. Mary had to be strong. She needed answers and she wouldn't get them by showing her weakness to her bully of a husband.

The kitchen door opened slowly, creaking on its hinges. Jack stuck his head around the wooden slats looking for her. Surprisingly, he looked nervous too. Husband and wife had not spoken for years and hadn't seen each other in the flesh since Mary moved in with Hannah.

Mary was shocked at the change in the man. He'd always been a short, stocky and muscular man. Father Time had not been kind. His hair had lost its thickness and now surrounded his pate like a monk's tonsure. What remained was grey and lank. His body had curved with time so that he couldn't stand upright. Jack did not stride with purpose anymore, he shuffled.

Jack made his way across the kitchen to the seat opposite Mary. Without asking, he lowered his crooked frame into the rocking chair and groaned as he eased his body into the most comfortable position. He stared across at his wife, possibly taking in the changes in her.

Certainly, Mary was no longer the woman he had married. Age had filled out her body, leaving her with the lumps and bumps of life experience. Her face was no longer soft but wore the jowls of a life hard-lived. She was tired and worn out with the travails of time.

"Mary," Jack nodded, acknowledging his wife.

For some moments the couple just looked at each other. Both took in the changes to their partner, assessing them. The silence gave Mary time to prepare her thoughts. Jack did not know what Mary wanted of him. He had been intrigued to get the message. A message out of the blue telling him his wife want to speak to him. Nothing more; nothing less than that. All he knew for certain was that Mary must have a reason. This was not a social visit. Mary had not come all this way for small talk.

As if she could read his troubled mind, Mary launched into her speech before she lost her nerve.

"Jack, I need to know the truth. My mind has been troubling me over recent months. I need to know why John died and I believe you can help me with that." Mary fixed her steely gaze on Jack.

Jack's face was a picture. Confusion, guilt, wariness played a struggling dance across his face. Which would win?

"What the hell do you mean, Mary?" Jack seemed to pull himself together as he cleared his throat. "He got sick. You were there. You saw him. What's this all about?"

"But why did he get sick? That's what is troubling me." Mary paused as she looked deeply into Jack's eyes, emphasising the seriousness of her need. "He was fine the night before. He felt alright when he left to help you with the lambing. He was fine when I came over with some food to break your fast. Then hours later he was so sick. His body was purging some evil from within. That's what I don't understand. What made him so sick?"

Jack looked angry now. "I don't know what it's got to do with me, woman. He was your husband and, as you pointed out, you brought breakfast over. So, if something made him sick then it must be your fault."

Mary could tell that Jack was floundering. The fact that he was angry was making her even more sure that he had something to do with John getting sick. She needed to know the truth and was not going to let it go now.

"Don't try and turn this round on me," Mary shouted. She was angry too with his typical arrogance. "If I recall it was bread and cheese. Nothing that could make him sick. Didn't you provide the ale?"

Silence reigned.

Jack shuffled in the chair nervously.

Mary's mind wandered back to that fateful day. She could see the two men sat in amongst the ewes and their new-born lambs, chewing on the crusty bread. Jack had pulled out two pewter flasks from his work bag. He had handed one to John, who had gulped down the contents immediately. The dust from the barn caught the back of one's throat, driving a need for liquid refreshment. As Mary searched her memories, she was hit with a realisation. Jack had knocked his flask over, spilling the contents across the floor.

"It was you. You bastard," she cried. "You put something in his drink. I remember now. You didn't drink from the flask. Only John did. What did you put in the ale?"

Jack stared back at her. He looked shocked, as if he was trying to decide whether to tell the truth or continue to spin the web of deceit. In his mind, he weighed up the risk of telling Mary. What could she do about it now? Would this be one more hurt he could inflict on his wife? Serves her right for ruining his life. He had done her the honour of marrying her when she was lost but how did she repay him? Mary and her useless children had made his life hell.

"Rat poison." The sneer on his face told Mary he was not bluffing.

Mary was agog, her mouth open as she watched Jack's face turn from a sneer to a wretched smile. She shook her head slowly as her mind tried to take in his words. Was he really confessing to murdering her beloved John?

"How else was I going to get into your bed?" Jack's laugh was full of hatred. "Oh, I think I had been patient. I had sat back and watched you and John weave your happy life together and what did I get? Just crumbs. John's leavings. All I could do was watch you and John creating your happy ever after family while I went home alone each night."

Mary gasped with the wave of sorrow which hit her. Listening to him rant with jealousy for her and John struck her deep in the heart.

"Why Jack, why?" she cried. "You could have found a woman to warm your hearth. Why did you have to have me? You didn't love me like John did. I know that now. You made my life hell and you didn't even love me." Her voice broke as a sob caught the back of her throat.

"I didn't want anyone else, Mary. I had wanted you before John Cozen came home, but you never saw me. Not after you set your sights on John. If we had married back then, perhaps we would have been happy. By the time I had you in my bed, you were gone from me anyway." Jack lent forward in the chair and reached out for Mary's hand. She pulled herself back from him. "You never wanted me, Mary. I was just someone you could play with. You loved being lusted over and don't you deny it. John was never enough for you. You had to have every man in the village at your feet. Poor, spoilt, little Mary Cooper. The girl no one ever said no to."

Mary sobbed again. Too much of what he was saying struck a chord. She had been spoilt. She had always got what she wanted. But did she really deserve the pain and suffering heaped on her by this man?

"John was your friend, Jack. How could you do that to him? If you had seen the way he died, his suffering, you would never have done such an evil thing."

Jack shook his head slowly from side to side. "I regret it, Mary. I do. John was the innocent party in all of this. I don't really know what I was doing. I never thought he would die. I thought he might just get sick. I don't know what I thought if I'm honest." Jack paused, shaking his head mournfully. "He didn't deserve to die. But bad things happen to good people."

Mary could no longer contain herself. They were sharing home truths and she wanted to hurt him as much as he was hurting her. It was to become a contest of hurt between the old couple. Who could strike with the nastiest barb? Her anger took over.

"Sarah was a good girl. Did she deserve to be raped by you? My daughter. You took her from me. She died because of you, just like her poor father."

Jack rested his head on the back of the chair, gazing up at the smutty roof. He sighed deeply.

Many a fire over the years had faded the paintwork, leaving swirls of dust across the ceiling. He knew where this conversation was leading now. With a weary acceptance, he allowed Mary to vent her anger. He had heard it all before. Words would not bring Sarah and her baby back. He really couldn't understand a woman's desire to pick the bones out of every drama in life. Bad things happen. Who was he to say why? It just happened. So as Mary ranted, his ears closed to her words. Her voice got louder and stronger as she spat out her anger.

After a few moments, his ears tuned into something new. Not the normal story of poor Sarah and her suffering. He thought he had heard wrong so stopped Mary with his hand raised.

"Hold on, woman. What was that you said?"

Mary had guessed that he wasn't listening and had thrown in the last sentence to catch his interest. She had had no intention of telling him, but sometime during her rant, she had decided he needed to be hurt as much as he had hurt her.

"I said, that is why I killed the baby." Mary spoke each word slowly with emphasis.

"The baby?"

"Yes, your bastard. That baby you put in my daughter," Mary spat out the words.

"What the hell do you mean? You killed it? How?"

Jack was confused now. Placid Mary, the woman he had bullied all their married life, had some fight in her. The babe died at birth so what the hell was she talking about? If she was trying to shock him, she had certainly succeeded.

"I made sure it didn't breathe its first breath. No one saw. A quick tightening of the cord and the poor brat was dead before it knew life." Mary exhaled slowly as she realised what she was saying. "I could not face the scandal. The whole village knowing you had bedded my daughter. Oh yes, we had a plan to cover the truth, but the truth has a frightening way of getting out. One day, that poor child would find out how she was made. It was better for her to never have lived than live with the shame of her parentage."

Mary slumped in the chair.

She had not intended to tell Jack everything. But she felt glad that she had.

She had borne the guilt for years, knowing that she had done wrong but not feeling any shame. She had done what was best to protect her family. The guilt had changed her. She had lost any love she had left for her life. Her life no longer mattered. She kept going for her children and grandchildren, without taking much pleasure for herself. Some could say she was acting the martyr, but she knew that the sacrifice she had made to her own happiness was worth it to save the family from shame.

Tom and Jane had rebuilt the business once Jack's fingers were no longer in the cash box. Tom had built a reputation similar to his father's and was respected throughout the county. Hannah had made a good marriage to John and was happy as the vicar's wife. Arthur was making a good job of managing Wood Farm and Jack's two daughters, Anne and Emma, were in service, out of harm's way. And of course, there was Jack junior; the baby born weeks before Sarah's child.

The baby who should have been a twin. Mary and her husband had planned to bring up Sarah's child as their own, alongside baby Jack. The deception they arranged which was supposed to protect Sarah's reputation. Mary would tell the world she had given birth to twins. But with the death of Sarah's baby, Jack had grown up alone, in a family which was damaged beyond repair. As soon as he could, he had left home for the army, where he was happy. Or so he said. Mary did not probe too deeply.

Jack grunted as he fidgeted in his chair. His eyes remained locked on hers and the stare was full of hate.

"For years you have punished me for Sarah's death, you stupid woman, when all the time you played a part. That girl would have lived if the babe had. She would have had something to fight for." He pointed his finger in her face. "You are to blame for your daughter's death. It's your fault."

"Oh, don't you think I know that," cried Mary. The tears had started to flow. "I have blamed myself as much as I hated you for what you did. Sarah has haunted me ever since. I can feel her anger at my betrayal."

"It didn't stop you treating me like the devil though, did it? You kicked me out of my own house, you bitch." Jack shouted.

Mary may have felt guilty about the baby, but she had no regrets in her treatment of Jack. "None of this would have happened if you had kept it in your trousers, you stupid man. And it was my house. Oh, you may think that by marrying me you could have everything of John's, but the inn is my son's." Mary spat out the last words.

Jack seemed to crumble. His anger dissipated in the face of her forceful comments. "I don't know why, Mary."

"What?"

"I don't know why I had Sarah. I think she reminded me of you when you were young. She was so beautiful and so feisty, just like you."

Mary sighed. Yet again he seemed to blame her for his attraction to her daughter. His arrogance was unbelievable. "She did not deserve it, Jack. She had her whole life ahead of her and you spoilt it all. Can you at least admit your fault rather than turn it round on me?"

"I am sorry, Mary. I do regret it. I was an idiot but you know what I get like with the drink. And she had a way of defying me which got under my skin. No excuses but she could drive me mad."

"Well, that is the first time you have admitted you were wrong. I just cannot believe that I blamed her for so long for getting with child. I was such a bitch to her in her final months. And I can't change that now."

Mary started to cry.

Her mind flooded back to those dreadful days. When she had discovered Sarah was with child, it was too late to do anything about it. She had railed at the poor girl, making her feel like a whore. If she had known what had happened, she would have treated her with more care. The fact that Sarah would not tell her mother what had actually happened was a shame she carried. The daughter, who John had cherished more than life itself, had been let down by her mother. She believed evil of her daughter rather than face the uncomfortable truth that she should have seen.

She had found out about Jack's behaviour by mistake. She had overheard Sarah telling Hannah just before the baby was born. Sarah had trusted her sister but not her mother. Further shame heaped on her shoulders. Mary had let her daughter down at the time she most needed her mother. The only thing left for her to do was to take the problem away for Sarah. Her daughter would not carry the shame of a bastard child.

Mary had thought it was for the best that the child didn't live. But perhaps Jack was right. Perhaps if the babe had lived, Sarah would have fought the fever. Mary remembered sitting by the bedside, watching the light go out of Sarah's body. She didn't want to go on and had let the childbed fever carry her off.

Jack had been silently watching Mary as she tussled with her thoughts. It was clear that she was far off and he didn't want to distract her. The light came back into her eyes as she raised them to look at Jack.

"Where is the child?" Jack's tone was softening. He reached across the cold divide and touched her hand. Mary clutched hold of it with an affection neither of them expected.

"I buried her in the back yard. Under the oak tree."

"Well, let her rest there. It will be our secret. There is no point in upsetting the family." Jack squeezed her hand.

"Why are you being so understanding?" asked Mary, looking confused. "I have been such a bitch to you over the years. Why are you being kind to me when you have the perfect excuse to wreak revenge?"

Jack sighed as he carried on holding her hand. "I am weary of fighting, Mary. We are old and worn out. Surely the time for hatred is gone. You said I never loved you. You were wrong. I loved you. I don't think I ever loved anyone like I did you." He studied Mary's expression, seeing the shock displayed. "I wish things had been different, but we deal the cards and play them as they fall. I have done you wrong. And you have done me wrong. I am deeply sorry about John. It is my biggest regret. I will pay for that when my time comes, but I think you have made me suffer for that and for Sarah all these years."

Mary wiped the tears from her face with her apron.

"I'm sorry Jack. We are both to blame for John's death. If I had pushed you away that first time then none of this would have happened. I think I enjoyed the attention. Having you lusting after me as well as John. I am ashamed by my wantonness." Mary smiled meekly at her estranged husband. "We are just wrong for each other Jack Whiting. Like two devils consumed by their own interests. We have hurt too many people and we will pay for it when the time comes."

Jack laughed. "Well at least we will be in good company down there in hell, woman."

Gallows humour broke the tension between them. Slowly they got to their feet, bones creaking as they did. Jack opened his arms and Mary shuffled towards him. The old couple held each other tightly. Neither of them spoke. They were both lost in their own thoughts.

Jack reflected on the woman he had lost because of his warped lust. He had forgotten why he had gone to such lengths to have her when she was married to John. She got under his skin and he just couldn't let it rest. He could have married another and put his fascinations aside, but he kept coming back to Mary Cozen, even though he knew it was wrong. He had committed the worst crime in his attempt to have Mary. Even when he had achieved what he wanted, the end result was not satisfying. Mary had not been the wife of his desires. Her heart remained with John. He had thought he could cope with that, but the cold bed of his marriage was not the passion of his dreams.

As she got older and fatter, he had seen the Mary he lusted for in her youth in her eldest daughter. His passion for Mary knew no boundaries. Sarah's wilful nature had attracted him as her mother's had done. He had to have her, to dominate her and bend her to his will. But his desire had destroyed the family for ever. He knew that Tom and Hannah hated him for what he had done. He was just thankful that his own bairns were too young to know the dreadful truth.

He had lost everything because of his lustful nature. He could have had a normal life, with a pliable wife and a brood of kids. But his fascination for Mary had driven him down a road full of deceit and evil.

Mary was overwhelmed with sadness.

She and Jack were like poison together. Between them they had wreaked havoc on their family, causing death and destruction. They had loved and hated each other and that tumultuous relationship had been the cause of their troubles. There were no excuses. She had blamed Jack for far too long. But responsibility also sat heavily on her shoulders.

She could have stopped Jack years ago. She made a mistake but she continued to make mistakes, despite the obvious risk to all she held precious. If she had put a stop to their passion, then John would still be alive. Sarah would have been safe from Jack's clutches. She would have lived a life, found a good man, like her younger sister had, and perhaps have a brood of children around her now.

And that poor babe. It would have been welcomed as a grandchild. It would be growing into a young woman now, with all the opportunities life could offer her. The child didn't stand a chance at life. Mary had snuffed out those chances and dreams before she had taken her first breath.

Mary had sinned. The blame could not just be laid at Jack's door. And the frightening thing was that her sins could not be striven. She could not confess them.

She accepted that. It was her punishment that she would go to her grave unshriven.

She was at peace now. She had made her peace with Jack.

The only thing left to do was to beg forgiveness of the poor babe.

The old couple stood in each other's arms for some time. They took comfort from the embrace. Where there had been hate, now there was understanding. Where there had been blame, now there was forgiveness.

It may have come too late in life to make a difference to their happiness but at least it provided them both with a closure of the hate and hurt which had dominated their life together.

CHAPTER THIRTY-SEVEN
JUNE 1875

The day was bright and warm with a gentle breeze.

Mary was sat under the oak tree at the entrance to the orchard. The oak tree stood proud and erect, guiding the way from the inn's yard towards the orchard. It stood sentinel. Behind it stretched numerous apple trees with the odd plum tree.

Mary had fond memories of her orchard. She had been the first to try making cider and her recipe had been handed down to Jane and Tom, who sold the beverage in the inn. She remembered how proud John had been when the first barrel was bottled and the first glass had been drunk at the May Day celebrations 1843. It had been the year Sarah was born and everything felt so special. Their world was full of joy and expectation.

How would life have been if things had been different? If John had lived to be an old man with her, how different would their family have been? Sarah would have reached adulthood. Perhaps she would be married now with a bundle of children flapping around her heels, just like the hens she loved to care for. John would be sat in his rocking chair with a grandchild on his lap. Their world would be full of laughter and love. Their family would not be dispersed and fractured. Indeed, four of her children may never have existed.

Mary shook her head as that train of thought worried her. How can you wish away your children's lives? She carried enough guilt for the way she had left Anne and Emma to grow up without her. Arthur never seemed concerned about his lack of motherly direction, but the two girls had been pushed into service far too early because Mary could no longer cope. And of course, poor little Jack. He had been bereft of motherly love throughout his life. No wonder he had been quick to leave home.

Her life had been tough. Her children's lives had been damaged by their parents' actions.

The harsh reality was that things don't always follow the path you desire. Mary had entered her marriage to John full of daydreams about her responsibilities as a wife and mother. The reality was very different. She had struggled with the daily grind of caring for the babies and supporting her husband. She had been frustrated by John's seriousness as the children came along. She was no longer the centre of his world and the spoilt girl in her had railed against his lack of attention.

It was that naivety and selfishness which had driven her into Jack's arms.

She had wanted to be attractive again. She had wanted someone to desire her, to lust after her. How stupid she had been. If she had just adjusted to married life and realised that fairy tales really don't exist, then the trouble in her life would have disappeared. John would be here beside her as they watched their legacy build. John should have been enough for her. To her shame, she had wanted more and paid the price for her selfish pride.

A robin whistled its beautiful morning call.

She looked up and saw the red-breasted bird sitting proudly on one of the lower branches of the oak. He sang with gusto, filling the silence with his trills. Mary smiled as she was absorbed by his song. An old wife's tale spoke of a robin's presence representing a loved one who has gone from this world. Could it be John, or Sarah or even the babe? She wished it was John, calling her to his side.

Reminding herself of the reason for her sitting under the oak tree, Mary reached down to place her fingers on the soil. There was a dip between two of the huge roots which wormed their way under the ground. The soil was moist with the early morning dew. Her hand reached into the soil, brushing the mud between her fingers.

"I'm so very sorry," she whispered.

Silence greeted her. Her words hung in the air. She did not expect an answer; just to be heard.

All of a sudden, the robin flew to the ground and rested next to her fingers. Mary froze, conscious that any movement would scare the bird away. The robin stood looking at the old woman, its head cocked to one side, mimicking a listening mode.

Mary repeated her words. "I'm so very sorry, child."

The robin danced around in a circle between the two roots, watching the woman intensely. Once it had completed the circle it ascended slowly, flapping its wings as if in slow motion. As it flapped, it watched the woman. He started to sing, a beautiful song of happiness and hope. Moments later it flew away, high into the sky.

Mary had an overwhelming feeling of peace. A calmness she had missed for so many years.

Was this forgiveness?

Had her visit back to Little Yaxley been the right thing for her to do before her days were over? The robin seemed to be reassuring her that it was. There was nothing left to fight against. It was time to rest and let the world move on without her.

As she sat in the sunshine, Mary came to realise that her time was now upon her. She would ask Tom to gather the family tonight and then take to her bed. She would say her farewells and drift into the arms of her husband.

Her fight was over.

Now it was time to be reunited with John.

CHAPTER THIRTY-EIGHT
JUNE 1875

Jane heaved the heavy kettle from the range, slopping boiling water into the teapot. She left the tea to brew as she joined the others.

The kitchen was crowded with family. It had been ages since the siblings had been together at the same time. Hannah's family were missing. There had not been enough time to get a message to her. She would not have made it in time. Hannah had realised, sadly, that she could not be with her mother at her passing before saying goodbye to her in Suffolk. Jack junior was also absent as he was in active service in Africa. Mary had been insistent that all her children be summoned.

Anne and Emma had been given leave. They were both shocked to see the changes in their mother. She had left the Crown and Hare in good health and returned an old, dying lady. Mary had been shocked to see her two younger daughters so grown up. She felt sad to realise how little she knew about their lives and loves. Earlier that morning she had laid in bed listening to the girls regaling her with stories of service. It had given her some comfort to know they were both happy.

The family was sat around the kitchen table as myriad conversations flowed, creating a crescendo of noise. Jane smiled as she made the tea, thinking how good it was to see everyone sharing happier memories of their mother. Death was a natural part of the circle of life and Mary Whiting was going to share the experience with those she loved and who loved her. The room was filled with love rather than sadness. The family would celebrate Mary's long life rather than wail with grief. This wouldn't be because the family would not miss their matriarch, but because they recognised her suffering and realised she welcomed the end. Her mind had been muddled for so long now and peace beckoned.

Meanwhile, Mary was not alone whilst her family caught up with each other's news.

Jack sat beside her bed, keeping her company.

He was quiet, watching the woman he had risked everything for, slip away. After they had talked a few days before, he had been a regular visitor. He and Mary had made their peace and, whilst there remained tension with his step-son Tom, that did not stop him from visiting his wife on her deathbed. Tom tolerated Jack's presence in his home. He certainly wasn't happy with him being there but for his mother's sake, was prepared to keep things civil.

Mary's breathing was becoming laboured. Every time she pulled the air in, a pain shot across her chest. She could sense her pulse weakening with each gasp of air. Her head felt crammed full of cotton. She struggled to grab hold of a thought and keep it for any real time. Her body felt almost weightless as she sunk back into the comfortable mattress. Tom had given her fresh stuffing for her mattress and the smell of spring grasses filled her nose.

She was not scared.

Peace filled her as she looked around her familiar surroundings. She searched the room as if she was trying to remember everything special to her and her family. Her eyes flicked back and forth. Suddenly they settled on Jack. He was looking away and didn't spot her gaze.

Mary was glad that she had spoken to Jack. They had spent too much of their life together to allow it to end in anger. All the bad things that had happened had taken over her memories in recent times. When they first married, they had been happy. It wasn't the passion of her and John, but she had felt cared for and supported at first. They had shared the joy of bringing Anne, Arthur, and Emma into the family. Jack had adored his babies, especially Anne who was the apple of his eye. Mary and Jack had rubbed along well at first.

They were happy once.

When did it all go wrong?

Was it just the drink? Or had she played a part?

Jack had always drunk too much but, as he got older, the ale made him angrier. The first time he laid hands on Mary, she was shocked. They had argued and he had slapped her around the face. He had been sorry but it happened again. And again. Mary grew to hate him in his cups. She protected the children from the worst of it, but obviously couldn't save Sarah from his evil nature.

How she wished things could have been different. If they had not behaved the way they had when John was alive, perhaps the guilt of their actions would not have haunted Mary and Jack's marriage. Jack became an angry man who disliked John's children and blamed Mary for all his problems. Mary become a bitter woman who hid the shame of her betrayal under a scold's bridle.

Mary watched Jack as he sat awkwardly, obviously uncomfortable in his sentry duty. He had told the children to leave them be for a while and now seemed at a loss as to what he wanted to do next. His face was troubled and he wrung his hands together. Emotion was not something Jack felt comfortable with. He had always hated it when Mary cried and his usual default position had been to shout and rage.

He had been such an angry man. Would things have been different if he had learned to control his temper?

Over recent days Jack had turned his thoughts back to the past. It had been a difficult thing for him to do, as he lacked emotional intelligence and very rarely would try and understand his actions. But the talk with Mary had unsettled him. He had done some truly bad things in his life, and watching Mary reach the end of her time was making him reflect on his own actions and responsibilities.

To his absolute shame, he accepted he had caused John's death. He hadn't really thought it through. He had acted on impulse to a problem and suddenly everything had escalated. Had he really wanted his best friend out of the way so he could have Mary whenever he wanted? What kind of evil had possessed him?

John had not deserved his fate. How he wished John had never returned to Little Yaxley all those years ago. Perhaps then he would have married Mary when she was a girl and none of this evil would have happened. It was typical of the man Jack was that he could blame John for his own demise. He had struggled all of his life to take responsibility for his own actions.

That was why he found himself alone and unloved for so long.

For years he had chased the prize of Mary, prepared to do such evil things to win her. And then when his fantasies had been fulfilled, the reality had been nothing like his dreams. Mary had not been the woman of his desires. All too quickly she had become a nag, dragging him down with her moaning. She had let herself go as the babies arrived, soon becoming a haggard, middle-aged woman rather than the beauty who had driven his dreams all those years.

Sarah had grown up during this period, becoming a beauty. She was the spit of her mother, the woman he had fallen in love with as a youth. Was that just an excuse for his dreadful actions? Blaming his step-daughter for her looks to cover his own evil. The drink had a part to play. He had spent too many years in his cups, drowning his sorrows. When he drank, his worst qualities came to the fore. And poor Sarah had paid the price. No wonder his family had turned against him. Could he ever recover their goodwill?

Or was it now too late?

He was somewhat jealous that Mary was surrounded by her family at the end when he knew he would probably face his reckoning alone.

He broke out of his reverie at the sound of Mary's gasp for air. Her eyes met his and he could see the panic flash momentarily across her gaze. She reached for his hand and gripped hard.

"The children," she whispered.

Instinctively Jack knew it was time. Pushing himself out of the seat, he went to the door and called for Tom. A clatter of boots was all he could hear as Tom, Arthur, Anne and Emma rushed up the stairs. Soon the room was filled as Jack moved away from the children. Now was their time with their mother. He stood on the periphery. He did not deserve to be with her at the end. That place was reserved for her children who were closest in her heart.

Silence filled the room. Mary's children sat around the bed, touching her arms, enveloping her with love. There were no tears. Brave faces greeted their mother as they watched her final moments.

Mary smiled as she took her last sight of her family. They were the good in her life. She would leave a legacy of which she was incredibly proud. Her only regret was that Hannah could not be with her, and she sent her thoughts across the miles to her beloved daughter.

She could see Jack away by the door, but her eyes were struggling with the gloom. It was right that he was there to guide her back to John. He had taken John from her and now Jack would guide her way back to her lover's arms. To share their eternal sleep together.

All of a sudden, she could see a bright light, and a feeling of absolute peace filled her. Someone was calling to her, willing her forward.

Squeezing Tom's hand, she uttered her final words.

"I'm going home now, love."

The End

AFTERWORD

Thank you for reading A Mother's Deceit. I hope you enjoyed it as much as I enjoyed writing it. The book is a prequel to my first novel, A Mother's Loss, so if you haven't read that novel then please do give it a go. I believe both books stand up independently or as part of a mini-series.

The book is based fictionally on our old home in Norfolk when it was used as a pub. After I finished writing A Mother's Loss I was keen to explore Mary's story. What were the circumstances which led her to marry Jack? Was he always a nasty character or was there more to him than his behaviour in my first book? Whilst it is hard to understand Jack's actions towards his step-daughter, unravelling Mary's story helped me to examine her part in the drama.

I had a great deal of sympathy for Mary but at the same time was frustrated with her actions and behaviours when she was married to John. She loved her husband passionately but for some reason he wasn't enough for her. This struggle with individual's morals feature quite heavily in my books. I like my main characters to be flawed in some way so that the reader fluctuates between supporting them and disliking their behaviours.

As an independent published author, reviews are important to help grow my audience. I would be delighted if you could leave me a review on Amazon or Goodreads. Your reviews will help me develop my craft and shape my stories as I continue on my writing journey.

I would love to hear from you on my social media and my website.

Facebook : www.facebook.com/crebisz

Twitter : @Carolinerebisz

Website: www.crebiszauthor.co.uk

ABOUT THE AUTHOR

Caroline has moved from her home in Norfolk which was the inspiration for A Mother's Loss and A Mother's Deceit. She now lives in Wiltshire with her husband and their cat. She has two grown up daughters who are the centre of her world. Family is incredibly important to Caroline and features strongly in her books.

Caroline worked throughout her career for a high street bank in a variety of roles. Her passion centred around leading teams and putting her communication skills to good use. Since taking early retirement, she has directed that passion to writing novels.

Other books in Caroline's portfolio include A Mother's Loss and A Costly Affair.

Find out more about Caroline and contact her via her website www.crebiszauthor.co.uk